Jim—

It's hard to say which is the more impressive achievement getting I 74 open to me or preparing those splendid students

Dan
2/17/72

In the Hands of Our Enemies

A NATIONAL COUNCIL ON THE ARTS SELECTION

In the
Hands of Our Enemies

STORIES BY

DANIEL CURLEY

University of Illinois Press

URBANA
CHICAGO
LONDON

ACKNOWLEDGMENTS: *Hudson Review*, "Where You Wouldn't Want to Walk"; *Perspective*, "A Very Small Grove" and "A Ride in the Snow"; *University of Kansas City Review*, "All of a Summer's Day"; *Epoch*, "The Tale of the Peasant Osip," "The Manhunt," and "A Story of Love, Etc."; *New Mexico Quarterly*, "The Day of the Equinox"; *U.S. Catholic*, "Look Homeward, Tourist," "A Day in Hamburg," and "The Moth, the Bear, and the Shivering Stars"; *Accent*, "The Man Who Was Drafted"; *Texas Quarterly*, "The Gingerbread Man."

To Helen

Thou are like to meet with in the way which thou goest, Wearisomness, Painfulness, Hunger, Perils, Nakedness, Sword, Lions, Dragons, Darkness; and in a word, death, and what not?

PILGRIM'S PROGRESS

Where You Wouldn't Want to Walk, 1
A Very Small Grove, 10
All of a Summer's Day, 18
The Manhunt, 24
A Story of Love, Etc., 46
The Day of the Equinox, 56
A Ride in the Snow, 70
Station: You Are Here, 83
The Tale of the Peasant Osip, 104
Look Homeward, Tourist, 116
A Day in Hamburg, 125
The Moth, the Bear, and the Shivering Stars, 135
The Man Who Was Drafted, 146
The Gingerbread Man, 163
In the Hands of Our Enemies, 189

Where You Wouldn't Want to Walk

"IF YOU DRIVE where you wouldn't want to walk," the ad said. I don't remember what it was that I was supposed to run right out and buy. Perhaps spark plugs. Perhaps snow tires—no, probably not snow tires. The picture showed a car stopped on a narrow road in the woods, not bogged down, just stopped. The hood was raised in the classic gesture of despair, and I imagined—as was intended—some logging road deep in Marlboro country, some trail between the trading post and the hunting cabin. And then I looked again.

Where I wouldn't want to walk? It was my favorite walk in all the world. I read once about a bum who was saving his money so that when he felt the end coming on, he could go into a whore house and die in bed with a woman, as, he said, a man ought. That's the way I feel about that walk. If you really could tell when death was coming and then set out as you ought, like an elephant, why, then, when I felt I could stand, good or bad, just one more thing, I'd set out on that walk and keep going until my heart broke with joy.

And it might happen at any step. There was scarcely a tree or a rock that didn't recall something to crack any heart. There was no lumber camp or hunting cabin around that bend at the back of the picture. And there was no trading post just behind the camera. No, around that bend, there was a big fir tree riddled from top to bottom with long rectangular holes, dim and weathered now around the edges, but bright and startling the day I watched the pileated woodpecker making them and littering the ground with shreds of fresh wood. I carried one of those shreds for a long time in my pocket. After all, I'd been looking for him for years so that coming upon him was like a vision of the grail, and the tree became forever a shrine.

Behind the camera, there was a break in the trees where you could see the marsh. I guess they didn't think the marsh was Marlboro enough, but it was where I saw the little blue heron, which makes it about the best country there is.

Anyone who knows anything about birds will know that it takes a good-sized tract to hold a pileated woodpecker and that a little blue isn't to be come across just anywhere. So was it really Marlboro country? No, it really wasn't. It was an Adirondack preserve that came right up to the edge of town, and what was really behind the camera was just about the best cooking you will find anywhere, clean quiet rooms, and half a dozen guests who came back every year or undertook to find guaranteed replacements—guaranteed simpatico replacements, people who wanted to read a little and take walks by themselves. Sometimes they worked—by themselves, quietly—at least their typewriters sounded like work. But they were the kind of people who used pads and towels to muffle the sound and who always asked if it bothered you and who always replied that it didn't and who never said what it was they were typing. I sometimes thought they were writers, and I sometimes thought they were blackmailers, but since I had been guaranteed, of course I never asked.

One, at least, was a poet. I found that out later but I suspected it at the time. She had a typewriter but she didn't type much, and she didn't type as if she had ever had to learn to get through pages and pages in a hurry. Slow and deliberate. And I used to visualize each letter black and distinct and solitary on the page. She also walked a great deal, and she carried bird glasses. We walked at about the same time each day, so it would have been easy for us to go together, but I couldn't force myself on her—I had been guaranteed not to. We kept our distance.

Then, one day, as I stood by the marsh, hoping for another

epiphany, I saw something glint among the trees on the hill opposite. I searched slowly. Another glint. Lost. Caught. Eye to eye, our binoculars locked for a moment. Then I continued my sweep. I was being watched. What kind of a bird was I, anyway? Was she spying for my wife, who was practically guaranteed not to be that kind of person, although really you never can be quite sure about wives? Was—ah, well that is all nonsense, cops and robbers, doctors and nurses, la vie de Boheme. Still, my eyes had met her flaming eyes, locked flaming, left flaming, something between us.

I began stalking her. It wasn't easy. She would set out in the afternoon and I would follow her. She didn't walk fast but I could never overtake her. She would simply disappear. Then I began to take an extra walk in the morning just to study the trail itself. I found all the spots where you could look back over the trail—across the marsh, for instance—and see if anyone was coming. I even found the place she had been watching from that day, and I felt a strange shudder because I hadn't realized how close the trail bent back to that side of the marsh. She could have been sitting there quietly as I passed almost at arm's length. One by one, I found her hiding places and watched her watching me. I triumphed over the spy. And then it came to me that she was the one who set out first each day and that she wasn't spying at all but was avoiding me.

I know now that she was very shy and so passionately devoted to her own privacy that she automatically faded from the face of the earth rather than invade another's landscape. I doubt very much that she ever allowed herself to look at me once she had gone into hiding, so that probably she wasn't looking at me at all the day I thought our glasses locked us to each other. Not that that makes any difference: I thought we were locked, I felt we were locked, and that's what counts and what explains the rest of it.

There were ducks on the marsh that day, the kind you never can be sure about, no gorgeous males to set you right at once. I pretended to study them but really I was trying to locate her among the undergrowth. I found her and went on taking out my Peterson and studying the plates. I can do that endlessly, and the great part is that I immediately forget everything I read, and it is all fresh and exciting day after day. Actually, I guess I was doing more than pretend to study the plates, but I told myself I was deceiving her. Any way you look at it, it seems pretty harmless. I moved on, glasses at the ready, bothered by dim thrushes among the undergrowth.

It would have been the easiest thing in the world for her to come out of that hiding place and be far away before I could get around to where she was, but I was convinced that her object was to lie in wait and get behind me. At that time, I still believed in the spy theory. Fortunately, the trail near her hiding place commanded the first view of a towering poplar with a dead top branch where more than once I had seen a hawk and once, when the light was fading, an enormous owl, which took a squirrel just beside the trail, a spot I still can't pass with quiet heart.

It was natural, then, that I should stop and study the tree at an angle kind to my neck. On my walks and in my room I had worked over dialogues for us to speak at some improbable confrontation, but I was surprised to hear myself say as I focused my glasses on the topmost limb, "Are you all right? Are you hurt?"

I hadn't seen her at all, but she stood up at once and said, "I'm just making some notes." And she had a pencil and note pad to show it.

"Inspiration?" I said, following my theory that she was a poet.

Perhaps she was so used to knowing she was a poet that it didn't strike her as odd that I should assume it. "Walking makes the rhythm come," she said and stepped out onto the trail with me.

We had broken in upon each other, so we continued our walk together. She told me she was sure the ducks were black ducks. She told me she had seen the heron several times but never the woodpecker. She envied me that, she said. She was very serious about birds and remembered everything she ever read about them. Her Peterson was fresh and clean and protected by a neat waterproof cover, and I doubt if she ever needed to refer to it. I found it rather intimidating. Mine is dirty and falling apart from my daily struggles through the same few pages, but she held it for a moment and considered it as if it were an object quite beyond price. She told me about Wordsworth's theory of the rhythm of walking and poetic rhythm and recited some of his lines as we walked. I never heard a line of her own.

I told her about my pilgrim's trail and all its shrines, about the tree chopped full of holes, about the place the squirrel died, silently, swiftly, before he knew he was in danger, the terrible shadow, and especially I told her of another place. "Here," I said, "under this drift of leaves. A year ago." I stirred the leaves with my foot, and they rustled sharply as they had that day. "It was autumn."

It wasn't the kind of thing easily explained. So much depended on what I had brought to bear, on the frame that set the scale for the action. For one thing, I was just out of the hospital. They had opened me up and pawed around, taking out this and leaving that, the soothsayers, and deciding in the end that I'd do very well provided I didn't die at once. I myself was much of the same opinion, although I was rather less optimistic and under the circumstances a good deal less interested. In fact, I was so uninterested that they thought it would do no harm if they gave me a roommate overnight, someone who would be dead by morning. He was a large man, very fat, and had been told, no doubt, again and again that he would have to lose weight and would have to stop drinking. He was blue and unconscious and was breathing like an engine. Ah. Ah. Ah. I must have shown some irritation, because they gave me a shot and told me to drop off.

Gladly, gladly would I have dropped off. It was no pleasure to listen to that breathing getting louder and louder and to see his wife standing at the foot of his bed hour after hour. I was far too close to it myself to enjoy it all as spectacle. Ah. Ah. Ah. Silence. The doctor and the nurse balanced the books. The wife turned and walked out of the room. Click. Click. Click. She was stupendous. Click. Click. Click. Measured and precise steps without the least faltering. Maybe that's why he drank and went on drinking. Why he ate and went on eating. Click. Click. Thud. They carried her away and almost at once they carried him away, too, in a wicker basket. It was not encouraging.

So I walked out slowly in the afternoon, stopping to sit down, leaning on my cane, still feeling as if at any moment my fortune might come tumbling out over my lap for all the world to read. I didn't go far, you can imagine, but right here, barely into the woods, I planted myself—what goes on four legs in the morning, two at noon, and three in the evening?—and rested. Suddenly there was a tumult in the leaves at my feet. I was still too unused to my arms and legs for them to run away unless I stopped and told them exactly what they were supposed to do. Even then they wouldn't always do what I wanted. Like my god-damned bowels. Imagine sitting down to reason with your bowels. It's an outrage.

There I was, picturing a rattlesnake at my very feet and faced with mutiny all over the place. Who can reason at a time like that? So I didn't run away and I didn't slash and smash with my cane. I could only stand and watch the revelation of something far worse than a rattlesnake.

A soldier spends his life drilling so he won't have to think when the chips are down. By the time a man becomes a sea captain, he knows what to say under any conceivable circumstances. Stave in his bottom. Out pops the right command. Chop off his masts. Stop his engines in a hurricane. Does he have to reason with his ship? He doesn't even have to tell his mouth to open itself so the computer can spit out the right message. Stimulus response stimulus response stimulus response. What rational being could ever imagine that he ought to spend his days drilling his arms and legs? Hup, two, hup, two. Biceps, pick it up. Hup, two, hup, two. Triceps, god damn it, look alive. Bowels, ATTENTION. You Bones, in there, what the fuck do you think you're in there for?

The leaves exploded into fury at my feet, two beasts locked in combat, the passion of monsters, each the size of my thumb. One got purchase for his back against the edge of my sole and rolled the other over. The earth trembled. The rocks screamed in agony. The horizon rocked and threatened to slip down over my ears.

"You must understand that it was over in an instant, all in the most absolute silence."

I would have sworn that I was listening to a battle soundtrack—but, of course, that was only my blood roaring in my ears—so that when one broke away and began to run, silence became suddenly oppressive. "He's making it," I said aloud. "He's going to be all right." There was no pursuit. The victor knew what losers never know and turned his back even before the other dropped in mid-stride. Charitably, my arms and legs and back and guts all got together and bent me down for a good close look.

"A hind leg twitching, two drops of blood on a leaf."

As far as the eye could see, great gouts of blood among the evergreens, here, there, draining down into the marsh, which was reddening from moment to moment. Half the sky was smeared, the firmament streaming with mole's blood and the endless scream of silence.

"The next day there wasn't a trace. There are those whose job it is to clean up. Even the blood was gone. As if nothing had happened. Not a trace."

My god, my god, who drinks up all the blood?

I had told her the best thing I knew—best? Most true, most moving, most terrible. And I had told it the best way I could, but I knew I had left out everything that made it best. I had only told what happened. As I heard myself saying it to her, I realized it could only be a story to someone else, an anecdote, the words wholly devoid of magic power. But whether she understood the story or whether she only understood the idea of magic, she took me by the hand and drew me into the woods to show me what was magic for her.

It wasn't far at all, quite within sight of my hawk-lookout tree, although I had never known it existed. There was a rock face in the hillside and a trickle of water from the rock, collecting in a natural basin about waist high. She looked at me and smiled and cupped her hands, dipped them and lifted them sparkling, and drank. She didn't have to tell me that this was the best thing she knew. Then she stepped aside so that I could drink. I cupped my hands and bent forward, believing completely that her best without any words could become my best, although my best had so failed in the telling. I reached and bent, but before my hands could touch the water, I dropped to the ground in agony.

"My back," I whispered, "my back."

She said she knew. And she must have, because she helped me flatten out on the ground, and she rolled up her sweater and put it under the small of my back, which is exactly what they did later in the hospital—not a sweater, of course, but a towel. And she bathed my forehead. And she went for help.

All I could think of as I lay there—because I could think if I was absolutely still and didn't move so much as a toe—all I could think of was how it would look to me if a girl came out of the woods and reported that a middle-aged man was lying in some secret place with a hurt back. It seemed to me that the least embarrassing thing for all of us would be for me to faint, so when I heard them coming with the stretcher, I rotated my ankle and passed out at once.

I was right enough in my fears. The doctors and nurses laughed at me in the hospital and made jokes about love. But what really broke them up was when I explained exactly how it had happened. I cupped my hands and held them out—very cautiously— and the hospital rocked with laughter. The gesture was so classic in back cases that until I left they would point me out to their friends, cup their hands, and have a good laugh all around.

I never saw her again. Her vacation in the woods was the last before she entered a convent. When I could walk, I went back for another look. There was the spot in the leaves that only I knew about and never could tell. The leaves were all green. The marsh glittered in the sun. The sky was flawless blue. I watched the spring in the rock and listened to the tiny drip. But I didn't dare put out a hand to it. I thought of kneeling so I wouldn't have to bend my back, but that was a fantasy like a posture in an erotic dream—I'd have had to kneel in mid-air and have a neck like a swan. There was her best, so close, untasted, although I could practically feel the shock of the cold. My teeth ached. My god, my god, what has become of us?

A Very Small Grove

As JACK WILSON crossed the archery range in the park, the sun dropped below the cloud bank. His shadow sprang out sharp and long before him, and Spring soothed his shoulders like a heating pad. For a moment he was so lost in a sense of sheer well-being that he forgot the ghosts of girls who had played and posed where he walked. He forgot the phantom wreathing of their arms and legs about him and the wind-soft panting of their breath against his cheek. But it was only for a moment that he forgot. Then came the ghosts of arrows, and then he was through with that part of his perilous journey home from his office. There was still the grove to come, however, a peril of a very different sort.

He could feel the heat spreading through his body like whiskey. His bursitis was miraculously relieved. The aches in his wrists and ankles vanished. He felt like a new man. The earth was different under his feet. The damp fields in the sun, the nearby groves were rich and heady in his nostrils. The song of birds was sharp as a dream. He was lost in another dream now, a dream of his own youth. He entered the grove.

It was not a large grove. You could almost see through it in winter but only almost. It had its own hush, its own sense of being a part of the great and endless grove no one need ever come out of. Toward the center of this grove he stopped beside a certain shagbark hickory tree he knew. He knew also that the sudden voice of the tree at his side was really a squirrel scrambling to keep the trunk between them. He leaned forward and exchanged a quick look with the squirrel, and then he leaned back and almost missed the squirrel's peek high above. The raucous cry of a flicker drew his eye off to the right, and the long sustained noise gave him a chance to locate the bird on the trunk of another hickory not far away. The tree tops were full of darting movement, mostly some very small birds he never had identified. A woodpecker that was either a hairy or a downy. He couldn't be sure. Doves flew over, gray and noisy. A cardinal flashed to a bush just down the path.

He stepped reluctantly forward. Somewhere within the next few steps he would have gone as deep into the woods as he could go and would have begun to come out. The exact spot was undefined but it was surely between the hickory where he had stopped and the bush where the cardinal was perched as if predicting the red buds of the bush a little later on in the spring. In the morning it was at the bush that he stopped for a moment.

At home there was no sign of life in the kitchen, which normally at that hour had all the clang and fury of a factory that isn't making its production schedule. "Hello," he called tentatively to the house at large, but there was no reply. "Hello," he called louder, "anybody here?" The house did not have the hushed air of a deserted house. In fact he could hear the muffled roar of the television, so he opened the door of the TV room and stepped in front of the set. "And now a word from your sponsor," he said and paused, allowing the white and strained faces of his children to shorten range and zero in on something less than seven light years away.

When he had all the attention he was likely to get, he said, "Where is your mother?" Silence. "Did she leave a note?" Silence. "Did she telephone?" Silence. "Thank you for your attention, and now back to your program." He stepped away from the set and left the room to the cadence, electronically magnified, of elephants eating dry breakfast food.

He picked up his paper and backed toward his chair. A glass

of beer, he thought. He reversed his motion and went down into the cellar to get a bottle from the drink refrigerator in the laundry room. He was startled to see his wife in an easy chair reading. "Oh, hello," he said.

"Hello," she said without looking up.

"Are you all right?" he said.

"Fine," she said.

"Forget what time it is?"

"No."

"Good book?"

"Not particularly."

"What's for supper?"

She shrugged. She was very clearly not interesting herself in supper and as clearly meant "Whatever you want to get."

He was baffled. He took a bottle of beer from the refrigerator, opened it and drank. "How'd that chair get in here?" he said.

"The gas man moved it in when he came to read the meter," she said. "My feet were hurting. It's nice in here."

"How about pancakes and bacon?" he said, letting himself off easy.

"That's good," she said. "Make a lot of batter. It will save time in the morning."

"Will do." He responded quickly to what looked like a re-establishment of communication, so he finished his beer and took another bottle from the refrigerator. "I'll call you," he said.

"Make a note in your pocket notebook," she said, and his notebook and pen were in his hands and his beer bottle clutched between his bent knees. "Call the phone company in the morning and tell them I'd like a phone down here."

"Got it," he said. He scribbled the message several times before he was sure he'd be able to read it in the morning. "Pancakes and bacon, coming up."

When he pulled the fuse to announce supper, the children came out of the TV room like miners carrying lighted candles although actually they all had flashlights for serious things like bathroom walks and night fears. They stuck their candles to the table and wanted to be fed. He told off the oldest girl to go down and ask his wife to supper. It really hadn't taken him long at all, because the kitchen help had been out from under foot.

The girl returned at once with a request for a tray for her mother. Jack Wilson prepared it without comment and fed the others. Then he went down to the cellar again. "Are you sure you're all right?" he said.

"I'm fine."

"Did you like the pancakes?"

"They were fine."

"You always like anything you don't have to cook," he said.

"That's right," she said.

It was late when he finished cleaning the kitchen and putting things away. He was tired and he was angry. "I'm going to bed," he shouted down the cellar stairs. There was no answer but he had committed himself and began to withdraw from the kitchen in the best order possible. Not the least of his problems was the light. If he didn't leave a light on, she would be offended when she came up and discovered that he thought she was crazy enough to stay in the cellar all night. If he did leave the light on, she would be offended when she realized he had expected her to come up—he couldn't conceive of her not making a tour of inspection after he was asleep. He compromised by leaving on the little light on the stove.

The light was still on in the morning when he came down stairs. There was no sign that anyone had been in the kitchen after him, but with breakfast to get and hair to comb and braid and lunches to pack he had no time for crazy women. Nor did he have any more time after he had got the children off to school, because by then he was already late for his office, and he was a very methodical man.

Actually it made no difference at all when he got to his office. He expected no one and no one expected him. Anyone who did want to reach him would know where he lived. Still, the violation of his routine upset him. The very nature of his business, formless as it was, made him feel obliged to hold himself rigidly to schedule in order to avoid total chaos: the dinner jacket in the jungle was his private concept of his own life.

His business was in fact almost no business at all. It was everything. It was nothing. He called himself an entrepreneur and left it to others to find uses for him. He picked up fees and commissions in all sorts of ways. People trusted him, and that was his biggest stock in trade. They trusted him to talk to experts they themselves didn't trust. He could take an old portrait of great grandfather hand painted in oil by a traveling artist named Smudge, and he could bring back from the city pretty much what it was worth—minus his commission, of course. He could talk with a contractor and find out if you needed a retaining wall or the contractor needed work. He could go halfway across the country and find out the value of the farm or the business you had inherited unexpectedly, and then he could find exactly the person who could be made to give just a little more once you knew how badly he wanted what you had to sell. Some people who moved in from a town where an entrepreneur pruned hedges put him to work gardening for them, and eventually he built up a stable of gardeners—and maids—for all occasions. Electricians or plumbers or carpenters that he recommended were much in demand. Although he hadn't yet figured out how to turn that into cash, he was tinkering with the idea of a Jack Wilson Seal of Approval for the local servicemen.

He shaved hurriedly and went down to the basement for a shower in that bathroom he kept dirty and unpainted in order to discourage its use by others. As he approached the door to the bathroom, however, he saw a sign in his wife's distinctive printing: Wet Paint. He opened the door cautiously and peeked in. The place seemed to be on fire. Then he recognized a particularly brutal shade of pink which he had allowed his daughters to select for their own room but which he had been unable to bring himself to use after he had put on a sample swipe or two. The cans had been in the storeroom ever since. His wife must have worked all night cleaning and painting.

She was asleep in her chair when he looked into the laundry.

His good paint brushes, gummy with paint, lay on a newspaper on the floor. Her hands and face were spotted with paint and she smiled as she slept.

He went upstairs and took a bath but even after that he was so furious with her that he fed his anger by telephoning the telephone company about the extension she had to have in the basement. Fortunately his discussion with the telephone company was all he could have desired.

"No," he said, "I don't want a beige telephone."

"No, I don't want white."

"No, I don't want pink."

"No, I don't want turquoise."

"No, I don't want blue."

"No, I don't want a phone that lights up nor even one that chimes the opening bars of the Star Spangled Banner."

"No, I cannot give you a credit reference other than the fact that I have done business with your company for twenty-five years."

"No, my father died ten years ago at the age of seventy-seven, and I am myself supposedly a mature individual, property owner, tax payer."

"Yes, I will be happy to repeat that to your manager."

Somewhat mollified he left the house wearing a suit that overnight had become far too warm. The cloth bound against his sticky thighs. His clean shirt felt soggy all over. When he stopped in the grove beside the redbud, he felt a chill go through him, and he had to begin moving again long before he was ready.

At his office that day he was offered a job that would take him into northern New England for a week or more. He was to fly over to look at various sites proposed for a new ski run. It was to be an ultraexclusive place, remote, inaccessible, guests to be flown in. Someone was needed to walk over the land, actually to see it and get the feel. Someone was needed to look into the future of the adjoining property and cover all the angles, because when you are going into business with the forest primeval as your selling point you want to be sure no one is going to set up an atomic plant on the back of your hill or start logging off everything in sight.

This was exactly the sort of job that appealed to Jack Wilson. Ordinarily he would have jumped at the chance, but now he asked time to think it over while he discovered—if he could— exactly what it was he had in his cellar. He tried calling his house but got no answer although he let the phone ring for fully ten minutes. He decided then that she must have come up and gone out, because she could never stand to let the telephone ring. It might be—god knows what.

He had no sooner put down the phone than it rang. "Hello," she said, "was that you trying to call?" He told her it was. "I thought probably it was, but I couldn't reach you until you stopped calling here."

"That sounds crazy," he said. "All you had to do was answer the phone."

"I'm downstairs," she said.

He was stunned for a moment. "All you had to do was pick up the extension. I see they got it in."

"It's not an extension," she said. "That's why I couldn't pick it up. It's a different line entirely."

"That is crazy," he said.

"If that's your attitude, goodbye," she said.

"Goodbye," he said. He hurried to get the receiver down before she got hers down. Then he remembered that he hadn't spoken with her about his trip. He dialed information for the number of the new phone and was told that it was an unlisted number.

"Unlisted be damned," he said, "that's my house and I want the number." This time he got nowhere, not even with the manager.

That night he discovered lettuce and tomatoes in the drink refrigerator when he went down for his beer and his talk with her. He was aware also that a pot of coffee was being kept hot on an old gas burner he had always meant to disconnect and take out of the laundry room. "You planning to live down here?" he said, desperately to the point.

"I'll make out," she said.

"I've been offered this trip out of town," he said, "but the children—"

"They'll make out," she said.

Not in the least reassured but hoping always for the best, he left on his trip to New England. There was just a chance that he might make out.

At the end of a week, he stood on a very high hill overlooking forest unbroken as far as the eye could see and farther even than the mind could reach, to the border and beyond. Behind him and far below, the plane and the guide waited on the river. In the brush at the edge of the forest a flying bird stitched a scarlet line, then turned at right angles and flew in among the trees. A ten-minute walk would take him to the place. The forest was dark and quiet without end. He needed only the first step and the second—he would make out.

But the very certainty of his making out turned his thoughts to his children, who only might make out. He watched a very long time for the bird and at last turned and went down to the plane.

Even outside the house he could smell supper cooking and he could hear the soft murmur of TV voices. He knew he had done well to come home. Then full of creditable thoughts about homecoming—mixed with a faint but unmistakable touch of self-congratulation—he entered the house by the back door.

The kitchen was dark and the stove was cold. He crossed quickly to the TV room—dark and silent. He turned on the light. The room was as always except that the TV set was gone. He stood in the doorway, baffled by the memory of the illusion of home that had reached him outside the house.

As he stood there he heard from beneath his feet the sound of elephants eating dry cereal. He tiptoed to the cellar door and stealthily opened it. One by one he identified their voices. He closed the door with infinite care and disappeared deeper and deeper and deeper into the house.

All of a Summer's Day

IT WAS warm, quiet, and still on the water. The sun stood clearly still just above the trees. The boat, although not anchored, hung softly over its unwavering image. Everything was suspended and withdrawn and asleep in a way I have not known since that time, the summer of my tenth year.

I heard a small hiss as another of my father's cigarettes hit the water, but I did not turn to watch the little pillar of steam rise amid the flotilla of soggy decomposing butts off the starboard bow. Neither did I look at the mutilated body of the big perch floating a little way astern. I looked only at the glazed water with my float hanging balloon-like among the trees and my own face staring back at me, striped by the stalks of river weeds.

I reached out to touch my face, my own familiar face peering through the weeds, but as my touch approached, it changed and twisted and was no longer my own but old and ageless, time-worn and timeless, changed and always changing, as if one flipped with incredible speed through an album of pictures of one person, the pictures identical in pose but taken at intervals from birth to incredibly aged death (and even beyond) and in the album arranged in no particular order, but changing, changing, birth and death and resurrection endlessly and meaninglessly and nowhere my own familiar face hiding among the rushes.

We had been fishing a long time when I caught the big perch. I was sitting there drowsing and half-watching my father endlessly casting upon the waters. My father stood braced in the boat whipping his rod about him and dropping the plug all around the little inlet in which we hovered. The plug plopped beside the lily pads and was reeled back in. Beside the fallen tree and was reeled back in. Beside the rock. Beside the snag. Beside a lazy splash in the middle of the inlet.

"Look at your float," my father said.

I looked just in time to see my float firmly plucked beneath the surface. I tensed myself but had no time to give a jerk on the line. The fish gave the jerk and set the hook and caught himself. I had only to pull the fish in on the strong twine and the sturdy bamboo pole.

"You were lucky," my father said. "If he had been a little bigger he would have caught you."

"Yes, sir," I said, knowing I had been caught asleep, an unforgivable sin for a fisherman.

"Just about the biggest red perch I ever saw," my father said, laying the now passive fish across his palm. "Must go twelve inches."

"Maybe fifteen inches," I said.

"Maybe," my father said.

I watched my father string the fish on a gill line and lower it into the water. It lay quietly gasping beside the boat. "Never mind admiring that one," my father said. "You can't claim any credit for it anyway. It did everything but jump into the boat. Get baited up and let's see if you can really catch a fish."

"Yes, sir," I said and threaded a fresh worm on my hook.

And we hung on the water through the warm summer afternoon. My father dropped the plug all around the little inlet: near the lily pads, near the fallen tree, near the rock, near the snag. And nothing happened. My father began looking out of the inlet as if trying to think of another likely spot. "There should be fish here," my father said. "I know there are fish here." I watched my father go from pads to tree to rock to snag again.

I watched the grim set of my father's face, and I knew that the fishing trip was not working out too well. I managed to draw very little consolation from the usually consoling fact that I had caught more fish than my father.

I stared again into the water but the ripples of the plug returning to the boat shattered my reflection, and the pieces of my face danced among the rushes. "There are fish here," my father said. "That fish of yours wasn't alone, you can just bet. We've seen them jump but they just won't bite for any bait I've got. I tell you what. If you let me use the belly off your perch, I'll try again and see if I can raise the granddaddy of all pickerel."

We both looked at the perch lying just under the surface of the water. It was not an unusual thing my father had asked. He always cut the belly off old roaches and shiners and sometimes even little perches. But today it was different. We had only the one fish to show for our day's fishing, and that one fish was perhaps the granddaddy of all perches, and I had beaten my father one to nothing.

"Well, what do you say?" my father said.

"Sure, I guess so," I said. I watched my father deftly slice the belly off the perch and trim it to a more or less fishlike shape with the two little belly fins on it. I saw my father toss the mutilated perch into the water where it floated just a little way off. "It's no good now," my father said.

I watched my father cast from pads to tree to rock to snag, and I watched the belly come swimming palely back to the boat, squirming through the water. Pads, tree, rock, snag. Again. Again. Cigarette after cigarette dropped hissing into the water.

So it was warm, quiet, and still on the water until the sun stood clearly just above the trees and just beneath the softly hanging boat. I did not watch my father and I did not look at the mutilated fish. I knew my father was standing with his back turned to me and the fish. I knew my father was casting farther and farther out toward the entrance of the inlet. I heard my father grunt under his breath, and turning I saw my father rest his rod over the side of the boat and sit down. "We better start back," my father said. "We'll free the line from the bush as we go. You reel up the line while I row toward the bush."

My father began to row and I began to reel. I reeled as carefully as I could because I knew my father was mad about catching the bush and might yell at me. But even though I piled all the line up on one side of the reel, my father didn't say anything.

When we got near the bush my father took the rod and quickly flipped the bait into the water and passed the rod back. I started to reel in the remaining line. "Let it trail behind," my father said roughly. "Let out more line."

I carefully let out a little more line and clutched the rod. This was the first time I had ever used my father's rod. I looked anxiously toward my father for an indication that I was doing right. "For God's sake, turn around and watch the line," my father shouted.

My father rowed back toward the pier and the refreshment stand, but not across the middle of the lake. He rowed along the edges following every indentation of the shore and rowing very slowly.

Although we moved very slowly, I knew that we were progressing inevitably toward the pier. The little whirlpools made by the oars swirled astern and dissolved. As the oar left the water the whirlpool was like thick clear glass, a little blue, and swirling very rapidly deep in the water, but as it fell back it swirled less rapidly and less deeply and at last it was only a small mild spot on the surface beside the gentle wake. Two or three such spots could be seen at a time, the most distant constantly disappearing and being replaced and disappearing and being replaced, always the same by the boat on the markerless water, but always different beside the implacable shore.

I stared at the spot where I thought the bait was, way back beyond the farthest mark of the oar. I imagined a pickerel, the granddaddy of all pickerel, sniffing the bait. I set myself for the strike and clutched the rod, but no strike came. I lapsed again into lethargy.

The strokes of the oars seemed to be slower and slower. The oars dripped and the boat gurgled softly as it slipped through the water, but otherwise there was no sound as the whirlpools slid relentlessly astern. I did not dare to look around to see how close we were to the pier. I lifted the tip of the rod and lowered it several times, inciting a hypothetical fish to strike by making the bait seem to speed from its very jaws. But no fish struck.

At last we were approaching the pier. I could hear the voices of men coming over the water. The boat slowly passed our car parked beside the lake with several others. I heard someone call, "Any luck?" But my father didn't answer. I clutched the rod, my father's rod, before the men on the pier and watched the line intently.

Even so the strike almost jerked the rod from my hands because I had no real hope of a strike. The reel hummed. "Set the drag," my father shouted and, knowing I didn't know what the drag was, reached over my shoulder and touched the reel. I held the rod toward my father. "I have to take care of the boat," my father said. "You'll have to land him." The clicking had almost stopped. "Reel in," my father shouted. "Faster." The line felt slack. I thought I had lost the fish. "Faster," my father said tensely.

I reeled as fast as I could, sick to my stomach for fear I had lost the fish. My father would be sure then that I was no fisherman. The thought of further censure brought tears to my eyes. I reeled as fast as I could.

Suddenly the handle of the reel was jerked from my fingers. "Let him go," my father said. I heard the clicking of the reel and felt the violent life of the pole, but through my dimmed eyes I could see nothing.

The clicking slowed. "Reel," my father said. I reeled the fish in and let him out and in and out, closer and closer, feeling more and more the sense of mastery and more and more the realization that I must not make a mistake now.

I made no mistake as I watched through my cleared eyes the

swirling of the water and the dim form of the fish. One last time I reeled in and my father made a swoop with the net and the fish was in the boat.

The men on the pier shouted when the fish came in. Someone blew a horn. My father slapped me on the back. And on the pier my father shared a bottle with the other men, but I had a coke all for myself.

The Manhunt

In the middle of the morning, Ken Marvin suddenly became aware that the stream he had been fishing since sunrise had already led him into the fringes of a swamp. He stood perplexed a moment with the water gently tugging at his boots. He thought at first of following the stream a bit farther, but when he tried to take a step he found himself up to his ankles in muck and sinking all the time. Although he had little difficulty in working his way back to better footing, he was shaken.

He sat on the bank to catch his breath and quiet the trembling in his legs. He glanced at his watch. Of course he hadn't wound it all week, but in any case the time was right for him to pack up his rod and take off across country for the logging road where he had left his car.

As he stood up, he noticed his billfold lying on the ground beside his pack. He reached for it and stopped with his hand extended: that might have been all that anyone had ever found to tell what had become of him, first the car and then this, and nothing more forever. That was rather more peace and solitude than he had bargained for when he came to the woods—certainly it was no improvement on the alternatives already facing him: to resume the role of the stranger who lies awake beside a peacefully sleeping wife and thinks of women, young and passionate, or to disappear into the disguise of the man nameless and hiding, afraid to claim even a profession for himself.

He picked up the billfold and he picked up the pack. There was still a long walk ahead of him. If he started at once he could take it easy and calm himself on the long walk back, and he could hold off until the very edge of the woods—and perhaps beyond—the haste and tension that usually accompanied his turning home.

For just a moment longer he looked at the stream and he looked at the trees. He listened to the water and the wind and a frog and a cricket and a blue jay.

As he left the stream, the undergrowth was thick but he shortly found a footpath going in more or less the right direction, and after a mile the footpath turned into a cartpath, and that quite gently led him into somebody's back pasture.

He was well out into the clearing before he noticed the large crowd around the house. He assumed there was an auction and thought for a moment of stopping to buy a present for his wife, just a little something to thank her for understanding how much he needed this trip by himself. But he still had far enough to go so that he was able to talk himself out of it before he got close. It would be awkward at best, out here in the Maine woods, to be the only stranger at a country auction. He might buy the wrong thing anyway. His wife might even resent not being taken to the auction herself—no, that really wasn't fair. After all she wasn't the one being driven crazy by her change of life.

But in any case it might be better if he didn't have to mention the auction at all, so he stayed as far away from the house as he could. Besides, he wasn't ready yet to come out of the woods, to start all that up again, to relinquish for good and for all the possibility of circling back to the brook in the swamp.

Although he was careful not to appear too interested as he was passing closest to the house, he was aware that a man was walking down to intercept him. The man was dressed in tan like a soldier and gave, even from a distance, the impression of authority. When Ken could no longer pretend the man wasn't there, he turned and saw him hung about with the signs of his trade: whistle, badge, handcuffs, and gun. He was a very large man.

"Good morning, sheriff," Ken said hastily. "Something I can do for you?" Ready or not, he was wrenched out of the woods.

"Routine matter," the sheriff said. "I see you been fishing. Mind if I check your catch?" His eyebrows twitched when he talked. They were enormous. Grizzled and tangled and wiry, they jutted a good inch and a half from his forehead, a positive thicket.

"As easily done as said." Ken smiled weakly. He had been very foolish to be alarmed. After all, sheriffs might appear anywhere, even here, little as he liked to think it. "I haven't so much as seen a fish," he said. "The streams are too high with all this rain. I've had a fine walk though."

"Well, that's something," the sheriff said. "But I might as well check your fishing permit while I'm at it."

"Of course," Ken said. "It's in my pack here." His pack was really his oilskins and sou'wester rolled up around his Spartan lunch and an elegant silver flask full of whiskey. It was a hip flask he found few opportunities to carry but always kept full against contingencies that never seemed to arise.

"Non-resident permit. Seems to be OK," the sheriff said. "And did you hike in or drive?"

"Drove partway," Ken said.

"Well, if I check your driver's license and registration I won't have to do it next time I see you out on the highway," the sheriff said. "Ah, yes," he said as he examined the papers, "that clears that up. Your car was spotted in the woods over in back of the ridge, and we thought it just might be stolen and abandoned."

"You sure keep an eye on things," Ken said, laughing without reservation.

"That's what we're here for," the sheriff said. "And if you're headed for your car now, you're a little out of your way—not much, but a little. That where you're headed?"

"Why, yes," Ken said. "I am."

"All you have to do is go on along here—oh, half a mile or so—and turn right at the crossroad. That will take you straight over the ridge."

"Much obliged," Ken said.

"Don't mention it." The sheriff stepped back to give Ken passage. "But wait a minute," he said. "If you've been fishing through there, perhaps you can give us a little help." His eyes swept over the country Ken had been crossing.

"Glad to—if I can," Ken said.

"Well, did you by any chance see or hear anything unusual in there?"

"No, I'm sure not," Ken said. "Something wrong?"

"The fact is," the sheriff said, "we're forming a big search party to go into the woods to look for a lost baby."

"Good lord," Ken said. He glanced toward the trees. They were close together along the edges of the clearing, and there was much underbrush. Flecks of darkness showed everywhere.

"Some of us have been out all night, but now we're trying to go at it more systematically."

"Yes," Ken said, "that's bad country, some of it. Rivers, swamps, cliffs."

"Did you see any animal sign?" the sheriff said.

"I'm afraid I'm not much of a woodsman," Ken said.

"There's not too much to worry about from animals this time of year. There are bears around, though, and bobcats aren't unknown."

"It looks bad," Ken said.

The sheriff shrugged. "Thanks anyway," he said. "Straight along here and right at the crossroads." He began to turn away.

"Wait," Ken said. "I wonder if you could use me to fill a place in your line?"

The sheriff stopped and faced Ken again. "Why, that's very kind, I'm sure. We need every man we can get. Come on up to the house and have some coffee. It will be a little while before we can get started. I have to radio my deputy to stop watching your car. We need him for other things now, but it was just possible that the thief—if there had been one—would have come back to the car. And you must tell me if you saw any other fishermen in there this morning. They might be able to tell us something." He led off toward the house.

"I'm afraid I can't help you there," Ken said. "I haven't seen anybody since I drove in yesterday. I went back to sleep in the car but I haven't seen a soul."

"Well, we'll just say you've scouted that section for us, and we'll start on something else."

The sheriff walked through the crowd of men to a police car parked on the lawn in front of the house. He unlocked the car and got in and began to use the radio. Ken had followed along in his wake and found himself close to the car and quite in the center of the group. As he waited for something to happen, it seemed to him that he was being stared at, but he decided that the men were really looking past him at the car. Even so, in order not to cross glances with them, a roughly dressed crowd, he magnetized himself to the car and stared straight ahead at an enormous red ear with a great dangling lobe. Among the messages relating to the search, Ken heard directions being given for taking the guard off his car.

Then the car door opened and the sheriff stepped out. He had put on horn-rimmed glasses while he was using the radio, and he looked rather like a professor who might have been a third-string tackle once upon a time. "All right," the sheriff said. "This field has got to be searched." He pointed to a large hay field south of the house. "Line up on the other side of the wall."

The sheriff started them off in a line that stretched all across the field. Ken was somewhere near the middle, and he could hear the sheriff close behind him exhorting them to keep the line straight and firm. They went slowly through the tall wet grass, silently except for the shouts of the sheriff. At the end of the field they crossed the road and came back through two smaller fields there.

As they approached the house, Ken could see the sheriff talking on the radio in his car. He hadn't realized until then how very silent the search had become, only the swish of the grass against his boots and a muffled oath as someone stumbled. The sheriff was standing beside his car when they gathered around. "They're sending an airplane," he said. "We'll wait for it."

"What'll we do till it gets here?" a man behind Ken shouted. Ken looked at the ground so no one would think he had spoken.

"Wait," the sheriff said without looking up from locking the car door.

The group began to disperse, and Ken turned, not knowing where to go, and found himself standing beside a knot of men squatting at the base of one of the large trees on the lawn. As he glanced down at them, their eyes flicked over him and were at once veiled. He was acutely uncomfortable but couldn't move without at least being able to give himself a good excuse. He looked unhurriedly away and studied his surroundings.

The farm gave the impression that it was gradually dying, that some vital force was drawing inward from the boundaries. The more remote fields were filling up with juniper and pine. The outbuildings were in various stages of disintegration. One, at some distance from the house, had fallen down so long ago that it was now only a mound of vines. Ken couldn't begin to imagine what it might have been. Another small stone building was roofless. It might have been a smokehouse. The farmhouse itself, however, a large house, had surprisingly been painted not many years before—say at just about the time somebody might have been putting in a lot of overtime in a war plant. There was surely nothing in the farm itself to explain such prosperity. Why, even the barn attached to the house had collapsed recently—at least it showed the same paint job as the house—and lay exactly as it had fallen.

Half a dozen men were poking along the edges of the jumbled timbers, which hadn't yet fallen so far they couldn't fall farther and snap a leg. A line of men sat along the edge of the porch swinging their legs and drinking coffee poured from blue enamel pitchers by women wearing men's jackets and sweaters. Ken wondered which of the women was the mother of the child.

None seemed right for the part—no tears or struggle against tears, no words or gestures from the men. More women were busy in the kitchen, but there too he could see no sign. If the thing had happened in his family, his wife would have been either the one organizing the work on the vegetables for the stew or the one at the table with the field telephone. But neither woman seemed young enough to be the mother of a baby. He gave up the futile speculation.

Under each of the large trees on the lawn a small knot of men squatted on their heels and plucked grass blades or scratched the ground with sticks. Others came and went around the corner of the house by twos and threes. And always more men were coming down the road to join the search.

They came from one direction only because, although the road didn't exactly end at the house, it did become the cartpath which became the footpath which lost itself in the woods near the swamp. He glanced involuntarily back over the way he had come. There was a small party of men just disappearing into the scrubby cut-over thicket near where he had come out.

"We can search the other field again." Ken, having completed his leisurely inspection of the place, looked down again at the group at his feet. The speaker was a bearded man, a young man with bright blue eyes and weathered skin. He wore a sou'wester like Ken's but he wore it with a sort of ramshackle authority that Ken knew he could never attain. "If we need something to do, we can search the other field," the bearded man said. "I went through it last night in the dark and twice this morning, and I know how it is to have to sit still. I was here all night, and I stood in that field after everybody went home, and I listened. If there were anything to hear, I could have heard it. I was listening down beyond the far end of the field in the brush just before daylight. There was fog off the brook down there. A buck walked out of the fog, and I put my hand on his side—right on his side—and I could feel him freeze, and then he was gone. Right on his side, he was that close." He was laughing with excitement and his hand was extended so that Ken felt as if he had turned just too late to see the buck spring out from under the reaching hand.

"Every time a new gang gets here, they search that field," the bearded man said. "If the man who's on the west end of the line is a woodsman, they find some big cat tracks along the wall way up in the northeast corner. Mighty big cat tracks. A bobcat will jump a man out of pure meanness. Then they swing around by the barn and find the garden, and that makes them think about the boy—teenager from the village—that was hired yesterday to work in the garden. And while they're thinking about that, they come to a place in the orchard where somebody's been digging. So they send up to the barn for a shovel, and they dig up a calf that died a week ago. Three times I've smelled that calf: it's dead."

"What about the pigs?" one of the other men said.

"Ah, the pigs," the bearded man said, like Socrates, as if he had been thinking about the pigs all along. Ken hadn't thought about them at all and still didn't know what everybody was nodding about.

"Knew a feller had a stroke and fell in the pen and had his leg et off," another man said.

This was such a revelation to Ken that he set off to look for the pigs without wondering at all if he had a good excuse for leaving. As he turned away, the bearded man was saying, "Looks like that gang's getting ready to do something. Guess I better take them through the field."

Knowing there was no point in volunteering for that search party because he'd never be good at finding cat tracks, Ken wandered around to the back of the house and poked self-consciously into trampled thickets and peered under a rickety board walk that ran from the kitchen door to the barn over a patch of marshy ground and some old foundations. He stayed a moment to watch a firetruck pumping out an abandoned well that had been remembered suddenly by an old man who had been a boy on that farm.

At last he found the pigs in the barn. He leaned on the

partition and looked at them. They looked at him. With a stick, he poked through their litter for a rag, a tiny shoe, a doll. They rooted around, turning over the straw in a frenzy of protest. He looked at them. They looked at him.

"I say," the man next to him said, "that a strange car up in here would be noticed and remembered."

"I guess you're right," Ken said as if he had at last been convinced although actually this was another entirely new idea to him. "If a strange car should ever find its way back in here."

"Which I doubt," the man said.

"It doesn't seem likely," Ken said, fighting to keep from putting on a phony Maine accent as he belatedly understood where the strange-car idea put him. It would clearly have been much better if he had gone on his way after the sheriff cleared him.

"Just what I say," the man said. "Mean-looking boar."

"Sure is," Ken said. He looked at them, and they looked at him out of their pig eyes, but he turned his head and went away because they seemed to know he didn't know which was the boar.

Crawling under the skeletons of tractors, climbing into the remains of truck bodies, he came to an orchard where two men were digging. The sheriff was watching glumly. A teenage boy was standing near the hole.

"It's only the calf," the boy said.

"Mmm," one of the men said and went on digging.

"I was right here in the garden all the time," the boy said. "She was talking to me awhile and then she went back around the house."

"Mmm," the other man said. They came to the calf. It was dead.

"Do you suppose," Ken said softly to the sheriff, "that if you took the calf out and dug under it—"

"I read them all the time," the sheriff said, "and I did that the time I dug up the calf: the ground hadn't been touched."

"It was a thought," Ken said.

"I appreciate it," the sheriff said.

"They say the pigs are a thought too."

"There're lots of thoughts," the sheriff said, brooding.

"It was nothing but the calf," the boy said.

"Mmm," one of the men said, scraping dirt back into the hole. The sheriff turned on his heel and started through the garden toward the house. The boy ran after him. "Any clues, sheriff?" he called.

"Not a one," the sheriff said. "This where you were working yesterday?" He stopped and studied the ground.

"Right around here," the boy said.

"She was out here, you say?"

"Her mother sent her out to bother me, and she was playing awhile on the grass under that tree." He pointed to the nearest apple tree. "And then she went around front."

"Around front?" the sheriff said. He looked off in the direction the boy indicated. The barn was between them and the house.

"She was bothering me, so I sent her around to her swing."

"I see," the sheriff said, "but you don't know if she ever got around front?"

"She was headed there," the boy said.

The sheriff headed there, followed by Ken and the boy, but once they were around the corner of the barn, they veered over to the well. A larger group of men was waiting near the pumper now. "How you coming?" the sheriff said.

"Should know pretty soon," a fireman said. "Don't know why they ever gave up this well. It's a corker."

The sheriff moved toward the barn. Ken went with him. The boy stayed at the well. "Think they'll find anything there?" Ken said.

"Not a chance," the sheriff said. "It took two strong men to move some of the junk off that well, and it hadn't been moved before in years."

"Why bother?" Ken said.

"Oh, you always pump out wells. People can see you're doing something, and a lot can happen in the time it takes to pump out a good well. I tell you, Mr. Johnson—"

"Marvin," Ken said.

"What's that?" the sheriff said. He stopped and turned toward Ken.

"Marvin," Ken said. He stood facing the sheriff. "You called me Johnson but my name's Marvin."

"Of course it is," the sheriff said. "I saw it on your papers. That Johnson business is just something we say around here. We're always saying, 'I tell you, Mr. Johnson.' I don't know why we say it, but we say it all the time, and we say it to everybody. I can tell you your home address, your car registration, and the name of your employer if you want to test me."

Ken didn't make any response because he had a sudden vision of the sheriff sitting in his car while the men were finishing the search of the hay fields; and the vision, like a dream, told him without words exactly what the sheriff was saying on his car radio and exactly what the answer would be when it came: K. Marvin, this city, guilty of three traffic violations in the past four years, two overtime parking, one red light. Ken could even see the headlines: Local Man Grilled as Sex Fiend Suspect. That would look very good on his record.

"Don't think we don't appreciate your wanting to help," the sheriff said, "but the truth is summer people just don't turn out very much—no offense intended."

"I've got kids of my own," Ken said. He didn't trust himself to try a longer speech. He had all he could do to keep himself from whipping out his billfold and frantically offering up the photographs.

"Well, I'll tell you right out," the sheriff said, "there's one hell of a long line of parked cars back along the road there, and there's only one car within miles that doesn't have a Maine number plate on it, and it's my business to know how many summer families there are around here."

"Yeah," Ken said cautiously.

"I'm sorry," the sheriff said. He laid his hand gently on Ken's arm. "Here I am blowing off to the wrong guy. Isn't that just the way life is? Hell, man, you're just the one who wouldn't want to face his own wife and kids if he didn't do his share up here on the mountain."

"Yeah," Ken said. "Especially since I know the area." The sheriff tried to be impassive but he didn't make it, and Ken knew at once that he had said too much. "I've fished through here a couple of times before." The sheriff managed to be impassive this time, but his eyes did flick toward the brush at the end of the field where the fog had been earlier in the morning. "Mostly on the other side of the ridge," Ken said and quit.

"Every experienced woodsman counts at a time like this," the sheriff said. Ken was through talking for a while, but the sheriff seemed not to notice. "I hope you won't mind if I ask a personal question," the sheriff said. Fortunately he didn't wait to see if Ken was going to be able to give the only possible answer. "I mean it helps in my work sometimes if I'm able to place a man by his accent and I don't get much chance to talk to people from your state, you see what I mean? I mean is your accent typical of your state?"

"Good lord, no," Ken said. He rushed ahead, sensing an opportunity to make himself a little less foreign. "Why, I'm practically a local boy, born and raised not thirty miles from Boston."

"That's what I figured," the sheriff said. "And I wouldn't mention it if I were you. Just a friendly tip, you know, but we're too close to Boston here and get a lot of the wrong kind of summer people—no offense. There was a lot of trouble last summer with a gang of queers that rented a place on the lake. They went around with lipstick on and like that. I got them out of town before anybody got hurt. But Boston just isn't popular around here if you don't mind. A man like you, trying to raise a decent family, knows all about that."

They had been standing between the well and the barn. Now the sheriff dropped Ken's arm and they went on together into the barn. People made room for them as they stepped up to look at the pigs. "Mean-looking bugger, sheriff." It was the same man who had said it to Ken before, only now he had a long stick and was scratching the back of the pig he obviously meant.

Ken looked at the boar, but the boar wasn't interested in him.

"Mean enough," the sheriff said.

"Going to butcher the lot or just him?" the man said.

"Not any of them for a while," the sheriff said. "Not until we get the well checked out anyway."

"Can't wait too long or it won't do any good," the man said. "You'll never know what they et." Ken was afraid he'd throw up, so he began to work his way out of the barn.

"Another hour won't matter," the sheriff said. 'I had the ag department on the phone last night. We've got plenty of time."

"Any strangers been noticed up in here?" the man was saying. Ken didn't hear what the sheriff said in reply. He was already out of the barn. He wanted only to keep on going and get the hell out of there altogether and find his car and go home, but as he came around the corner of the house he saw how impossible it would be to sneak off.

The lawn was now entirely covered with men. Women were serving coffee and doughnuts on the porch. Ken wanted a cup of coffee but he didn't take it because he was too flustered to be able to tell if it would look funnier if he did or if he didn't. Everyone seemed to be pretending not to watch him. He drifted back to the group around the bearded man.

"Henry knows pigs," the bearded man said. "What do you say, Henry?"

"No," Henry said. He was dressed all in heavy denim and wore knee-length leather boots. His hair curled over his collar like a woman's.

"See?" the man with the beard said. "Henry says no."

"No blood," Henry said. Everyone waited. "A pig will toss," he said, "and a pig will shake, and a pig will splatter blood all over the walls. Rats, snakes, a dog one time. Always blood. No blood, no."

"There's a winter's eating on those pigs," the man with the beard said. "These people will be awful hungry by spring if we kill their pigs. Poor bastard lost enough on the hay we trampled. Kill his pigs too and he'll really have something to come home to

—no pigs, no hay, lost kid, wife out of her head up there." He raised his eyes toward an upper window of the house.

"Where is he?" Ken said in spite of knowing he ought not to open his mouth.

"Hospital," the man with the beard said.

"How come?" Ken said.

"Cut off his leg with a chain saw," one of the others said.

"They better lay off the pigs," the man with the beard said. He started to get up.

"Sheriff knows it well as I do," Henry said.

The man with the beard stood up and turned, as if it had been his intention from the beginning, to watch a small yellow airplane that flew low over the house and out over the south field, slewing heavily through the air like a car in snow.

The sheriff appeared at the corner of the house, striding toward his car. He unlocked the car and reached in for the handset of his radio. "It's about time," he said, looking at the plane as if the pilot could read his face as well as his voice. "The well is dry and in another ten minutes it would have been the pigs and then god knows. Have him stay low and in sight of the house as much as possible." He put the handset away and locked the car. "Now there's one thing we haven't tried," he said, "and it's something they can't cover from the air. I mean the fence rows."

"OK," the man with the beard said.

"No," the sheriff said. "I want you to stay here, George, and be ready to lead a party at a moment's notice. This field's about played out."

"Gottcha," the man with the beard said. "That cut-over land due north of here up to the foot of the cliffs. We stayed out of there because it's too thick for a man to force his way through very well, but a child down low might get through. There was a bear in there last fall."

"Henry—" the sheriff began.

"Power line right of way," Henry said.

"Right," the sheriff said. "But not until I give the word. You'll need two big parties and I'll need a small one. Hey, kid,

come on and make yourself useful. Earn that cup of coffee."
He spoke this time to the boy who had been working in the
garden.

"I'm with you, sheriff," the boy said. He came over with his
coffee cup in one hand and a stack of doughnuts in the other.

"See that you stay with me," the sheriff said. "I may need
messages carried." He looked to see who else to take.

"I'll go with you, sheriff," Ken said. He didn't know what he
thought he was thinking. Perhaps he wasn't thinking at all. Perhaps he just couldn't bear to discover that the sheriff really
would pick him after the kid.

"OK," the sheriff said as if it were a matter of no importance
to him. He barely glanced at Ken before he went on picking his
men. One of his men was the man who had twice called the
boar mean-looking.

"Why me?" the man said. "Why not some of these guys who
haven't been out once even. Is that fair?"

"No," the sheriff said, "it's not fair. But that's the way it is.
There's nothing fair about a kid being lost in the woods and god
knows what else besides. And there's nothing fair about the
stores that are closed today and the farm work that is piling up,
but there are a lot of men who know that fair or not they've got
themselves to shave tomorrow morning, and that's a pretty
tough job when you can't look yourself in the face."

The man flushed. "OK," he said, "so I'll raise a beard." He
was obviously trying to make a joke of the whole thing.

"Ask George Booth about beards," the sheriff said. "He'll tell
you how much trouble they are." He laughed.

"I feel like a jerk," the man said under his breath.

"So what," the sheriff said, "as long as you aren't a jerk?"

Ken saw now that he had gained nothing by volunteering and
wished he had forced the sheriff to make a move and perhaps,
one way or the other, put an end to all this cat and mouse. Well,
he wouldn't stand for any more of that. He knew how it would
be in the woods, men straggling off in all directions and at all
paces until he was left alone. It would be a simple matter then

to straggle over to his unguarded car and be clear of the state before he was missed. Then he would very shortly be talking about this day with somebody, his wife perhaps, telling it as a funny story, perhaps, reducing it to words—but could he really, to his wife, of all people, ever say actually, "In Maine they thought I looked like—well—like a degenerate"?

The kid stood beside him while they waited for the sheriff to get ready. "I seen it all," the kid said, "only there wasn't nothing to see."

Even when the sheriff had his men picked out and had given final instructions to George and Henry and had inquired when the stew would be ready, he still hesitated. He said to Ken, "Look, I feel like a bastard, you having been so cooperative and all, but the truth is, not knowing you, you see what I mean, but what I did was let the air out of one of your tires. That was before we knew whose car it was, and we didn't want it going anywhere while we weren't looking. I feel bad about that now, believe me, and what I'd like to do is have one of my men go by there and put on your spare for you."

"No, no," Ken said.

"No trouble," the sheriff said. "I've got to send a man over past there anyway."

"Please, no," Ken said.

"It would be very kind of you," the sheriff said, "to let me do this in order to make up for what I thought—in the line of duty, of course, but still I feel pretty rotten about it now."

"What can I say?" Ken said aloud to the sheriff and repeated silently to himself. At least the deputy would be finished there long before Ken could walk back to the car. It would still work out.

"Thank you," the sheriff said. "I'd have felt very bad if I couldn't have done anything."

"No," Ken said automatically, "thank you."

"I'll need the car keys," the sheriff said, "to get the spare out of the trunk. Don't worry, my man will be back with the keys long before we get out of the woods."

Ken silently handed over the car keys. It was just possible that the sheriff meant only what he said and that he wasn't simply confiscating the keys.

The sheriff turned with the keys in his hand and crossed the lawn to what looked like a state trooper. The two men spoke together. Ken couldn't hear what was said, but he saw the trooper nod and start back up the road toward another police car. The sheriff came back empty-handed.

The sheriff led his group to the corner of the wall near the garden. He put two men on each side of the west wall and started them off to the north, and he put two men on each side of the south wall and started them off to the east. Ken was on the south side of the south wall with the kid. The sheriff himself stayed on that side of the wall.

When Ken got to the end of the first field, the sheriff was waiting to offer him a cigarette. Ken took it and the sheriff held out his lighter, snapping it as he reached toward Ken's face. The lighter didn't work, and the sheriff withdrew his hand, peering at the lighter and continuing to snap it. "Must be the flint," he said. He put his hand into his pocket and pulled out a fistful of change and disintegrating Kleenex and keys. Among the keys, Ken saw the keys to his own car.

"A dime will fix it," the sheriff said, and picked a dime out of the mess in his hand.

Ken didn't trust himself to say anything. He was afraid his voice might show his terror or, even worse, his triumph as he thought of the secret key stuck up inside a bumper guard.

The sheriff tried his lighter again. It flamed at once. They both lighted their cigarettes. "You people continue along here," the sheriff said. "I'm going to go over and see how they're making out along the other wall."

Ken nodded. All he had to do now was lose the kid, and he'd be off. He could change the tire in five minutes—if it really was flat—unless, of course, the sheriff was making it too easy for him to make a move. It might be just as well to wait a bit and see what way the wind was blowing. And when he did make his move, the sheriff, with the keys safe in his pocket, would never be looking for that particular move.

It would be easy to lose the kid, Ken discovered, once they got started again, because whenever the going got in the least rough, the kid would make long detours away from the wall. He'd miss fifty yards of wall in order to avoid a briar patch or a blow-down. Ken, who found himself caught up in the search, was irritated that he wasn't free to come down on him sharply and doubly irritated because he supposed the kid thought him a fool for looking carefully in even the most impossible places.

The going got rougher and rougher way down in back where the fields had long since been allowed to revert to woods—except for the walls there was no way of telling they had ever been fields. In fact they had had time to grow a crop of timber and be cut over and grow up again in brambles.

He crawled and climbed and bulled his way through, often walking on top of the ruinous wall. Stones rolled under his feet, logs crumbled, vines wrapped themselves around his legs. He was soaked with sweat. He took off his windbreaker and began to get chilled. His legs were trembling when at last the entire party reassembled at the farthest corner of the last conceivable lot. Just beyond that wall the land dropped suddenly into a swamp.

The sheriff didn't look at the swamp, but he did look at his watch and said, "I guess that's it. The stew should be ready by now."

Ken was surprised that he hadn't made his break before this, but at the moment he was too exhausted to strike out by himself. The search had led them off in quite the wrong direction anyway, and he'd have to go back past the house to reach his car; so he stumbled along behind the others.

The firetruck was gone from beside the well. The barn stood empty. Ken ducked into the barn for a good belt of whiskey. The pigs lay sleeping in their pen. Someone had dragged an old-fashioned grindstone out into the middle of the barn floor. As he tilted his head back and looked along his flask he saw the worn and darkened handle and part of the freshly burnished blade of a knife projecting from a timber not a foot from his head. Still holding the flask, he took the knife and hid it among some boards stacked off to one side. Then he had another drink and went around to the front of the house.

There was a long line of men waiting for stew, but Ken was able to get a cup of coffee without waiting, and he sat down to eat his sandwiches. He knew when he leaned his back against the tree that he'd had it. He was afraid he might not be able to walk all the way back to his car even if he got his chance.

Around on the other side of the tree, the sheriff was talking with the bearded man. "How'd it go?" the sheriff said.

"Just fine," the bearded man said. "They began going home just after you left. Can't be more than a hundred still here."

"Did you search over north and along the power line?"

"Didn't get to it."

"Then we've got that to do this afternoon," the sheriff said.

"Some Boy Scouts brought a St. Bernard."

"After all this rain?"

"It would just make a big circle in the field and keep coming back to the barn," the man with the beard said. Ken looked instinctively toward the barn where several men poked thoughtfully at the fallen timbers.

"That's an idea too," the sheriff said. "Things quiet otherwise?"

"Just fine." The Boy Scouts filed past with their mess kits full of steaming stew.

"Here comes my old lady," the man with the beard said. "She's going to scalp me for all this time up here."

"Hello, sheriff," a woman said. "You getting any work out of him?"

"Couldn't do without him, Mrs. Booth," the sheriff said. Ken, who had lately felt a passion for scrutinizing other marriages, turned frankly around to see what the bearded man's old lady would look like. She was a very pretty woman, a little older than he would have guessed, which only meant he had been fooled by the beard into thinking the bearded man looked older than he was. Except for a gingham apron she was dressed for the woods: boots, jeans, and jacket.

When Ken turned around to look at the woman, the sheriff spotted him. "There you are," the sheriff said. "Feel up to tackling the power line this afternoon?"

"I'm afraid my legs are shot," Ken said. "I'm afraid I've had it."

"I tell you what," the sheriff said, "if you still feel like helping—"

"Of course," Ken said as quickly as possible.

"What I need is to have somebody stay at the radio this afternoon, somebody steady and reliable. I'll show you how to work it, and you can rest all afternoon and still be a big help, OK?"

"Of course," Ken said. "Glad to do what I can." At least he'd have a few hours, while he sat in his goldfish bowl, to try to make some kind of plan, to decide whether it would be worse to ask for a lawyer too soon or too late. He was already certain he couldn't prove his innocence of any charge that might be brought against him.

"I'm going to bring George some stew," the woman said. "How about you, sheriff?"

"Much obliged," the sheriff said.

Henry, the pig expert, was going off around the corner of the house together with the man from the barn—the one who had twice called the boar mean-looking—and half a dozen other men. George's wife was already coming back with a bowl in each hand when everyone heard a horn blowing in the distance. At first it sounded like a short-circuited horn, but then they could tell it was someone making a racket. The car was clearly coming all the way to the house. They could hear the racing motor now. Men began moving toward the road to see. Some began running. Ken was literally unable to move. The sheriff stood up and came around the tree until he stood beside Ken. His bowl was just at Ken's eye level. It was a very real bowl of stew, steaming hot. The random size of the chunks of potato and carrot and meat was convincing. The color of the liquid was genuine, never made with food coloring. It looked like the stew they used to have at home.

A small black car careered up onto the lawn. An old woman was leaning out the window screaming, "The child is found," as if she had been waiting all her life to scream something out the window of a speeding car.

There was no more time. The steam from the sheriff's bowl drifted gently between Ken and the car. "Let it be a bear," Ken said.

"What did you say?" the sheriff said.

"The child is found safe," the woman screamed.

There was a cheer. "Lucky kid," the sheriff said. He cheered. The kid stopped gobbling his stew long enough to cheer briefly. The man with the beard cheered with one arm around his cheering wife. Ken cheered. He picked himself up.

"Your keys," the sheriff said digging in his pocket and bringing out Ken's keys. "Your car's all ready to go. My man even took the flat in and blew it up, so you're all ready to go."

"Thanks," Ken said. He felt expansive now that he had beaten the sheriff at his own game, besides there was nothing to be gained by calling the man a liar.

The old woman ran tottering from the car to where the sheriff stood. "The child is found safe," she gasped. "Just walking out of the woods. On the other side of the mountain." The old woman turned and waved her arms over the crowd. "Safe," she screamed, "safe, safe," and subsided without transition into an elegant Victorian faint.

Women rallied to her and hid her completely. Ken and the sheriff were elbowed into the background. "I almost forgot," the sheriff said. He reached into another pocket. "When my man was fooling around with the jack, this fell out of somewhere." It was the secret key.

"Thanks," Ken said with a difference.

"It was the least we could do after the way you pitched in," the sheriff said.

"Anytime," Ken said.

"Lots of people don't look at it that way. They don't like to get mixed up in things."

"Anytime," Ken said. But he was deathly afraid.

A Story of Love, Etc.

I WAS THINKING about the Depression and discovered things had gone so far that even I could scarcely believe there had ever been such a time. I found myself wondering if maybe I hadn't read it all in something by Chekhov or Gogol or Dostoyevsky.

I was thinking about the story of How Father Lost the Store, which is a story everybody knows, and about How I Lost All My Teeth at the Age of Twenty-five, which isn't really a story at all but a kind of blackout tableau, a quick dark hole in the face. Did you ever notice, by the way, how Chekhov's peasants always seemed to have plenty of teeth for whatever black bread they got? That's remarkable, isn't it?

But I was thinking about these things only as a warm-up for thinking about Bill and Ellie Martin, which is something I take on from time to time when I feel particularly strong.

Now, what I know is this. Bill Martin was a master carpenter, and if there was work he got it. He was sent for from all over—when there was work. Mostly there was no work. He was the only man for counties around who could hang a spiral staircase the way they did in the old New England houses. Things like that. He learned his trade from Ellie's father, old Charlie Grant, who before he went totally blind used to be the man who was sent for.

Old Charlie went blind over a number of years, and he would grope his way to the ten-cent store from time to time to find a pair of glasses he could see with, but that may be another story, and we see him here only as a neat old man sitting in his daughter's kitchen, listening to the ball game on the radio and goddamning just about everyone he ever worked for, all those bastards who got rich while he wore out his sight and cut off his fingers and laid down in his bones a reserve of aches to last him to the grave. So there he sits, a noise in the background, but a man of sweet disposition—except on one or two subjects—a man who would be indignant if he suspected anyone had ever found in him the least resemblance to any of those stinking Reds.

Still, he crept in by way of the hanging staircase, which was no longer of any practical use to him nor for that matter was Bill Martin making much on it either in those days, as you can well imagine. Bill was lucky if he got a few days' work patching a roof for somebody who had been too poor in the beginning to have his chimney fixed so it wouldn't fall through his roof. Bill would fix the chimney while he was at it, and if any wiring had been carried away in the avalanche, he'd set that right too—that is, if the power was still on in the house, for everything comes back to the fact that it was then the Depression.

They all lived together in a house they themselves had built. It was a very good house. If God had been heard muttering in the night, "My wrath be upon the town so that one house and one only shall remain standing," we would all have crowded into Bill Martin's house because everyone knew that Bill Martin's house would be the house to withstand floods, earthquakes, and tornadoes of divine wrath. Those men built like that.

Old Charlie, who was no more a dirty atheist than he was a stinking Red, had often been heard to say after a few beers, "Heaven and earth shall pass away but my work shall not pass away." A learned man might call that blasphemy but he would be wrong. Charlie had no desire to usurp the powers of God. He had powers of his own and he knew his powers and he found them good.

And Bill learned carpentry from him. And Bill also knew his own worth and the worth of his work, but he was in no way given to rhetoric. Perhaps if he had been given to rhetoric this story would have been different, not the meaning, I should say, but the events.

Bill was a good man and he saved money when he was working. Charlie had saved too in his day, and when he had to come to live with Bill and Ellie he made them take him to the bank, and he drew out all his savings. He put the money in their hands and said, "When this is gone, I guess you'll have to shoot me."

"First thing I'll do with the money is buy a gun," Bill said. Charlie knew exactly what he meant, and Ellie knew exactly what he meant, and even the bank teller—that was Roger Ames, by the way, the same that is now president of the bank—even the teller knew what he meant, but Bill himself didn't know. The words frightened him. He was a very serious man. First thing in the morning he took the money to the bank and put it back in Charlie's account. Charlie never learned about that—and a good thing too, because he wouldn't have stood for it. He was a serious man himself and only the rhetoric made it look otherwise. This is something Bill never quite understood.

Charlie wouldn't have stood for it because he would literally rather have died than consider himself beholden to anyone. Bill ought to have known this because he was the same way himself. On the other hand perhaps this is exactly what he did know and mean to make manifest (darkly) by putting the money back in the bank just in case something should happen to him and Ellie.

Bill's savings lasted a long time. A man who is prudent about saving is also likely to be prudent about spending his savings. Nobody was hungry but everything was careful. Bill and Ellie planted a big garden, and Ellie canned everything she could get her hands on. They ate a lot of dandelion greens and wild berries. Bill fished day after day, and while he fished he invented details of jobs to tell Charlie about, because Charlie thought he was working pretty regularly. When he told Charlie about these jobs, Charlie would nod and say, "That's right, you did exactly right." There was nothing else he could say, because, of course, Bill had learned everything he knew from Charlie. And it was good.

What is easy to suppose is that there came a time when prudence was no longer enough. At least I've never met anybody who claimed he got through the Depression on his savings. Berries, greens, and fish are all very well, but they don't heat the house or put shoes on anybody's feet, and in these parts furs from muskrats, skunks, and rabbits don't make much of a money crop either. They barely kept Charlie in pipe tobacco. Bill gave up smoking. Doctor's orders, he said, the same explanation he gave for the way they were eating although actually they were eating pretty well. They even had meat on the table a lot of the time, because the garden really outdid itself and produced a rabbit almost every week and pheasants when the tomatoes were ripe and once in a very great while a deer. But there was no way the garden could grow any cash because everyone else had a garden too. So it is quite clear that the savings must have given out.

About now somebody is sure to bring up the matter of Charlie's savings although I don't quite see why. It seemed to me that I had made it clear that Bill was a serious man.

There is also the matter of relief. Everyone was on relief, so what's the harm? That's the way the logic runs. But you can't have been listening very carefully if you haven't heard old Charlie say, "I will not be beholden to any man," and "When this is gone I guess you'll have to shoot me." And of course you haven't heard tell, as I have many a time, how Bill Martin walked off the schoolhouse job, saying to the assembled School Board and the Selectmen and the General Contractor, "I don't kiss anybody's ass." In the evening Charlie said, "You did exactly right," although that was a job that would have seen them through a hard winter.

In the end what's so hard to believe, perhaps, is the fact that deep into the twentieth century there were two men who fundamentally lived by such incredible slogans as All men are created equal and A man's house is his castle and Death before dishonor —at least that's how I translate the remarks of both men. This is what makes the story difficult—that there were two such men. And a woman.

It must have been pretty obvious that I wasn't saying much about the woman. There was good reason for it, believe me, very good reason. What I was talking about before was what I knew and what I could suppose without much trouble. If thinking about how Father lost the store and how I lost my teeth is a warm-up for thinking about Charlie and Bill, then thinking about Charlie and Bill is no more than a warm-up for thinking about Ellie, because there is a good chance that she turned out to be the most serious of the lot.

She didn't have Charlie's rhetoric and she didn't have Bill's silence. She sang in the house and she sang in the garden. There were those who said her house was no cleaner than it ought to be, but no woman in town ever got out of sickbed or childbed to find her house the worse for Ellie's having stepped in for a few days or a few weeks. The children weren't even spoiled although it was commonly agreed that Ellie liked to be in a house where there were children. Those were innocent old times so nobody found anything nasty in Ellie's loving the children she couldn't have, and they were quite right. Probably if Charlie and Bill had known about *Honi soit qui mal y pense,* they would have believed in that too.

As for Ellie's gardening, it must be said that whatever she planted came up. It prospered and multiplied. She scattered seeds about and sang. She pulled a weed and sat in the sun on a little stool and sang, and whatever she planted came up. This is not in the least to be considered proof of anything at all, because whatever Bill planted came up too, and he had been known, when it came planting time, to go to his toolbox and get a piece of string and a piece of chalk and then chalk the string and solemnly snap a line on the ground as if he were getting ready to put up a partition or lay a course of shingles.

They must have seen the moment coming for a long time, but Ellie went on singing—at least in the house—and Bill went on fishing and telling Charlie about the cabinet work he was doing in the high school principal's house. That was work that had actually been talked of at one time, although nothing ever came of it, which is a great pity, because Bill wasn't under pressure of any other work and made a very fine thing of it, a thing the principal could have sold the next day to any solvent museum in the country. Charlie, of course, saw it and felt it and smelt it and said, "That's right, Bill, that's just right."

Probably the moment was put off more than once by a day's work here and there. For instance, I can remember about then seeing Bill at work on a simple set of steps for Roger Ames when his big old porch fell off and left his side door six feet in the air. You can be as sure as you can ever be of anything you haven't seen with your own eyes that was one job Bill got paid for.

But the moment must have come at last when there not only wasn't any money in the house but there wasn't any gas in Bill's Model A pickup truck so that even if he did get a chance to work he wouldn't have been able to get to wherever the work was. Yes, there must have been that moment. Both knowledge and imagination insist there must have been that moment.

The trouble is, however, that the moment has no scene. Obviously it must have had a scene. Perhaps in bed late at night or down at the end of the garden. Perhaps in the truck with the rain drumming on the garage roof.

The trouble is that the scene has no dialogue. Bill never did have much to say, and this must have been one time Ellie wasn't singing. Still, there must have been dialogue. Ellie must have said something and she must have found some way of making Bill agree, because another fact begins to loom up ahead, a fact to be approached by way of the imagination, which at least gives us the last bit of dialogue in the hidden scene, a line to be said by either of them or both, together or alone: "It's not right, it's just not right."

The fact we have arrived at has plenty of scene, and it tells us that in the town there lived—or had lived—a boy fortunate beyond the men of his time. He had a job. From seven in the evening to seven in the morning he worked in a restaurant in a nearby city, every night without fail. He washed and polished and scrubbed and cleaned and cooked a little too and had every night a belly full of broken meats. He had a place to sleep back by the storeroom, a clean uniform every night, and even a few dollars every week to put in his pocket. There was no reason why he should be singled out for prosperity. His prosperity was simply a fact, but it isn't that fact we are getting to.

The boy himself isn't the fact either. He is simply a part of the scene like a tree on a stage when there must be apples or a park bench when there must be love or a murder. The rest of the scene includes the usual cheap restaurant sort of thing: a counter with stools, some tables and chairs, some slogans like WATCH YOUR COAT AND HAT and IN GOD WE TRUST ALL OTHERS PAY CASH. There is also a big window that looks out on a shabby street, the kind of street that runs parallel to Main Street in towns just big enough for one big street.

One night just as the boy was settling into his routine, he looked out the window and saw pulling up to the curb a Model A pickup truck he'd have known in a million. His heart suddenly burned within him because it had been a long time since he had gone home for a visit, short as the distance was. He was about to run into the street when he observed that as Ellie climbed down from the truck she was crying. He hesitated.

Then he did run into the street although there were surely a thousand men within range of a shout who would have been quite willing to work from seven to seven every night without fail, eat broken meats, share a place near the storeroom with rats, and never once run into the street. This is not to say he felt himself ill-used. At the time he was as aware as any of the other thousand of his good fortune. Later he came to believe that his good fortune had kept him from discovering a lot that gradually loomed up as desirable knowledge. Things like what he would have done if he hadn't had that job. Would he have gone on relief? If so, what would have happened to his character? How, finally, would he have been able to come in the end to say, "That's right, that's just right, I was never beholden to any man"? He seems to have been another serious one. Perhaps everybody was serious in those days.

When he ran into the street, however, he wasn't thinking of discovery or anything like that. He ran because he had to, and then he did what he had to do next, thinking only years later how it might have looked if he had been caught. He stalked Bill and Ellie like a birdwatcher, like a boy birdwatcher.

He wasn't close enough to hear if they spoke, but they didn't seem to be speaking. They walked close together without touching, but there was nothing to suggest there had been a quarrel. Quite the contrary. Under a street light Ellie made Bill stop while she wiped something off his face. Just the way they stood together suggested she was wiping off lipstick.

He followed them until they stopped in front of a movie theater. Bill stepped up to the ticket window. Ellie waited to one side, and the boy waited at a distance. He was ready to go back to the restaurant. He was baffled but by no means as baffled yet as he was going to be, for when he expected them to go into the theater together they exchanged a look and parted. Bill went into the theater and Ellie continued along the street.

In his mind he gave up his job and followed her. It turned out that he didn't lose his job because he had friends in the restaurant who covered for him. He hadn't thought of that. He had done favors for them in the past but had never been repaid because he had never before thought of anything he wanted.

He hadn't followed her a block when a man stopped her and began to talk. Soon the man was wiping her face gently with his handkerchief, and they went on together. They went around a corner and into the Hotel Bazaar, a shabby building whose hidden splendor used to torment the boy as he lay listening to the secrets of rats in the wall. He peeped through the lobby window until Ellie and the man disappeared into the elevator. Then he ran back to work.

Each night for a week he followed. Each night it was exactly the same: tears, silence, movies, the Hotel Bazaar. Each night the Model A truck disappeared at some moment when he was engaged in a frenzy of washing and scrubbing and polishing and cleaning. He would look out and it would be gone.

So he began counting his money by day. At last, disguising his voice, he called the Hotel Bazaar and inquired the price of a room, double. At work he cleverly led conversations into channels where he picked up invaluable concepts of value: two-dollar job, five-buck deluxe. He counted his money and asked for a night off.

To his own amazement, however, he found himself buying a movie ticket and following Bill into the theater. All night he watched from the dark how a red exit light dimly illumined one side of Bill's face and made a thin red shine that remained constant through both the tear jerker and the comedy. When Ellie came and found Bill and they went out together, the boy did not follow.

But there was still one thing he had to know, so he traded shifts with a man who had some desperation of his own, and he went home for a day. He cleverly listened and led, and he found that Ellie still came in for a few days or a few weeks when there was trouble and children were still loved but not spoiled, that Bill still fished, that Charlie still smoked his pipe and listened to the ball game. Although it meant a two-mile walk in each direction, he passed the house and heard with his own ears that Ellie still sang in the kitchen. When he went back to work, he left all his spare cash for his parents.

Shortly after this there began to be more work, and the Model A stopped coming into the city. The boy went on to other things and with the passage of time became, I suppose, a man, but there was no passage of time that could save him from a memory. Let him only come across a Model A, an exit lamp, a certain song, a woman's name, and once again he felt the anguish of a thing he had only thought and never done, that no other person had ever known, fresh and sharp as the moment when he had first seen himself for what he was, neither better nor worse, probably, than most people, who certainly, when you come to think of it, do far less evil than they might.

As for Ellie, very likely all this makes her a whore except, as I said at the beginning, it all seems like a Russian novel; and everybody knows that in the Russian Novel Sonia Marmeladov, who is a whore, is also Jesus Christ crucified and saving the world. And if there are springs of Grace in the Russian Novel great enough to accomplish this mystery, I, for one, can't see why I shouldn't hope that our life, too, springs eternal with power to save Ellie —who also saves—and I think I can even hope there will be Grace for Bill, or what's the point of it all anyway? And finally for the boy, who found himself not to be so serious as he had hoped, I can at least pray although surely it must be that our trespasses are not forgivable except in the perpetual blood of a lamb.

The Day of the Equinox

Iᴛ ᴍᴀʏ ꜱᴇᴇᴍ ꜱᴛʀᴀɴɢᴇ that Michael Pegnam was glad he was
asked to work on Saturday for no pay except a meal on the
company. But he was glad. It was something different, something that would set this week apart from all the other weeks
of his first winter in New York, and might even divide the
winter from the spring.

He was automatically aware of the weather when he came
out of the subway that morning. It was obviously a fine day,
and he looked on this as a hopeful sign. The sun was higher than
it had been at nine o'clock for a long time—or at least he guessed
it was by the glow in the sky and on the buildings. All winter he
had watched the glow getting higher and higher each day and
brighter and brighter as the sun approached the end of the
street. All winter he had waited for the morning that the sun
would rise squarely in the end of the street, but somehow he had
missed the day. Perhaps it was that rainy week. Perhaps he was
late and in a hurry. Perhaps he just didn't notice. And now the
sun was rising behind the buildings to the north of the street,
higher and higher each day at nine o'clock, but each day farther
and farther to the north of the street.

As soon as he turned from the street into the empty building,
he felt strangeness and expectancy. He had been instructed to
use the freight elevator, but even so he felt like a conspirator.

The freight elevator was bound up in his mind with being late for work and trying to sneak in without being seen and then in the afternoon sneaking out for a quick one just to get over the horrible butt end of the day after the three-thirty deadline.

When he opened the door to the Webster Corporation's fourteenth-floor offices, he thought at first that the great newsroom was empty, but then he heard the soft clear voices of Jimmy Schuyler, his boss, and Joe Black, the district supervisor; and as he came out of the short end of the L-shaped room, he saw them standing near the files talking to a group of girls. Joe Black looked at his watch when he saw Pegnam, undoubtedly a pure reflex. "Right on the dot," he said.

"That's my boy," Jimmy said.

Pegnam felt ridiculous to be so patted on the head, and some of his joy in the day vanished. They seemed to forget about him, however, and went on explaining the exact procedure to be followed in weeding out the files.

He didn't try to understand what was being said because he was there only for the dirty work. The only thing he had to hear was that he was supposed to make a pile of the old reports at the end of the hall near the freight elevator. He went out to take a look at the place and stayed to smoke a cigarette. He looked up and down the elevator shaft and up and down the stair well and out the window at the fine spring day. He couldn't see the sun itself, but he could see the buildings to the west shining, and even the deep small streets were bright with an indirect light.

By the time he finished the cigarette and got back into the office, the girls had already filled their wastebaskets with discarded material, and the floor was littered with paper. He never did catch up all morning, and the only thing that saved him at all was that every once in a while the girls would remember they were working in the office, and they would pick up their purses and twitch off to the ladies room just as if all the reporters were sitting at their desks to look up after they had passed. Pegnam looked up, of course, and went on snatching reports from the floor.

By noon he was soaked with sweat, for he had literally moved a mountain, and he was ready for a break when Joe Black said, "Let's get cleaned up for lunch, everybody."

Joe Black herded them all into the freight elevator and directly across the street into the bosses' restaurant. He talked over their heads to the head waiter. "The big table," he said. "The big table for my big family." That was a part Joe Black didn't know how to bring off, but he didn't know it so there was no harm done.

"Yes, sir, Mr. Black," the waiter said. "This way, please." They followed him into a kind of back room with one big table in it. The room was so dim that they could barely see at first, and Pegnam found himself at the foot of the table beside Nancy Hatcher, a reporter from the construction news division.

Nancy was beautiful. He saw her every morning through a glass partition while he was sorting the morning mail, and he couldn't be mistaken about that, but he just didn't believe in beautiful women. When he was a kid he had believed in them. He had looked at magazines and seen movies and told himself, That is what it will be like to be grown up: there will be women like that. (He had also thought there would be money like that and success like that, but those were other stories although they ended up the same way.) After he grew up he looked around for those women for a while and then forgot about them. Of course now he saw them every day on Fifth Avenue and in Rockefeller Plaza and almost everywhere he went, but he didn't believe in them. He didn't believe in Nancy either although he had known from his very first day with the company that she was not only a beautiful woman but a good kid as well, because she kept suggesting things for him to do so it would look as if he were taking hold.

Even knowing she was a good kid, he had never allowed himself to think about her, but now impulsively on this strange day he believed in her, if not as beautiful, at least as a woman.

"Hello, Micky," she said.

"Hello, Nancy," he said. He was going to ask her to call him Mike, but Joe Black was rapping for attention.

"We're all going to have a drink while we study the menu," Joe Black said, and everyone applauded. The waiter began taking orders for drinks.

"When he comes around," Nancy said, "tell him I don't want any."

"Don't let me down, buddy," Pegnam said. He had seen Nancy stop in with the boys for a couple of quick ones after work.

"My mother says I shouldn't drink before four o'clock," she said.

"Where'd she get that?" Pegnam said.

"She read it in a book," Nancy said. "She thinks you shouldn't drink so much either. She worries about you."

"Bless her heart," Pegnam said.

"I tell her everything," Nancy said.

"What's yours?" the waiter said to Pegnam, perhaps because he was wearing a sweater with no shirt.

"Bourbon," Pegnam said. "Water chaser. The lady will have the same."

"My mother won't like this," Nancy said.

"You aren't even going to see it," Pegnam said.

"I mean," Nancy said, "she isn't going to like to hear what a sot you really are."

"Janitors can drink any time," he said. He was already high just on the thought of the drinks and the general excitement that accompanies drinking. Joe Black looked almost pleasant. Jimmy was laughing and joking with the girls, who were gentle now, somehow attractive. And Nancy—well, she was still Nancy. And they were all of them such wonderful people that Pegnam wanted to make a speech before he had had even one drink. The tears were beginning to come to his eyes foolishly.

"Nancy," he said, "what does your mother think of McSorley's?"

"McSorley's?" she said.

"Where I drink my ale. Two-hour lunch hours on working days and noon to midnight on Saturdays."

"Oh," she said. "McSorley's. I'd like to see that place."

"No women," Pegnam said. "They don't allow women."

"Is that why you go there?" Nancy said. Then she reddened. Her eyes opened just a little and her lips parted as if she were about to put her hand over her mouth.

"I just like it there," Pegnam said a little shortly.

"My mother thinks a man should spend a certain amount of time at his club," Nancy said, and Pegnam knew that a girl whose mother was that intelligent must be more than just beautiful. "But she doesn't think a man should overdo it."

"Moderation."

"Moderation in all things, my mother believes, and no drinking before four o'clock."

"I'll see you then," he said. The waiter set her drink in front of her. Pegnam downed it at once. He was ordinarily a leisurely drinker although often in the long run immoderate.

Joe Black stood up and everyone was quiet at once. He said, "For your loyalty and co-operation, to you." He raised his glass. "My big family." He had to do it.

Then Pegnam jumped up. He didn't know why. It wasn't the kind of thing he did. He wasn't really like that. "To you, Joe Black," he said, "and all these beautiful people." He didn't ordinarily make that kind of fool of himself. But at least he tossed off his drink and sat down without suggesting For He's a Jolly Good Fellow. Joe Black waved across the table at him, and Jimmy grinned openly and indeed even foolishly at him.

The waiter was going around taking orders. You would have thought the office girls were all pregnant the way they were ordering the fruit salad bowl that Joe Black ordered. But Pegnam was listening to Jimmy, so Nancy and he had the roast beef special. Good old Jimmy. Good old Nancy.

Just as the waiter was leaving, Jimmy called, "Another round for everybody while we're waiting."

"Make his a double one," Joe Black said, pointing at Pegnam. Pegnam waved at him and he waved at Pegnam.

So all in all Pegnam had five shots on an empty stomach, and he felt so wonderful that he hated to begin his lunch. But Nancy poked him in the ribs and said, "Eat something before you fall into your plate."

"I feel wonderful," he said.

"Eat up," she said.

"Your mother wouldn't approve, would she?" he said.

"Oh, she always says, Better a happy sinner than a sullen saint."

"Good old mother," he said. "Let's go see her." He started to get out of his chair.

"We've got to work," Nancy said. "Eat your lunch."

"Yeah," he said. "Sure."

"Eat your lunch, Micky," Nancy said, so he began to eat his lunch.

"Feel better now?" Nancy said.

"No," he said. "I felt wonderful."

"You shouldn't drink so much on an empty stomach," Nancy said.

"Does your mother really want to know why I drink so much?" he said.

"She's sincerely interested," Nancy said.

"Let's go see her," he said, but he didn't have the drive to get even half out of the chair.

"Not now," Nancy said.

"You come with me tonight," Pegnam said, "and I'll tell you everything while we eat. Then you can tell your mother."

"Fine," Nancy said. "I'll call my mother and tell her not to expect me." He was still drunk enough so that it all seemed perfectly natural. If he had been sober he would never have asked her.

Even after Joe Black paid the check and they were ready to go back to work, Pegnam still had enough of that good feeling left so that he hated to let it go. "You go on ahead, Nancy," he said. "I'll catch up. I have to get cigarettes."

He got cigarettes and another double shot at the bar. That really held him right up there, so he moved another mountain and sweated another gallon without being particularly aware what he was doing.

At about three o'clock he went down for another drink because he didn't want to lose that fine casual feeling he would have to have to ask Nancy to slip out for a quick one at four o'clock. But as it turned out he could have been cold sober. He was rushing around to get a little ahead so he wouldn't be missed when he saw her ringing the buzzer by the freight elevator. She held up four fingers and he heaved his trash box at the pile and went with her.

"Your mother would be proud of your self-control," he said.

"No," she said, a little sadly it seemed, "she expects it." They had one and then a cigarette and then another one and went back with the comfortable knowledge that they could last until five.

And last they did, very handsomely, but five minutes past five found them back again at the same spot. Nancy was paying for her own, and it was just as well, because Pegnam never carried too much money on him.

Almost the first thing they did was decide to go to Chinatown for dinner, but it took them a long time to get started. Nancy had to call her mother and one thing and another. They ate potato chips and boiled eggs and pickled pigs' feet and herring and the sort of stuff you can find in bars to hold you just a little longer.

"Tell me, Micky," Nancy said. She showed no signs of being ready to go to Chinatown or anywhere else. "There's something I'd like to know."

"What's that?" he said.

"What do you do when you ride me home on the subway and then stay on after I get off?"

"You really want to know?"

"When I called my mother this is one of the things she particularly asked me to find out for her."

"Bless her heart," Pegnam said. "Well, I tell you. I just ride to the end of the line and get off and walk around. Then I find a place to eat and have a couple of beers. One Friday night I was in a diner with some truck drivers and they gave me a ride to Manchester, New Hampshire, and back the next night. Some nights I ride over to Jersey or Brooklyn with some of the other guys. I've seen a lot like that. Two nights a week I go right home after work and write letters."

"And on Saturday you go to McSorley's, right?"

"As soon as I get up. I usually get there between eleven and eleven-thirty for a big corned beef and cabbage feed, and I stay until they close up at midnight."

"I'd sure like to see that place," she said.

"No women allowed," he said.

"I know," she said. "I guess that covers it."

"I guess it does," he said. "How about you?"

"We've got to decide what to do after we finish here. I don't really feel much like eating."

"Me neither," he said, "and it's just as well because we don't have much money. We could do something cheap like go to Coney and walk on the beach."

"Not tonight," Nancy said. "Some other time but not tonight. How about the Staten Island Ferry?"

"Is that good?"

"It's one of New York's most famous cheap dates," she said.

"Sounds OK to me," he said.

"First, we have to get to the Battery," she said, pushing back her chair and starting to get up.

"Wait till I look at my map," he said. "The Battery isn't in my territory." She settled back and he took out his city map— he never took a step without it. "From where we are," he said, "it looks easy."

"It is easy," she said. "Let's go."

But if the Battery wasn't in his territory, Staten Island wasn't even on his map. At the bottom of the map was only a dotted line that ran right off the edge. Printed beside this line was the legend: To Staten Island.

As they stood at the rail waiting for the voyage to start, he said, "It's wonderful already." In his mind's eye he saw the ferry boat plunging off the edge of the map. Then the boat began to move and they were indeed cut off from the land.

"There's nothing like a sea voyage," Nancy said.

"Nothing," he said. "Smell the salt spray."

He inhaled deeply and flung his arms out wide. In dropping his arms he let one of them fall, as if by accident, on Nancy's shoulders. She wasn't in the least deceived and leaned against him. "It's about time," she said.

For some time after that they said nothing but remained in the classic grouping at the boat's rail, their backs to the land and even to the boat, their faces looking, not at horizons, but down at the water sliding directly beneath them. It would have been nice if there had been the arched backs of porpoises and phosphorous reflections of stars and hammered moon path, but there was only the black water sliding hypnotically below, carrying unidentifiable objects into their narrow range of vision and swiftly out again.

Nancy turned her face against his shoulder. "The water almost put me to sleep," she said.

"Me too," he said. He looked down at the top of her head. He had long forgotten that she was the most beautiful girl he had ever seen. It was dark. She was in his arms. He felt strong, gigantic even, protective, yet on the verge of tears.

"We should be looking for the Statue of Liberty," she said without moving.

"Hush," he said. "I'm too comfortable." That was an outright lie. His feet were killing him, and he was getting a stitch in his side from maintaining his position, but he had no intention of giving her an occasion to move away.

"Yes," she said. This time she straightened and took her arm away from around his waist. "Yes, we must. We must always say goodbye to the old lady on the outward voyage."

"We really must," he managed to say although he actually wasn't at all happy about this turn of events. The pain in his side and having lost his grip on her did nothing for his disposition. He would much rather have sulked, but fortunately it was so dark that his sulky attempts at dissembling succeeded.

When they raised their eyes and looked outward, they couldn't very well miss the Statue. "Goodbye," Nancy called, waving to the Statue.

"Goodbye," Pegnam shouted. Nancy began to wave her handkerchief and dab at her eyes. Pegnam shredded a couple of Kleenex and let the pieces float over the side. Then he tore up a cigarette package and threw the pieces into the air. He held the last few cigarettes in his hand.

Near them somewhere a great whistle cut loose with a blast that shook the whole boat. They looked at each other. He could see her laughing but couldn't hear her. He was laughing too. She made a little gesture with both hands and he jumped at her. She met him—at least—and they kissed very hard. The hand that was holding the cigarettes freed itself behind her back simply by opening and letting the cigarettes fall into the water.

At that moment, however, another couple came toward them. Nancy saw them over his shoulder. At first he was glad she saw them, and then he was a little resentful that she should have seen anything just then. She drew away a trifle—just the trifle that made the difference between passion and romance.

"What's all the shouting?" the girl said as the couple came up.

"We were just saying goodbye to the Statue of Liberty," Nancy said.

The boy and the girl turned toward the Statue, which was by then almost out of sight. "Goodbye, goodbye," the boy said.

"Goodbye, aloha," the girl whispered.

"Aloha, aloha," the boy whispered. He drew himself up as if he were about to sing an aloha song the way they do in the movies, but he only kissed the girl, and for the rest of the crossing they stood there hung at the lips, eyes closed, oblivious. Nancy and Pegnam could have acted as if there was no one there at all, but for some inscrutable reason they chose to hold tight to each other and whisper together making fun of the other two. When they tiptoed away and got off at Staten Island, the boy and the girl were still standing there.

Once they had landed, Pegnam discovered that Nancy had no more idea than he did where they were. She had never before got off the ferry but had always ridden directly back across. All around them people were running toward buses lined up in the terminal. "What shall we do now?" he said.

"I don't know," Nancy said. She drooped a little against him.

"Well, let's go," he said and pulled her arm until she was running along with him. He passed up the first two buses because they were almost empty and jammed her ahead of him into the third bus. "All these people have to be going somewhere," he said into her ear. He had one arm around her to hold her up because there was no grip for her anywhere. She just stood there with her arms down and her head against his chest. He would have been completely embarrassed except that he hadn't—and he didn't think anyone else in the bus had—ever seen such a pretty girl acting like that in public.

Now it was his turn to keep his eyes open, for she seemed scarcely aware where they were. "Are you all right?" he whispered.

"Are we in heaven yet?" she said. He flushed, for she said it quite distinctly and several people near them smiled.

Fortunately his rash guess about the crowded bus paid off when several people got off at a kind of square where in one quick glance he could see a diner and a drugstore still open. He helped her off the bus, and when they were alone he shook her gently and said, "Are you all right?"

"Yes, Micky," she said. "I'm floating."

"Call me Mike," he said.

"Yes, Mike. I'm floating."

"OK," he said. "Let's get something to eat."

"We don't have enough money," she said, which was a strange thing for an enchanted girl to say.

"Lots of money," he said because he had a reserve fund in the bottom of his billfold, a ten-dollar bill that was so much an emergency reserve that he had once walked from 7th Street to 92nd Street rather than break into it. He hadn't really lied to her before when he told her he didn't have any money. He just never thought of that ten-dollar bill as money, but now he took it out and showed it to her.

"Let's eat then," Nancy said. He led her into the diner because she was still not exactly all there. Then she said, "But we ate just a little while ago."

"That was on the other side of the water," he said, "and besides it wasn't really a meal. Do you know what you want?"

"Yes, Mike," she said, but she didn't say any more about it.

"Give us two of your special ham and eggs," he said. "Hash brown potatoes, toast, and coffee."

"So much?" she said.

"This is the best time to eat," he said. "If you can't sleep, you got to eat." So they ate.

He swabbed the last of his toast over his plate and ordered more coffee. "Now, Nancy," he said, "what are your plans for the evening?"

"I don't know, Mike," she said. Her plate was as clean as his.

"Will your mother be worrying?"

"When I talked with her on the phone, she said she was going to take seconal. She hasn't been sleeping well lately."

"I'm sorry," he said.

"She'll be out now until noon," Nancy said.

"Then we can do as we please," he said.

"Yes," she said.

"Well, then," he said between sips of the hot coffee, "let's see about finding a place to stay."

Discreet inquiry at the diner and the drugstore uncovered a rooming house in the next block. And most discreet rapping at the door resulted in the porch light's being turned on and the door's being opened on the chain. "Could we have a room for the night?" Pegnam said into the opening of the door. "We're exhausted from sightseeing and can't make our way back to our hotel or the place we parked our car." He put that last in so that his accent would suggest that he was a traveler from Boston or— if the person behind the door was naive enough—from England. At all events no one could mistake him for a native of the place.

A streak of old face with no teeth and white hair in curlers appeared in the opening of the door. "Step back both of you so I can get a good look." They stepped down two steps and stood still. The door opened and the old lady said, "Come in, come in. It's my business to know good people when I see them even if it is late and they are tired. Come in, come in. I have a bed all turned down for you."

She led them up the stairs to a large room with a connecting bath. "This used to be our room," she said, "but I don't need such a large room any more or such a large bed." She pressed lightly on the bed to show the softness of the mattress. The whole bed shook gently but didn't creak or rattle.

"We are very sorry to have disturbed you," Pegnam said.

"It's quite all right," the old lady said. "Sleep well." She left quietly.

When they at last woke up in the morning and thought about getting home, they had little to say to each other. After paying for the room, they had, deducting the bus, ferry, and subway fares, just enough for two cups of coffee and one doughnut. That was nowhere near enough, for Pegnam was ravenously hungry. As a result of his hunger he was disagreeable—or would have been if he had had to say anything—but the normal sadness of such a morning made it easy to avoid talking, although he meticulously put his arm around Nancy on the ferry and even gave her a little squeeze as they passed the Statue of Liberty.

"Hello, Statue of Liberty," she said. "We're back."

"Hello," he said. But they didn't wave or shout, and no one came out to salute the Statue.

"Do you have money at home for your breakfast, Micky?" Nancy said without removing her head from his shoulder.

"Yes," he said.

"Well, why don't you come home with me for breakfast anyway?"

"I don't want to meet your mother like this," he said. "You're going to have trouble enough."

"It's all right," Nancy said. "I live alone. I don't have any mother."

"But—"

"It's all a game," Nancy said.

So they went to her house for breakfast. Then they lay down for a nap and decided to get married. In the long run nothing came of it, but that was what they decided that day.

A Ride in the Snow

O N NEW YEAR'S MORNING I drove through the snow across Massachusetts toward Albany. Although the road was well plowed, it was a little slippery in spots, so since Mac and Leo were asleep in the back seat, I never got up over thirty even when the land flattened out a little. It was just as we were coming into Williamstown that I hit the bus.

I had got around a lot of curves tougher than that one, but perhaps I saw the bus across the open curve and tensed up. That would have been enough to do it. I felt the car go right out from under me. The bus driver saw me coming and pulled over as far as he could. Trees and telephone poles and the bus kept twitching past my eyes as I sat there staring straight ahead, spinning the wheel first one way and then the other into the skid while everything I had ever heard about accidents went through my mind all at once. I hit the bus square in the middle with a terrific crash. Everything was quiet for a second while I sat there still alive and quite unhurt.

Then Mac and Leo came up from the floor in back, and the bus driver came around, and we all got out to look at things. The water from the radiator was steaming on the snow. There was glass on the snow. The right front fender was torn in two. "Back it off if you can," the bus driver said, "so we can see the bus." Mac backed the car off and ran it over to the side of the road. There was almost no mark where I hit. The bus driver ran his fingers over the side of the bus.

The bus driver took my license and copied everything down. Then he asked for the registration, but he had to wait for that until Mac walked back to us. "His car?" the bus driver said.

"We rented it," I said.

"I hope you're rich kids," the bus driver said. Then he noticed the Alabama plates on the car. "Going to win today?" he said.

"By four touchdowns," Leo said. "Those are my boys."

The bus driver got the rest of the information from Mac. "I'll have to report it to the police," he said.

"Will you have to tell about him?" Leo said, nodding toward me.

"What do you mean?" the bus driver said.

"You know," Leo said, "about the way he is."

I turned open-mouthed toward Leo. "Give him a break, Leo," Mac said.

"I've seen him drink twice as much and not show it," Leo said.

I still couldn't say anything. "He did everything he could to save the car," Mac said.

"But it was an accident," I managed to say at last. "I wasn't drunk."

"It may be so," the bus driver said. "These other rapscallions seem to have been too drunk to sit up."

"Why, sir," Leo said.

"Go on, the gang of you," the bus driver said. "I wouldn't believe any of you, but I can tell a drunk. You say you're going to win today?"

"A pushover," Leo said.

"Happy New Year's," the bus driver said. He went to make his call.

"Happy New Year's," we all said.

"What were you trying to do, Leo?" Mac said. "Get the guy thrown in the clink?"

"A joke," Leo said. "The bus driver knew it was a joke."

"A fine joke," Mac said. "The guy was wetting his pants."

"That's the best kind of joke," Leo said. "When they wet their pants."

"I better go and call a wrecker," Mac said. He ran after the bus driver.

"A wrecker?" I said. I guess I hoped we could just go on and get the others in Albany and go on to school before we had to do anything. I guess I thought we could go miles and miles across states and states and not have to do anything.

Leo and I stood beside the bus smoking, and the people in the bus kept looking out at me until the bus driver came and took them away. "If Mac tries to get money out of you, don't give him a cent," Leo said.

Mac and Leo and I stood there in the cold. Nobody said anything for a long time. Then Mac said, "I was sound asleep and I felt the car going and I looked up and there he was wheeling away like crazy and then bang." Perhaps he was trying to be kind and tell me that he didn't blame me for what happened. There was something of that in his voice, but I would have felt better if I could have remembered what I did with my feet while I was steering the car into the skid. It's one thing to remember to steer the car right, but it goes against all instinct to keep your foot off the brake when you can see hell and damnation coming at you all of a sudden. I knew I steered right but I couldn't remember about the brake and that worried me: I didn't know whether I had really done the best I could. Mac tried to tell me I had, but I couldn't be sure myself.

The wrecker picked us up and towed us in while we sat stiffly in the car, tipping backwards and riding silently and softly except for the lurches of the car against the suspending tow chain.

We went to get something to eat while the mechanic was patching up the car so that it would run. The place where we ate had the game on the radio so we drank coffee and listened. It was bad for Alabama from the start.

The mechanic had the game on too. "Where's Alabama?" he said before we were well inside the shop.

"They haven't got warmed up yet," Leo said. "My boys have to be hot."

"Wait until the end," Mac said.

"I got about fifteen more minutes here," the mechanic said.

Mac and Leo and I huddled around the stove made from oil drums. "I can pay him now out of the money you guys gave me for the ride," Mac said, "but then I don't know what I'll do when it comes to paying for the rent of the car, let alone fix it up good."

"I'm cleaned," Leo said. "The holidays cleaned me."

"Me too," Mac said. "I had all I could do to hang onto the car money."

I didn't know what to say. I might be able to spare ten or perhaps fifteen dollars. I still wasn't sure what I did with my feet when the car was skidding.

"If I can just get a little time," Mac said, "I can get it out of my mother easy. But it takes a little time."

The mechanic rolled out from under the car. "All OK now," he said.

"How much for the job?" Mac said.

"Cost you twenty dollars," the mechanic said.

"I'll be twenty dollars light with the Drive-It Company," Mac said.

"I got twenty dollars," I said.

"Let me have it for a month," Mac said. "I can work my mother easy."

"OK," I said. I had been offering to give him the money. In a month I would need it for textbooks.

As we drove out of the shop, things still looked bad for Alabama. The team just couldn't seem to do anything right. They kept fumbling and tripping over their own feet.

Leo was asleep in the back. Mac was driving. I was sitting up front with him. I had never seen the Taconic Trail before that day because I had slept all through there on the way home. "We're getting close to the state line," Mac said. "We go into New York just this side of the summit." The piles of snow left by the plows were getting higher and higher until we could barely see over them. We came around a bend and looked across and up to a bluff that seemed like the end of everything. "That's the summit," Mac said. "The state line is about in the middle between here and there."

"What's that up there?" I said. "Up in the road there?"

"Cars," Mac said. "They look just about in New York. Suppose they haven't got their roads plowed in New York?" As we got closer we could see two cars slewed across the road. They were just sitting where they had stopped. Mac blew the horn loudly and went ahead as fast as he could. He squeezed past the first car without slacking speed while my heart was in my mouth, but as he was getting back into the middle of the road, I could feel the rear wheels start to go out from under us. He steered into the skid and gave it the gas, but the wheels only spun and we lost momentum rapidly and began to slide at an angle toward the outside fence. I hung on tight and looked way down there what looked like a mile down. We hit the snow bank with scarcely a jar and stopped. Leo hadn't even waked up.

"Three hundred more yards and we'd have been in the clear," Mac said. "You can see the bare road up by the bluff where the wind gets at it."

We all walked up the hill to the car ahead. As soon as the man stuck his head out to see what we wanted, his hat went sailing over the side and way down into the valley. It went beautifully away in the snow. After his first futile snatch at the hat, he didn't pay any attention to it, but only turned up the collar of his overcoat. "What do you think?" he said.

"Maybe if we all push we can get you up the rest of the way," Mac said.

"This car is much too heavy for that," the man said. We were standing in some ruts he had made trying to get the car squared away. "We'll have to take all the cars back down the hill and try to go by another road."

"Well, let's get the man from the other car," Mac said. "Then we'll see about getting you out of here." I leaned tentatively against the big car. It felt as solid as a house.

"It's going to be better to take out the car farthest down the hill first," Leo said. "Then we can horse the others around as much as we please without banging into anything."

"Good idea," the man said.

"Do you have a shovel?" Leo said.

"Let's take a look," the man said. He reached in and took the keys from the ignition. Over the car radio we could hear Alabama being penalized fifteen yards. I backed off down the ruts.

The man's wife moved over to the door of the car. "Come in here," she screamed over the wind. "Come out of the snow this instant." He shook his head. "Come in here," she screamed. He went back along his car, ignoring the ruts, floundering and slipping, fighting the deep snow and the wind. He got in and closed the door. We stood still a minute.

"Let's look in the Ford," Mac said. "They always have something."

The man in the Model A got out and ran around to open up the back so we could have a look. I was still standing in the ruts left by the big car up ahead while Leo and Mac plowed through the snow around to the back of the car. "Here's an orange crate," Mac said.

"Empty out the books and break it up," Leo said. Mac kicked the crate to pieces while the man tried to stack the books in the back of his car.

We each took a slat from the orange crate, and then we all looked instinctively up toward the warm car, for the wind and the cold were wearing us down. "What about him?" Leo said.

"Maybe he was waiting to see if we got anything to work with," Mac said. "Let's go see."

We climbed up to the other car again. "Ready to go to work?" Mac said when the man lowered the window. The man didn't say anything.

"Tell them," his wife said. The man shook his head and sat

with his hands gripping the wheel. "What's so bad about a rupture?" his wife said. "Lots of people have ruptures, don't they, boys?"

"Yeah," Mac said. "Sure." Leo and I nodded our heads. I felt sorry for the guy with no chance to get out and help.

"So he has to take it easy," his wife said.

"He can drive the car out," Mac said. "He can do that."

"Yes," his wife said, "and that will help." The man just kept gripping the wheel. "Do you want to get in back and get warm before you go to work?" his wife said.

"We want to get out of here before dark," Leo said.

"Say," the man said suddenly, "I've got some Scotch in my suitcase." He started to get out.

"Stay in," his wife said. "Give them the keys."

"It's in the big pigskin," the man said, slumping back again.

Leo dug up the fifth of White Horse and we all took a big drink. He gave the bottle to the man. "Keep it handy," he said. "We'll be back."

We went down the hill past our own car. "Motherlover got no more rupture than I have," Leo said.

"He wouldn't just say a thing like that, would he?" I said.

"Maybe he's afraid of the snow," Mac said.

"Maybe he's afraid of his wife," Leo said.

We slipped and slid down the hill, our overcoats flapping and flying around us. Leo and Mac had both dug earmuffs out of their pockets to my great surprise, but I was completely bareheaded. I tried walking with my hands over my ears, but it was too hard to keep my balance in the ruts, so I had to let my ears get colder and colder all the time.

Leo and Mac went around to dig out a little behind the wheels of the Model A. Then the driver gunned it while they pushed against the rear fenders and the doors. The driver gave a surprised look at me, and I stepped hurriedly out of the rut into the knee-deep snow and put my shoulder against the radiator. With Leo and Mac beside the rear wheels shoving sideways when the car began to slip, we had that one back over the state line within half an hour.

When we gave one last shove, the car just went away from me suddenly and left me on my hands and knees in the snow. I was too weak for a minute to get up and I stayed there breathing hard. The driver came back and helped me up. "That wasn't bad," he said. "You're strong. At first I didn't think you were going to be much help. Why don't you try tying your scarf around your head?" I would have tried anything.

"It was just stepping into the snow at first," I said. We scuffed through the snow up to our car. Mac got in to start it.

"Motherlover sitting up there with the woman and the Scotch and the heater," Leo said.

"He's really ruptured," I said, "or he'd be down here with us."

"You believe everything you hear?" Leo said.

"A man wouldn't lie like that," I said.

"How stupid can you be?" Leo said.

Our car was tougher to get out. I was mad at Leo and I almost killed myself being strong. Once toward the beginning, the car moved so fast that I couldn't keep up and fell flat in the snow. When I looked up I saw that the others had stopped to rest even before the car moved. "Come on, come on," I shouted, rearing up on my knees. "We could have had it." But the car had slewed across the road again.

When I got up I found that my knees were trembling so with fatigue that I could scarcely stand. I was grateful that Leo called a break and went up to the big car for the Scotch. The man from the Model A got in the back of the car with me. "Scarf doing any good?" he said.

"I don't know," I said.

"They may be frozen," he said. "Rub them with snow."

"In a while," I said.

"Save yourself on the pushing too," he said. "They'll let you do it all if you're willing."

I was willing but I said, "Yeah."

When Leo brought back the Scotch, the man said, "Give it to the horse first. We got to keep him in shape if we're ever going to get out of here."

"First time I knew he was a whole horse," Leo said, but he gave me the bottle. Although I have never liked Scotch, I took a big drink and smacked my lips, but the heat of it never reached my ears or my hands or my feet. "They scored again on my boys."

"It's a long way from over," I said.

"It looks bad," Mac said. He had the car started.

"Now look," Leo said. "The first thing this car is going to do when he guns it is to slide sideways over against the snow bank. That will straighten it out all right, but if it gets all the way over it will jam against the bank and we'll never move it. You stand by the rear wheel, you horse, and when I yell you try to hold it off the bank. The rest of us will be pushing on the front. You're the pivot man for the whole thing."

"OK," I said. I took my overcoat off and threw it in the back of the car. Then I took my position.

"Get in there, horse," the man from the Model A shouted. He and Leo pushed. Mac gunned it. The rear end slid sideways down the camber of the highway toward me. I could hear the grunts and cries of the others as their feet slipped and they fell.

I took a quick look over my shoulder at the bank and the gray sky beyond it. Leo's head popped up over the hood. I dug my feet in and held. "Push," he said. The front end of the car came away from the bank and the car began to back down the hill. It was still at an angle because it couldn't climb up onto the crown of the road, but it was going quite fast crabwise. I ran alongside of it for about ten yards, plowing through the snow, and then it lost momentum and began to slide toward me again. I threw myself against the fender, but my feet kept slipping and I couldn't do any good. Mac kept spinning the wheels and the car just walked me backwards toward the snow bank. I kept slipping to my knees and getting up and pushing with my body almost parallel to the road. Then my feet hit the snow bank, but by the time I could collect myself for a big effort the car had pushed me all the way back and mashed me right into the bank.

I couldn't even move my hands. I was stuck like a pole in the snow. The others peeked at me around the ends of the car. "Are you all right?" the man said. He had come around to the back and was right near me.

"I guess so," I said. "I don't feel hurt."

"In that ice box you wouldn't feel anything," Leo said. I began to wonder about the parts of me under the snow. I couldn't move a muscle. "Get the whiskey," Leo said. Mac went into the car and tried to reach the bottle out the window to me, but he couldn't get it into my mouth.

My friend from the Model A came floundering up the bank and over to me. He took the bottle from Mac's hand. "Take a good one," he said. He held one hand behind my head as he raised the bottle and gave me the drink as if I had been a baby. "Take it easy now, horse, and we'll get you out." He dug out my left arm with his hands and then I was able to get my right arm out myself, but I was still stuck almost to the armpits. They all began to dig behind me with the orange-crate slats.

"How about me trying to move the car away from him?" Mac said.

"How about you get an ax and chop him off at the top of the snow?" Leo said. "What do you think that wheel would do to his legs if it hasn't already?"

"I think he's all right," my friend said.

Leo took hold of me and began to work me back and forth the way you work a post you want to pull out of the ground. They pulled me out and I rolled down the bank into the road. "Are you all right?" Leo said.

I got up and walked around. "I'm all right," I said.

"At least you kept the wheel from going right into the bank," Leo said. We all had a small drink because the Scotch was getting low. "OK, horse," Leo said, "up front with me. And you other one take the back."

When we got our heads down by the radiator ready to go, Leo

said. "Take it easy, horse. Don't kill yourself. We got this guy out. Let him sweat to get us out." Mac started up and we pushed against the bumper which was about all there was solid up front. Leo didn't push very hard, but he kept grunting and every once in a while cursing. I couldn't help giving it everything I had left. "Save yourself, horse," Leo would say. "You did a good job to-day but you got to know when to let the peasants do it."

The car worked slowly down in fits and starts. When it got stuck, the man in back would yell, "One, two, three." Or he would chant, "All together, now." Then Leo would grunt like mad and maybe push a little or maybe just duck down behind the radiator. I would charge against the bumper each time until once I got caught flatfooted and just stood there. Then Leo clapped me on the back and said, "You're catching on now." The next time the man in back called I just sat on the bumper and kicked my feet.

After a while we hit the ruts of the Model A, and the work was easier, but I kept falling down in the snow, and sometimes I couldn't catch up until they stopped to rest. I kept falling down and it was harder and harder all the time to get up. In the end I was just following along.

"How about him?" Mac said, jerking his thumb up toward the big car.

"Leave him there," Leo said. "Let him really rupture himself."

"Leave the motherlover," I said. I fell off the running board of the Model A.

"Old horse is all shot," my friend said. "Let's put him in the car and go back and see what we can do with that other one."

"Don't come to me for help," I said. "Once I get in there I'm not getting out until I get where it's warm."

"Sure not," my friend said. "But we can't leave them sitting there. We got at least to give them a ride back in one of the cars."

"That's right," Mac said. "We got to try."

I got in the back of the car and took off my shoes and socks. I discovered that I had lost one of my rubbers. I took the snow from the other one and rubbed my ears and my feet and my hands until they began to hurt. I could hear the others talking outside. Leo opened the door and stuck his head in. "Here's something I saved for you." He gave me the bottle with a little left in it. "They still want to help that motherlover."

"The motherlover," I said. I piled the blankets on myself and pulled them up over my head. My hands and feet and ears were hurting, and a tremendous pain was building up in my groin as if I were ripped open. I let out a consoling groan and wet my mouth with the Scotch.

It didn't seem very long—or I may have slept—before I felt the door open at my head. "I want to see him," a woman said. "I want to see the boy who got hurt saving us." I could feel her fumbling with the blankets.

"Leave me alone," I said. She kept fumbling with the blankets, and the cold air blew on my hand. She opened my fingers and closed them over something I couldn't feel very well. After she went away I pulled my hand up to my face. I could smell money.

Then the car began to move and I lay still under the blankets. In the dark I could see my hands flashing before my eyes as they spun the wheel, and the bus crossed back and forth across my field of vision, and I could feel my feet pressing hard against the side of the car. I said to myself almost aloud, See, I am pressing the accelerator just as I should. But it could equally well have been the brake and I knew it.

Someone patted the blankets gently. "How are you, horse?" Leo said.

"All right," I said. I didn't move and stayed under the blankets.

"We scored," Leo said. "How about that?" I didn't say anything.

"He really was a horse," Mac said.

"Yeah," Leo said. "He's my boy."

The car kept going along and my hands kept spinning and my feet kept pressing and I hurt so much and I smelled the money so strong and I could just see that guy sitting gripping the wheel of his car up there on the mountain and I said under the blankets, Motherlover.

The next thing I knew I was propped upright in a corner of the back seat. It was daylight but I couldn't see anything but rain and mud. The car was stopped and gasoline was pouring into the tank. A man said, "Where was Alabama?"

Leo said, 'They were lucky all year. They were never really good."

Station: You Are Here

Mason first saw the canal from the top of a double-decker
bus. He was crossing from Swiss Cottage to Kensington and
riding on the top deck as he always did in order to look about
him. As always he was careful to pick an hour when it might be
possible to find a seat away from the inevitable pipe or the
Gauloise stench of burning socks. Somewhere in the middle of
the journey, the bus bobbed over a little bridge, and Mason,
looking idly down, saw the canal, a street of brown water, curving away between the walls of warehouses and lumber yards and
the corrugated fence of a building site. Beside the canal, on the
left as he saw it, there was a path, and on the path a man was
riding a bicycle.

The bus roared over the bridge and on its ordinary way, but
Mason had his picture. The man, wearing a dirty gabardine raincoat and tweed cap—and bicycle clips—rode on in a silence that
became more and more dense around him. He pedaled slowly
without ever leaving the bridge. Space receded from him and he
acquired supernatural volume, rounder than life if not larger.
The curve of the canal opened into the curve of the earth and
would never be done. But Mason and the bus had appointments
in the direction of Kensington and arrived inexorably there.

The bicycle rider did not desert Mason, however, but appeared
from time to time, silently pedaling and bringing with him the
smell of pond water. He was particularly present when Mason

read in the *Times* that a section of the canal at Regent's Park
was being opened as a public walk. Mason remembered now
seeing the canal at the zoo, and he quickly found the place and
walked there. No one was about. Birds sang in the thicket on
the Park side opposite. The water was filthy but fish were rising
among the litter. He passed under bridges and felt his path going tranquil across the torrents of traffic. A man on a bridge
shouted to him, "How do you get down there?" Mason gestured
back the way he had come and passed on. He felt silence thick-
ening around him and space hollowing out to accommodate his
bulk, but the new benches were already chalked with obscenities
and the new stanchions marked LIFE PRESERVERS already showed
only the bitter end of bright orange rope, and he came to the
end of the walk and had to return to the street.

Now the canal became an obsession with him. He went back
to Regent's Park and tried the PUBLIC FOOTPATH again. Again the
birds sang and the fish rose. Again he passed impervious to
traffic. But a gaily painted water bus from LITTLE VENICE passed
on its way to THE ZOO and half a dozen disgruntled passengers
glared at him. Again the bits of orange rope dangled from the
ravaged stanchions. And this time he knew that just under that
bridge and around that bend he would come to the barrier. It
was time to try something else.

He stood on the bridge at last and looked down at the spot
where he had seen the bicycle rider. Although traffic was roaring
behind him, he seemed to catch a hint of silence near the water
and of expanding, receptive space. He studied the buildings and
fences along the towpath but could see no break, no gate or
gap. He went to the nearest corner and began to follow the street
that paralleled the canal.

It was a deserted street, a devastated street. His footsteps
echoed in the vacuum, and the high fences and boarded windows
crowded in on him. An alley led him toward the canal but
brought him up against the blackened brick wall. Another alley
connected with a foot bridge, but the stairs and the bridge were
so stoutly fenced in with so high a fence that he couldn't even

see the water, and on top of the fence there were ornamental chevaux-de-frise and graceful spirals of barbed wire. Once, he got into the yard of an old warehouse that had a slip of its own, and through an arch he could see the canal but could find no way of reaching it. At the next bridge he stood long and looked down at the canal. In a muddy spot on the towpath he could plainly see the marks of bicycle tires. So there had to be a way, he told himself.

Immediately, however, he was forced to go a long way away from the canal in order to get around a gas works. He felt he had lost contact entirely when he came to a wide field, a park probably. It seemed to be completely flat but must have sloped up away from him, because at a great distance a soccer game flowed silently back and forth on the sky line, a frieze of figures remote and lovely.

Inevitably he was drawn toward them—grubby schoolboys stumbling through their games—and past toward what appeared to be a church of some kind with stubby towers and an enormous arched window in the end. Then he stopped amazed. There was a whole crowd of churches, all alike. He realized then that he must be standing in Wormwood Scrubs, looking at the prison. He veered off sharply, held at bay for a time by a railroad embankment, and at last found his way back to a bridge at which there was a well-worn path leading down to the canal. By then it was almost dark, however, and he was exhausted by his day's search. After carefully noting his position in his *London A-Z* (p. 59, map coordinates, F2), he injected himself into the transport system and was efficiently returned to his accustomed life.

Mason's accustomed life was a quiet one, extemporized from various literary odds and ends when in the middle of his life (45) he unexpectedly inherited a modest income. He immediately gave up his job in a New York advertising agency where year after year he had done very well what he was paid to do while wave after wave of young beards swept over him to glory and oblivion. He left his job with no more emotion than he had pursued it and turned his back on New York, which he actively detested, and settled in London on the modest fringes of Hampstead. He was convinced he was very fond of the English, but in truth he didn't know a single Englishman any more than he had known a single one of the New Yorkers he detested.

Each morning he had his letters and his *Times* at breakfast, although for a while he felt betrayed when the *Times* took the personal ads off the front page and looked like any other paper. He shopped around among other papers for some weeks but finally came back to the *Times* as somehow closest to itself. Each morning he lay dozing until he heard the clang of the mailbox, and as he sat up in bed he blessed postal inspector Anthony Trollope, whose noble conception it was that every Englishmen is entitled to have his letters every morning with his toast. Often in his gratitude he resolved to write a strong letter to the *Times* attacking the plan to replace the familiar pillar boxes, another of Trollope's conceptions, with some new thing. Often, when he felt in a remote way that his life might after all grow thin, he thought of dedicating his skills to humanitarian causes such as saving the pillar boxes.

After the letters had been considered and after the carefully annotated *Times* had been set aside to be thrown out at the end of the day, he was ready to write his own letters, always after a two-week delay in order not to seem too eager or, as he put it, not to impose too soon the burden of a reply. In spite of the fact that he had no real friends in New York, he did understand who would like to hear first-hand about the newest plays and who would like cameo reports of old buildings, Roman ruins, a minute detail discovered in Westminster Abbey, a vignette of pub life observed from an obscure corner, a walk on Hampstead Heath, a visit all at once to the graves of Karl Marx, Herbert Spencer, and George Eliot. The walk by the canal at Regent's Park and the search for the passage to the true Grand Union Canal would be, in fact, the subject of a new series of letters.

Somehow, no matter how much or how little the *Times* might

hold on a given day or how long or how short his letters, he always finished the letters precisely in time for lunch, which was invariably (and literarily) bread and cheese, although he allowed himself a good deal of latitude in the matter of cheeses and indulged, in the English manner, in a good deal of butter on the bread, having picked up the habit by watching people in restaurants. And black coffee, of course, Italian style, which he had actually come to like. While he ate, he read Henry James, the choice of novel often being dictated by James-derived plays he had seen or was to see, for lunch led to a walk in the afternoon, which led in turn to a theater in the evening.

It was a very efficient life, input and output balancing in a highly satisfactory manner—or so it almost always seemed to him when he considered his own ways. Sometimes, it is true, he vaguely felt there might be more, as when he contemplated his campaign to save the pillar boxes. Sometimes on Hampstead Heath or at the grave of Karl Marx he found a phrase that simply would not do for a letter and that clogged the channels of his prose the next morning. But these occasions were rare. A brisk walk quickly cleared his brain. It was a very good life.

Still half in a dream, he knew that something was different, but he automatically drifted into his morning ritual: "In winter I get up at night and dress by yellow candle light." Each morning was thus begun with pleasure, the recognition of life imitating art or at least justifying it. Wallowing in the pleasure of getting up in the dark, he lay in bed and listened for the mailman. Then he turned on the light and stood up. Today really was different. Today there was page 59, coordinates F2.

The mailman had not yet come when Mason passed his *Times* in the hall and went out into the street. At once he saw that getting up in the dark was one thing but going out into the dark street was something else again. There was nothing about that in the rhyme. Nothing to tell him that it really was dark, without even the suggestion of morning gray in the sky, the street lights still as bright and healthy as at midnight. Nothing to tell him that day was going on just the same as if by perverted instinct, children hurrying to school, traffic building up to its peak, small cars darting and stopping, nimble as fish in a stream. It was as if a perfectly ordinary day had been treated with a perfectly ordinary enchantment and not as if something awful were really happening to the sun. Train after crowded train swept through the station as he waited, but his outbound train when it came was empty except for a few schoolboys in uniform, and he was quickly taken to page 59, coordinates F2.

The day had achieved its full gray by the time he actually stood on the towpath of the canal. A lighter gray smudge on the sky stood for the sun. Day after day he had sat at his desk and watched it slide along the ridgepoles of the houses opposite, like a drifting gull, keeping pace with the cats on the garden walls. He daily expected it to go away like a cat at last and not come back. But now he had something else to follow, and it was only after he had instinctively turned toward the bridge where he had first seen the bicycle rider that he realized that the canal, unlike the sun, went in both directions and that he might have elected to go off quite differently. He was convinced, however, that he had chosen well.

The canal itself was no different from the canal at Regent's Park. The water was neither more nor less dirty. The floating litter was subtly different, however. It had the look of having been hurled in rather than blown in by the wind. There was less paper and more wood, fewer milk cartons and more bottles. The debris was at once more industrial and more personal, bits of styrofoam packing and gaudy plastic bottles for household use. There were also more contraceptives, which he looked on as a favorable omen because it reassured him that the pill had not after all rendered his memories and his hard-won techniques obsolete. Sullen bubbles rose through the water, suggestive of decay deep down, but fish still broke the surface and, as he bent to look closer, the black sheen of the water was turned white by the sudden flight of a school of tiny fish. He walked on in good spirits.

To his right was a high fence and beyond that the web of tracks of a railroad yard. To his left, beyond the canal, birds sang in a thicket. Beyond the thicket was the high brick wall of a cemetery with several gates facing the canal as if even a hundred years ago it had still been possible to expect the funeral barge of the Lady of Shallot to drift into view. Farther on, the railway yards gave way to the gas works and the cemetery to a succession of factories. He noted with pleasure that often there was a patch of flowers on the canal bank beside some obscure door in the back of a factory. He noted a laborer burning trash in a factory yard and tending a fishing pole propped at the canal's edge. He noted a block of houses backing on the canal as if in Venice, washings flying over the canal and back-porch secrets open to his view. And there was one moment when he stood exactly where he had seen the bicycle rider and watched a bus pass over the bridge. These were the things his letters were made of. But by noon he found himself wandering among warehouses at Paddington, having suddenly run out of canal.

For the next two weeks his letters were splendid—and got better—as he bent London over and spread its cheeks. It was with sincere regret that he wrote the last letter he could write on the subject without risking the danger of two of his correspondents comparing notes. He prepared to put away his *London A-Z* and the big street map he had bought to keep his memory within bounds—in fact, he had twice gone back to check the accuracy of his reports and pick up any lucky details beyond the reach of invention. He closed the book and folded the map and stared at them with regret as he ate his lunch. There should somehow be more than inconclusiveness at Paddington. Then he remembered what he had seen and not regarded as he first entered square F2 on page 59. The bicycle tracks went on under the bridge in the way he had not taken. There had been a sign that read BEYOND THIS POINT PRIVATE FISHERIES. And a man fishing. And a squadron of swans keeping him under surveillance.

There was no fisherman that day, but the swans came to him. The swans paddled beside him and hissed softly. He found that he could reproduce the sound by opening his mouth wide and blowing a *ha* along the roof of his mouth. The swans tired of the game more quickly than he did and swam off about their business, which seemed mostly to be making sure that the circling gulls weren't really on to something. Although there were only a few hours of daylight left, he was in no hurry. Conceivably there was no end to the canal. He did make a note of the time when he came down to the towpath so that he could always know how long it would take him to get back to F2 if there were no other exits. He quickly discovered, however, that at nearly every bridge a wire mesh had been beaten down for access, at every building site there was a loose panel in the fence, at every abandoned warehouse there was a way through a frameless window, a doorless door. He felt he had this time picked the right way. He felt the towpath stretch before him endlessly, so there was no hurry. He could never walk it all. The realization made him so happy that when he saw a pub near a bridge he climbed up and got a pint before 3:00 closing.

The pub was small and grubby and almost deserted. It was very different from his local, the Washington, where he felt as if he had wandered by mistake into an enormous cocktail party and was the only stranger in the place, a pariah even, so that he no longer so much as tried to speak to the barmaid but just pointed to the tap as if he were dumb or a foreigner. But here in this strange pub he risked the two words he was confident of. "Pinta bitta," he said. "Right," the barman said and filled the mug and eyed it and let it settle and filled it again and eyed it again. Mason didn't think it was so clear as it should be, but "Wot th' bloody 'ell you think you're serven?" was not exactly his style, so he was silent—and he might have been wrong. However, the barman set it aside and took a fresh glass and tried a fresh tap. "Right," he said as he set it before Mason. "Right," Mason said. The barman returned to his game of darts with the two customers, taking bottles of Guinness all around as he went. Mason, well content, chose a chair from which he could see the dart board, for he had acquired considerable connoisseurship of darts at the Washington and in his first enthusiasm had even bought a dart board and practiced anxiously in private. In public, however, he had never touched a dart. When the Guinness was drunk and the game finished, the customers went out a minute or two before the barman would have had to announce closing. And Mason followed at once.

The canal was now passing between back gardens of a very respectable sort. Men looked up from their flowers and eyed him coldly. Occasionally a street came down to the canal, and once a street turned and became the towpath for a block. Swans paraded the street and inspected the front gardens opposite, and a woman came out and threw them scraps over the fence. The swans hurried to her like hens in a coop, especially the mottled brown swans which Mason judged, by analogy to gulls, to be young ones in their first-year plumage.

It was already dusk when Mason heard footsteps behind him on the gravel. The steps were heavy and quick. He was tense but not seriously alarmed. He was just approaching a bridge where there was a lot of traffic and during the afternoon he had got pretty well used to the people he was likely to meet on the towpath. The better-dressed men seemed lost in thought, but women smiled distantly when he stood aside to let them pass on their bicycles. The men that Mason thought of as working men seemed open to greeting and usually were. Once he had stopped to watch a boy fishing. "I never see anybody catching anything," he said. "You have to know where you're fishing and what for," the boy said, contemptuously glancing toward some boys fishing in a happy group and, as Mason had noted in passing, quite without success. "There are fish all right," the boy said. And he pulled out a tiny fish to prove it. "A stickleback," he said. Mason bent to take a good look. He had read about stickleback nests. But the boy wrapped the fish in his handkerchief and gently disengaged the hook and dropped the fish back into the water. "What did you do that for?" Mason said. "The handkerchief, I mean." "To protect the fish," the boy said. "I wondered," Mason said. "I was taught to wet my hand." He looked at the water doubtfully and went on his way.

The footsteps came on with a rush, and a man fell into step with Mason. Out of the corner of his eye, Mason noted that the man was much smaller than he, which ought to have been a consolation but wasn't because Mason had no knowledge or experience of violence to draw on. "Just off work, mate?" the man said in a heavy Irish accent. "Right," Mason said and was at once appalled by the course he had taken. To be sure he had inherited a classic Irish face—so classic that he often passed for a Jew—but he had been brought up to scorn—and to fear—the bog-trotting Irish. "The pay is all right but it's far from home," the Irishman said. And having once got away with it, Mason again said, "Right." Mason stood up taller and threw out his chest, but then he remembered once in an Irish pub in Camden Town hearing a barmaid wish that Muhammad Ali would stop in to chat up the boys as he had done the night before in a pub in another part of the city. "But on second thought," she said, "I wish he wouldn't because if he did there'd be sure to be three or four little Irishmen who thought they had to prove something." Mason shrank into his collar and into his shoes. He telescoped himself at the knees and settled gently into his pelvis. They were about to pass under the bridge. It would be very dark there. Loud traffic noises above. "Will I see you at the Lion?" the Irishman said and sprang up a path to the bridge. "I'll be going on," Mason called after him. It sounded to himself as if he were mocking the Irishman but perhaps the noise of the traffic covered his words.

Somewhere beyond the bridge Mason stepped into a thicket to piss. As he hiked up his zippered jacket and fumbled at the heavy corduroy of his trousers and carefully planted his stout walking shoes—Sears' best work shoes—he suddenly saw himself as an object, even to the great smear on the shoulder of his jacket, the nameless smear he always got on his clothes even when he crossed on the best ships. "Just out of work, mate?" he said to himself. "Right," he said. "Jesus."

Next morning in his impatience he took his breakfast standing up and left the house in the dark without having bothered to shave. In the first light of day he hurried off page 58. Then he toiled across 39 and 38, cut across the corner of 56 and passed beyond the grid of the *London A-Z*. The stench of kerosene, the burning in his eyes, the repeated howl of the jets told him he was on a true course for Heathrow Airport, but he kept on, trusting that the canal would bend around the airport—or the airport around the canal—as it had bent around railway yards, gas works, blocks of flats, factories, warehouses—or they around it. For a few moments he was very happy as he stopped to rest where the canal sailed like a Roman aqueduct over a busy motorway. He waved to some children in a car. They must have thought him some kind of railway worker. Who would ever guess a canal up here? Who could control his car if he saw the sails of a boat passing high over his head?

But there were no boats. Not since he saw some houseboats at Paddington had he seen any sign that the canal was in use. The great freight doors of the factories were obviously never opened. Weeds grew in the docking areas. Mooring rings were disappearing in the sand. Many warehouses were ruinous. He saw a crew of men dismantling one, salvaging steel beams and sheet-metal roofing. Now, however, he began to see the deep, cleated track of a large wheel, wider by far than a bicycle, too heavy even for a motorcycle. It led him to hope that something was pulling barges along the canal—he hadn't actually hoped for horses. And presently he came to a dredge loading barges with muck from the canal bottom. He was encouraged.

The prospect was now more pleasing. It was a narrow prospect to be sure, along the canal and between dense thickets. He seemed to have got out of the traffic pattern of the airport. Even the water seemed cleaner. Then he thought he saw—and, yes, he did see—framed in the little arch of a distant bridge, a number of barges tied up in regular tiers as on the Thames itself. Gulls swept over the water. A bird sang in the bush beside him. He stopped and waited. "Sing again," he said, but the bird wouldn't sing, nor even fly from its hiding place. Fish broke the surface of the water beside him as he went on. Swans patrolled the approaches to the bridge up ahead. He hissed at them with open mouth. "Bird in the bush, bird in the bush, sing again," he said to his own surprise and realized he had been silently repeating "bird in the bush" to the rhythm of his footsteps. Wordsworth was right, he said to himself. Walking does make the rhythm come. And he passed under the little arch and found he had come to the end of his canal.

Or to be more exact his canal made a T-junction with another canal. The barges tied up opposite were at a repair yard. There was even one on a way ready for a sidewise launching, a reassuring sign of life. Others were in drydock. It was not exactly boxes and corded bales but it was highly reassuring. The yard stretched away toward his left, so he was drawn in that direction and went on. After all, how *could* he choose?

The towpath soon became a sort of sidewalk sunk a couple of feet below a street. The houses opposite all had signs NO TURNING IN THIS DRIVE. Some even had wires stretched across the drive. But the pub at the next bridge served a very decent ham roll to go with his bottle of Guinness. He lingered over a second bottle and listened to the daily reports of old men living their children's lives.

After lunch the rhythm was insistent. Bird in the bush, bird in the bush. But so was the beer and there was no bush. In desperation he stopped under a bridge and pissed into the water. The clatter under the arch was magnificent. "Sing again," he shouted. "Sing again."

Then there was a lock. It occurred to him that this was the first lock he had seen all the way from Paddington. Of course there was the aqueduct but such a level stretch was remarkable. He admired the great gates and the jets of water spurting from the cracks. He was surprised by the sweeps by which men obviously had to operate the gates. Perhaps he had been too pessimistic in not expecting horses on the towpath. He was delighted with the cobblestoned area at the sweeps where the men would work and with the radiating lines of raised stones against which they would brace their feet. He looked down the canal for a barge to watch so he could see it all and perhaps even help out and get the feel, but there was nothing in sight. The lock attendant called across to a woman just passing on a bicycle, "Anything coming up?" "No," she said. "They broke in again last night," he said, jerking his head toward what seemed to be a lock keeper's cottage, although perhaps now unoccupied. "Pity," she said, standing astride her bicycle. "See?" he said. "Don't mind if I do," she said and rested her bicycle against the fence, not without a glance at Mason, and walked briskly across the top of the gate to the other side. She looked back again at Mason, so he moved along.

He passed two more locks and came in sight of another quick pair. He began to think it would be a good idea to keep count of them, but when he had come to the pair he couldn't remember whether five was the count including the pair or whether the five he said when he first saw them referred to the lock he was then passing or even whether five was the number he had been carrying in his mind up to that point. So there were five or seven or nine, and he went on having the same difficulty. When he came to the end of the locks, he settled on ten as a likely number and then changed it to nine for credibility.

The landscape steadily deteriorated as he came down along the locks. The most interesting thing was a plaque commemorating a pile-driving competition years ago. Fields of sparse brown grass looked utterly useless, waiting only to be laid out in streets of sparse brown houses. A close-cropped green field supported six wretched horses, one so lame that it hurt Mason to put his feet down on the towpath. He passed under a motorway and recognized the tops of buildings that are landmarks on the route from the airport. He passed under a very high brick bridge rather like an aqueduct. He stopped to study a weir—WARNING WEIR AHEAD KEEP RIGHT—and found it to be only a spillway, a cement wall over which water flowed to a stream below in order to maintain the constant level of the canal. Hardy's weirs didn't sound at all like this, but he would have to check them again when he got home. And suddenly there were barges and warehouses and all the bustle he could desire. The towpath led through warehouses. He had to BEWARE OF OVERHEAD CRANES. Corded bales of Ovaltine were coming out of the hold of a barge as he passed. He had also to beware of a field trip of girls in school uniform. "All right, you chaps, all right," the mistress said, "line up by twos." The towpath ended. The canal went on between sheer warehouse walls. Around the nearest corner Mason found a way to a wharf and the Thames.

His A-Z, his street map, his transport maps, much inquiry, and a little luck brought him back to the T-junction of the Paddington Branch and what he supposed to be the main line. He had come by bus and by train and by underground and would have used a cab if he could have caught one. He had come through strange cities where the men wore turbans and the women wore saris, where the neatly uniformed children who swarmed onto the bus were very brown and dark-eyed and spoke to each other in a tongue that might have matched the psychedelic alphabet on the shop signs. But finally he passed the driveways where no one was to turn and came to the boat yard and the junction. Darkness was not far off as he crossed the hump-backed bridge over the Paddington Branch and took his first new step.

His first new step was not a light step, however, for he was by now very tired. He walked with his head down and followed the marks of the tractor as if he were hunting it, and as if he were a hunter he observed, to his own amazement, that the marks after the puddles were very wet, water draining slowly out of the depressions made by the cleats, scattered bits of mud still wet as if just dredged. Now he hurried on, peering ahead.

At the next bend he caught a glimpse of the barge just passing under a bridge and out of sight. By the time he got to the bridge it had disappeared, but the reassuring tracks insisted that there was, after all, nowhere for it to go but on. He lost it twice more. But each time he saw it it was closer. Finally he overtook it on a long reach. His pace was so close to the barge's that he walked a long time beside the man standing at the tiller, watchful but relaxed, smoking an easy pipe but constantly correcting the direction of the barge. When Mason first came abreast of the rudder, the man took out his pipe and waved a greeting with it. Mason waved back as if there had been roaring seas between them. They continued to glance at each other in a friendly way until Mason slowly drew ahead.

He was definitely bored with the barge before he was done with it, and then there was the long tow rope vibrating beside him as he gained on it fist over fist against the torrent of noise from the little tractor, which was, after all, only the kind of thing to give at Christmas to the man who has everything, useful for plowing a drive or mowing the back forty-foot square. Mason looked ahead, timed his pace, and overtook the tractor at a place suitably wide and dry. He passed in a burst that made his legs hurt and his heart pound. The driver, lost in the fury of his machine, was looking back at the barge over his other shoulder as Mason passed, so Mason never saw more than the back of his head. Then it was night.

Darkness was a two-dimensional trick. Strings of yellow lights went from left to right or up and down but never receded. Flaming founderies and the torches of refineries were higher or lower or brighter or muted but never nearer or farther. Small specks of light near the top were supposed to give the illusion of depth and even tried to improve on the illusion by appearing again along the black streak of the canal. Mason crawled across this surface, black and invisible, toward a red spot low down that gradually worked its way up, accelerating alarmingly toward the end until it nearly bent him over backwards and stood over him, a neon tube at the corner of a bridge pub.

He was very tired and very hungry as he opened the door, and he read only automatically a sign that retreated before him as the door swung. He was inside the room before he realized he ought not to patronize a pub that announced NO CARAVAN DWELLERS WILL BE SERVED HERE. But he was in the room. The air was thick with noise and smoke. Everyone seemed to be talking at once, and every face as it turned toward him was talking, laughing, convulsed with animation about the mouth but about the eyes very still, as if looking at something in a test tube. Mason was used to that, however, and made his way through the crowd toward the bar.

He couldn't get very close to the bar and lurked one and a half persons or so back and tried to catch a barman's eye. "Pinta bitta," he called twice when he thought it might be his turn. Then he tried "Bottle of Guinness" with no better result. It was very tiresome. People got their drinks and stood at the bar or passed them back over his head, but he never got any closer and he never caught a barman's eye. He felt very tired and very old—they were all so young, so vigorous, so loud, so smoky that he felt he might just as well creep away and find a cafe suitable for old men down on their luck. He was about to turn away when a woman took him by the arm and said, "Let's get out of here." So he went.

They went fifty yards down the street to another pub that was just as crowded and noisy and smoky as the other. The people were just as young, and they put him just as much in a test tube, although a number of them spoke to the girl by name, Edith, as she worked her way to the bar. Mason got a pint of Guinness to sustain himself because there didn't seem to be any food, and a whiskey for the girl—no, he had decided out of the corner of his eye and in bad light as they changed pubs that she wasn't a girl. Her skirt was very short, although with her heavy legs her skirt suggested more courage than discretion. Her embroidered coat, her dangling earrings, her loose blonde hair all were girlish. But she was clearly no girl. She had that same pale blue, wide-open scientist's eye, rather quelling he thought. Insolent, he would like to say. It must be what he had read of as a machine-gunner's eye and had never understood

before. At first he had supposed it went with a certain educa-
tion—Singing, Dancing, Drawing, and Glance slightly extra at
Miss Pinkerton's School. But it was far too common for that.
Perhaps the result of some historical process, the eye of Woman-
on-a-pedestal in the face of Votes-for-women on the body of
Single-standard-if-any.

They fought their way to a corner and found it relatively free.
Everyone seemed to be trying to stand in the exact center of the
room as if they were playing some discrete version of King of
the Mountain. "This is more like," Edith said.

"Yes," Mason said, "isn't it?" He still had most of his Guinness but he didn't begrudge those portions of it that had gone
down people's backs and into their pockets.

"You should have got it in a thin glass," Edith said. "They
have no business serving Guinness in those bloody thick mugs."

"I hate to ask," Mason said. "I'm afraid they'd think I was
putting it on, trying to be in."

"Bloody great fools," Edith said. She got her whiskey in her
sights and downed it in a single burst.

"May I?" Mason said, reaching for her glass.

"My round," Edith said. "I pay my way. Not one of those
girls."

"I insist,'" Mason said. The situation was going to his head.
"I'm a rich American."

"Truly?"

"In actual fact, no," Mason said, coming on very British this
time. "But let me anyway."

"You are American, though?" Mason nodded. "That explains
a great deal," she said and held out her glass. "I'll look after
yours," she said. "It would never survive another trip through the
eye of the storm." They exchanged glasses, and he went to
the bar.

Mason's wheels had been going around furiously while he
worked his trip to the bar and back, and he came up with a be-
lated question. "Explains what?" he said as he handed her the
whiskey.

"Explains why you couldn't get a drink at The Swan—bloody fools—and why I knew they were making a mistake."

"Ah, yes," Mason said, and he reclaimed his mug.

"No," she said, "you don't see. I can tell you but you won't see. It takes a lifetime to know the signs. It's how you dress and what you drink and what you smoke. Things you wouldn't dream meant anything. Give me a cigarette."

"Sorry," Mason said. "I'll get some. What kind?"

"Never mind," she said. "I've got my own. I just wanted to prove something. For example, if you'd pulled out a blue pack of Gauloises, I'd have known you were a person I wanted nothing to do with—if you were English, that is. Only a certain kind of Englishman smokes Gauloises, a kind with pretensions, a kind you don't want to have anything to do with."

"It's the smell I can't stand," Mason said. "I visualize someone going around Paris in the spring and collecting socks people have been wearing since the beginning of winter and grinding them up dirt and all to make those cigarettes."

"Don't be too sure they don't," she said. "They'd do anything."

"It's what it smells like anyway," Mason said. "For a long time I thought I was smelling feet."

"Disgusting," Edith said. With marvelous reflexes she shot down another whiskey she wasn't even looking at. Mason congratulated himself on the healthy state of his petty cash and on the reserves prudently hidden about his person.

"Guinness is an all-right drink. I wouldn't recommend it for a serious night's drinking though. Too heavy. But suppose you go into a pub with a chap you've just met and you say Guinness, and he says Mild and brown, you know all you need to know. You chat him up, have your drink, and never see him again. See what I mean?"

"Yes," Mason said, and he really did have a very clear picture even if it wasn't exactly what she meant. "Shall I get you another?" And he did.

"Of course," she said, "for you it's different. You can wear what you like, smoke what you like, drink what you like. The same things don't mean the same things. But you do have signs, I suppose, the way you know each other. Dogs know how an ass hole ought to smell, if you pardon my French." Mason took it as a general observation, applying equally to what she had said about the English, and perhaps he was right. It was beginning to look, however, as if he was going to have to invest more than money.

"Americans are a marvelous people," she said. "I see you're a Wasp so I can speak freely." Mason wanted to rush off to the Gents to take a good look at himself in the mirror, but he settled for rubbing his hand over his face. It felt unchanged, although he really needed a shave, worse luck. "A wonderful people, standing alone against Communism, doing what's right in the face of world opinion."

"We aren't exactly united at home," Mason said.

"Keeping your own people in line at home. Oh, we admire you and we study you to be ready when the crunch comes here. They're coming in every day and taking our jobs and lowering our standards and demanding more and more all the time. They think we're soft but they'll see. Believe me, they'll see."

"Colonial chickens come home to roost," Mason said mildly.

"We'll pull the roost right out from under them."

"I tell you what," Mason said. "I haven't had anything to eat all day. Could we find something to eat somewhere?"

"Come to my place. I'll give you bacon and eggs."

"That would be a nuisance. Let me treat you."

"Do come. I like to pay my way."

"It's probably your breakfast you're offering," Mason said.

"No, not at all." She got her glass in her sights but seemed already to have riddled it in some abstracted moment.

"Let me bring something to drink, then."

"If you want to," she said. "We can stop at the off-license and get a bottle." She reached up and put her glass on a sort of moulding or plate rail that ran around the room and that was already lined with glasses.

"Are you sure it's all right?" Mason said.

"All right?"

"Proper, then," Mason said.

"My god," she said. "This is the Permissive Age, man."

"I didn't want to take advantage of you."

"You wouldn't." Their eyes met and Mason knew he wouldn't.

"Or compromise you."

"Haven't you heard? Everything is permitted. Sin is permitted. It's bloody all permitted."

"Then OK," Mason said. He put up his glass and followed her. What luck it was to have been brought up when skirts were long so that now these legs, these glorious legs everywhere, silken and long and whispering, whispered to him Touch me, Touch me as they never could (he supposed) to boys to whom a glimpse had never meant everything.

Mason woke up very slowly. For a long time he was aware of his arms and legs, of his back and sides, of his stomach. He was scratching himself. Something seemed to have spilled on him. He was all wet. He got quickly out of bed and hurried to the bathroom. Cockroaches scuttled for cover as he turned on the light. He tried to lift himself off the floor and hover before the mirror. He was terrified when he saw himself covered with blood, but then he found he had only scratched the top off several of the great insect bites that covered him from head to foot. The light from the bathroom showed him the bed. The wall beside the bed was seething with bedbugs. Edith slept undisturbed. Brought me home as a decoy, fresh meat for her pets, Mason said to himself as he collected his clothes and took refuge in the bathroom where the cockroaches, he theorized, would at least try to avoid him.

He inspected each article of clothing as he put it on and hoped passionately that her resources were limited to bedbugs and cockroaches. He left, by way of revenge, a five-pound note on the kitchen table and with great care let himself out of the flat.

His watch had stopped but it was still very dark and there

was no one on the streets. A cold wind made him think of shelter, and he began to walk briskly. A series of signs directed him to the railroad station but the station was closed. In front of the station was a large map in a glass case. In the middle of the map a light burned and beside the light a label proclaimed, STATION—YOU ARE HERE. On the frame below the map a row of buttons suggested destinations for him. He tried UNDERGROUND STATION, and a light flashed on in the wilderness of streets in quite another part of town. But that would be closed. He tried HOTEL and that was near at hand, but between it and him his bloated unshaven reflection hovered in the glass. He tried PARKS and got a fine pattern of points of light, mostly in distant places, but they seemed hard to find. If only the route would light up on the map. In any case he was too cold for a night in the open. Then he noticed that just beside the light marked STATION there was a strip of blue marked CANAL. He followed it with his eye, flowing serene to the edge of the map where there was a notation TO BIRMINGHAM. To Birmingham, then. Days of walking. And where beyond? No limit. None at all. Within a minute he was on the towpath.

Late in the night he tired and took shelter in a village church. At least there was no wind. He sat nodding in a pew. And he saw himself standing by the map, pushing the buttons. Only the map didn't light up—he did. A network of shining nerves. A tree of veins. A chandelier of bones. He was lovely.

He woke with his head and both hands on the back of the pew in front of him. He straightened himself and studied his hands. One was red and one was blue. He looked toward the stained glass. The light was very strong. He tried to intercept it with his hand to see what color his face was, but he kept failing and had to give up.

The Tale of the Peasant Osip

You'll think I'm crazy trying to tell a story about a Russian peasant. I'd think so too in your place. What's the matter with him? I'd say. He must think he's Chekhov or Turgenev. Delusions of grandeur. Stick to what you know, I'm always telling my students. And what do I know about Russians, peasants or otherwise? Of course I love the Russian writers and give their books my fullest response, but I'd never pretend I really understand the Russianness of *The Hunting Sketches*, say, or *Ward 6* or *The Insulted and Injured* or that I really dig the authors, that pack of Frenchmen as Avrahm Yarmolinsky used to call them. Oh, I see all the Russian films I can find, trying to flesh out my imagination. But that doesn't help much. Even after seeing a troika who could imagine one? I'm afraid that, as I read, Russian gentlemen are still galloping around in something like a hansom cab—with three horses, of course, very obscurely harnessed—and that peasants still ride to town in old Mr. Luddy's tipcart. It can't be helped. The films are very interesting, full of fantastic details I'd love to use and full of fantastic Czarist types, who must be kept locked up at the studios because any right-thinking cop would liquidate them on sight as an offense to public decency. But what's the use? I'd somehow get it all subtly wrong. Telling a story about a Russian peasant is crazy.

Except it's not a story. It's a dream. It came to me fully formed. Of course it's slipping away now. I can't write fast enough to keep the plot and characters in place. And there's the difficulty of viewpoint. It seems to me that I was a woman in the dream. I suppose, really, that by taking thought a man could add a cubit to his stature or imagine his way into the nature of a Russian peasant. But a woman—good god. That's beyond being crazy. So there I am in the dream, a Russian woman. This is clearly to be a story of maximum technical difficulty. Not only that but it has to be based on a technical lie, because the only woman in the dream—and I must assume that's who I was— knew something that is to be reserved for the end, that gives the meaning a sudden twist. Since the knowledge must constantly be in her consciousness, it is dishonest not to make it accessible to the reader as well. At least this is what I believe and drum into my students. If I were writing this story, I'd have to change the point of view, let everything be seen by someone who cannot know the secret, her husband, perhaps, or a stranger—a government inspector, say, or a traveling portrait painter. Yes, he could be painting her portrait as the tragedy unfolds. Oh, very good. Just right.

Unfortunately, I am not writing a story but reporting a dream. I can't start off Once upon a time, the way I like to do, and then change it after I have lulled myself into the story. I have to start off, wham, there they are, all talking at once. No point of view at all. I don't even know who they are. I can't find out which one is supposed to be me. Naturally I'm not surprised that they are all dressed as if for the TV version of *The Forsythe Saga*. Nor does it surprise me that they are talking Russian—ah, there's one in a peasant blouse just like *A Month in the Country*. There's no problem with language because I never hear anything they say but know what they're saying. Subtitles or simultaneous translation may be the device. There are one, two gentlemen. I thought there were more. A lady. And the peasant. Am I the peasant?

Yes, I should like to think so. He is a man of vigorous middle age. He has been educated—at least he reads a good deal. Perhaps he is clerk or overseer of the estate. No, his coloring and general frame suggest something more active. Perhaps game-keeper or miller. He must have been bred as a clerk but didn't like it. As he gained his master's confidence, he was able to get a transfer to a job where he could be more solitary. He thinks a lot and has strong ideas, although it is not clear whether they are religious or political. It might be nice to be this man. Osip is his name. It would be interesting to learn that this is my secret image of myself.

The older of the two gentlemen is about Osip's age. There is ancient familiarity between them as if they had been boys to-gether on the estate—perhaps I'm thinking of Faulkner here, though. But if I am, I'll have to keep an eye on Osip for signs of secret Blackness. That would be an interesting image of myself. This gentleman has spent much time in Europe but has been drawn less to the usual German spas and to Paris than to London where there is political economy. He does not love political economy, however. Quite the contrary. He sees it as a sort of plague infecting Russia, and he seeks an antidote, an inoculation. He reads constantly in *The Little Blue Book of Adam Smith* and constantly shakes his head in despair. I should not be surprised if his name were Fyodor Mikhailovitch, but I hear him addressed as Pyotr Petrovitch.

The younger gentleman is engaged to his daughter, who for some reason does not appear. Well, I'll tell you why she does not appear. This is an afterthought, though. The truth is that my oldest daughter is getting married shortly. After all, this is a dream and takes a little explaining. She lives in another city and the arrangements at long distance are difficult and often ex-asperating. Day by day she has forced on me the knowledge that she is not here but elsewhere. It is for this reason, perhaps, that she is banished from the dream. The young man, on the other hand, poses no problems, although he is by definition a problem, so he can be admitted to the dream but must be expected to make trouble. When she was little, she liked to be called Ivanna and to hear her name and mine rolled out together in the Rus-sian manner. In fact, all the children liked that, and in play I would often call them Ivanna Danilovna or Katerina Danilovna and so on. Well, that was a long time ago. A very long time ago. Ivanna Danilovna. It's hard to believe.

The woman is called Marfa Petrovna. She is the wife of the older gentleman. She is the mother of the missing daughter. She is the prospective mother-in-law of the younger gentleman. Her relationship to Osip remains to be seen. I would bet a good deal, however, that she has never been his mistress, or, not to confuse matters, because she owns him lock, stock, and barrel and is in that sense his mistress, I will change my bet and say he has never been her lover. There's something there, but that's not it. I am finding it very strange that I should know so much about the others and so little about Marfa Petrovna. Strange, that is, in light of the fact that as the action develops—if that's the word for it—I discover that I am Marfa Petrovna.

That's really amazing, but not without precedent. I remember dreaming once that I was Perry Como. I was being introduced on a stage. Everyone was smiling and clapping, expecting me to do something. But what was ridiculous was that I didn't know who Perry Como was. Still don't, as a matter of fact. I mean, I really was Perry Como and could do whatever Perry Como does. There was a piano on the stage and all kinds of musical instruments. Microphones, of course. I needed only the faintest clue and I would begin to play the piano or the saxophone or to sing or tell jokes and everyone would scream and faint and tear off their clothes or my clothes or whatever it is Perry Como makes people do whenever he does whatever it is he does. So there I stood, feeling vaguely perplexed, and everyone went on smiling and clapping until the end of the dream. Or maybe the floor opened and swallowed me up.

And there I was being Marfa Petrovna without the least idea who Marfa Petrovna was. You can imagine whether I was paying close attention to see if I could sort things out. Everyone was talking at once. They were all excited, waving their arms, spilling their tea—being very Russian, in short. It was an uproar. At the same time, it was crystal clear. I might have been looking at an exploded drawing of a complicated machine, the circulatory system, say. Each speech stood apart, each speaker spoke in a different color and in a different area. I could have been reading it off a ticker tape or listening to exchanges in a string quartet. And yet, of course, it wasn't clear at all. Not in so many words, not any more than the quartet.

The young man wanted something. He was making trouble, exactly as I expected. He wanted to borrow the peasant Osip. That's it. The others were going away on a trip, and he wanted to borrow Osip while they were gone. Now it comes out that Osip was a carpenter. That is consistent. He was a master of his craft and an ingenious workman. Pyotr Petrovitch could have sold him a dozen times and named his own price, but he valued Osip as a workman and as a man. It would be foolish to say that the prosperity of Pyotr Petrovitch's estate rested on Osip, but it would not be very foolish, only a trifle poetic, perhaps. And it was not only the prosperous appearance of the estate—the fine repair of every house and barn and fence and well curb—that was owing to Osip the carpenter. There was something else owing to Osip the man, the respect in which he was held by everyone from Pyotr Petrovitch—yes, and Marfa Petrovna— down to the lowest goose girl, to the oldest woman sitting in a doorway watching the girl watch the geese, out to the most remote gamekeeper, to the ferryman himself, who was only half in, half out of the estate. So Osip was a jewel and Pyotr Petrovitch knew he was a jewel and would not part with him even for a day—unless Osip himself wished it, of course.

And Osip in this case did not wish it. There was enough work on the estate to keep him busy. It was fall or it was spring, and there was the fall work or the spring work to set in train. There was a new greenhouse he hoped to have ready against Marfa Petrovna's return. It did her no good to protest, to suggest priorities. Osip knew what needed to be done. He had established priorities.

Furthermore, it was not for a day that the younger man—it's curious that he has no name. I've just noticed that. Not even at the utmost stretch of politeness do the others address him by name. Osip gives him "your honor" until he frowns with impatience, but he must go down as having no proper name. What he wants is quite right and proper, very logical and natural. He wants to borrow Osip to build a house for his bride, for Ivanna Petrovna. What could be more reasonable? He wants only the best for her, a splendid new house on his own estate. It's a compliment all around, to Ivanna, to Osip, to Ivanna's parents, and to Osip's master, to his own taste and judgment not least of all. But Osip will have none of it. Even if Pyotr Petrovitch and Marfa Petrovna are going on a journey, the estate is not going anywhere, and their very absence only makes it more necessary for him to keep an eye on things, to carry out some schemes for rebuilding their private apartments. Not so much as a day can he spare. Not an hour. Not even for Ivanna Petrovna, may she prosper. No matter how long the journey, his work is longer.

The journey may be a very long one. They are going to Germany, because this time it is not a matter of political economy but of Marfa Petrovna's health. She is not really ill, but she is certainly not well. Some certain female complaint. Curiosity upon curiosity. When I thought I might be Osip I was watching him for signs of secret Blackness. Now I find that not only am I a woman but that I have a bona fide female complaint. A bona fide complaint of a certain age. Ah, if you just let the words fall long enough, they'll sooner or later tell you something. Of a certain age, that is, of an age curiously like my own age.

A certain male complaint of a certain age, that is. I'll not go into details, though. Men of a certain age will understand, and wives, particularly young wives, of men of a certain age will understand. There's no good trying to explain it to others. They'll only say, Impossible. It can't happen to me. I'll hang myself, they'll say, when that happens. I can remember saying that myself, but I haven't hanged myself—not yet. So I'll just leave it alone. If you know, you know. If you don't know, the news will get around to you fast enough.

In the beginning I was surprised to discover that there were only two gentlemen (and a lady and Osip) making all that noise and spilling all that tea—for some reason Osip was drinking tea along with the rest of them, glass for glass. Now they seemed like a dozen. The young man was very angry. Pyotr Petrovitch was deeply disturbed, and when he became excited his voice got higher and higher and finally almost falsetto, which is very strange, because that is a characteristic of my own, and I am Marfa Petrovna, who for a sick woman was all this time performing splendidly, holding up the part of a dozen ladies, balancing the illusory dozen gentlemen. She flashed her eyes and her teeth and her gleaming dark hair, her rings and her earrings, her bracelets and the lacquer of her fan. Her dress glinted in mysterious folds. Her bosom glittered as her passion rose. At the hem of her dress something on her little shoe gleamed and was gone. No wonder she was a match for any two men pretending to be twelve.

Osip was not included in the uproar, of course. He was not a gentleman to begin with, and as the others became more excited, he became more wary. He hadn't been a peasant all his life for nothing. He limited himself to No, your honor and to No, your honor, it can't be done. He even stopped drinking tea and hid his glass within his large red hands. Suddenly everyone was quiet and looked toward Pyotr Petrovitch.

The young man had offered to buy Osip. Pyotr Petrovitch could name his own price. The young man would have Osip and no other build the house for Ivanna Petrovna, the very man who had built for her and carved for her all her life and knew what would most delight her heart. Anything else was impossible. This wasn't the first time Pyotr Petrovitch had been offered his own price for Osip. But always before he had known what to say: he would as soon sell Ivanna Petrovna as Osip. And that was the end of it. Now, in a sense, he had sold Ivanna Petrovna, and he had got a fine price for her, too, and it was the very man who had bought her who now wanted to buy Osip. There was a mad, disturbing logic about it. He looked toward

Marfa Petrovna, who was now all dark, and toward Osip, who was silent. They might have been pillars of salt, but they were graven pillars, and the message was still No, Pyotr Petrovitch, your honor, it cannot be done. With deep regret and humblest apologies, Pyotr Petrovitch relayed the message.

Matters were now very grave. Everyone was silent. They sipped their tea with great gentility. Even Osip raised his empty glass to his lips and pretended to drink. The young man selected a bonbon from a silver dish and popped it into his mouth like a cad and began to speak with his mouth full and with great elegance. He managed to give the impression that he had just taken a pinch of snuff. It was, he regretted, now impossible for the marriage to go on. Such a failure of confidence on the part of a prospective father-in-law—

Marfa Petrovna fainted. Or it is much more likely, since there is no gap of intelligence in the dream, that she pretended to faint in order to gain a little time. Pyotr Petrovitch, with cool and practiced skill, found her smelling salts in her reticule—a word you don't get a chance to use every day—and applied the vial—another—to her nose. She rolled her head to escape the fumes. In my sleep I feel the cold tears on my cheeks.

Pyotr Petrovitch took advantage of the time his wife had gained for him. Through the blur of her eyelashes she saw him grinding at the problem. It was jewel weighed against jewel. His hands, as he worked with her reticule and her salts, were light and sure, delicate in their touch and sensitive in their judgment. It was jewel against jewel, and as he thought about one and then the other, first his right hand and than his left hand sank inexorably to his side. Marfa Petrovna closed her eyes tight, and the frail tissues of her lids turned her brain red. She sighed and opened her eyes. Pyotr Petrovitch's eye sockets were pools of blood.

"It shall be so," he said to the younger man. The younger man nodded gravely and had the good grace not to smile. Marfa Petrovna sighed again, although by now she was fully conscious. Osip came forward and kissed Pyotr Petrovitch's hand but said nothing. Pyotr Petrovitch, deep in conversation with the younger man, did not even look at him but went on talking as before, and the younger man started for a moment when he thought he was being told to prepare his things for immediate departure.

"It shall be so," Osip said. He kissed Marfa Petrovna's hand and vanished.

Marfa Petrovna now took up her station at the samovar, although what she did there is not very clear. Everyone was longing for a good glass of tea, and soon all two dozen of them were talking at once and spilling tea and being very Russian. Marfa Petrovna held her sugar between her lips—of course, it should be her teeth—and sipped her tea and then sent the sugar to Osip as a great mark of her esteem, which was very odd, because there was no one there to carry the sugar, but go it did.

Even more odd was the knowledge that arrived by no agency whatever, that was not spoken, but that was known equally by all. Suddenly, they were merely two gentlemen and a lady, sitting and looking at each other as angels who know the heart's secrets must look at each other in hell. Osip had hanged himself.

Now the terrible gaze that enabled each to look at once into the eyes of two others made Marfa Petrovna's secret knowledge common to all of them. Osip was not Pyotr Petrovitch's to sell in the first place. Many years before, Marfa Petrovna had given him his freedom, and so great was his value of the gift and so great was his love of Marfa Petrovna for giving it that leaving her was completely out of the question. So Osip had had jewels of his own, and he had weighed them and had made his choice, which was to refuse to choose between his love of freedom and his love of Marfa Petrovna. The truth was that he could not be sold, but if any explanation were to come it had to come from Marfa Petrovna in the moment when she was fainting or appearing to faint.

What is not immediately clear is why Marfa Petrovna had ever freed Osip in the first place and why she had to keep it secret from Pyotr Petrovitch, who would have freed twenty Osips for her if he had had them. The idea keeps suggesting itself that Osip had been her lover. That would very nicely account for why Marfa Petrovna could never tell Pyotr Petrovitch that she had freed Osip, and it would give a lovely reason for Osip's preferring death to a revelation of Marfa Petrovna's secret. But looked at in any other way, the theory is nonsense. If Osip had been Marfa Petrovna's lover, she never would have freed him. She would just have kept him—as she seemed to do —or she would have sold him out of hand long ago or she would have bet him in a card game she was sure to lose against a landowner with vast estates in some distant province. There's no logic nor romance either that will sustain the case for Osip's having been Marfa Petrovna's lover.

Of course, none of this came up in the dream. Things just happened so. I knew what it was necessary for me to know, and I woke up to find my face wet and cold with Marfa Petrovna's tears and to discover that I was so wrapped up in the bedding that I couldn't move, the sheet under my shoulder and hard across my throat. I fought my way free and sank back toward sleep. "Ivan Danilovitch was right," I said very distinctly inside my head, not realizing at first that I had given a name to the nameless younger man. "No one but Osip should have built the bride's house. And Osip was right to insist that his first obligation was to his work on the estate. And Pyotr Petrovitch was right in trying to be just both to his daughter and to Osip and in finally deciding to inflict the hurt he had every reason to expect to be the less. And Marfa Petrovna was right in freeing Osip—" And then for a moment I was less asleep. It was the second time I had assumed Marfa Petrovna was right without so much as a shred of evidence.

I began plotting to complete the pattern. Osip, it seemed, was in fact the father of Marfa Petrovna's daughter. What had happened was that after five years of marriage, Marfa Petrovna became convinced that her husband could never give her a child. Worse than that, he became convinced of it, too. He seemed to lose all pleasure in life and all interest in the future. At that time, the peasant Osip was building a summer house on a wooded knoll overlooking a great sweeping bend of the river, and every day Marfa Petrovna rode out to inspect the work and to command Osip to impregnate her. This happened sixty-three times before she knew she was pregnant, and then she stopped altogether and with considerable relief because in order to avoid the possibility she might have any pleasure in the transaction she had taken the precaution of wearing a hair shirt whenever she went riding. She had selected Osip because she had known she could trust no gentleman in such a delicate matter, and when she saw her husband's joy in her pregnancy, she freed Osip out of sheer gratitude.

Well, that is just the kind of thing that occurs to you when you aren't quite sure whether you're awake or asleep. Perhaps in 750 pages it could be made convincing, but, as it is, Osip, who in the dream was almost saintly, becomes in this version open to the charge of hanging about hoping that Marfa Petrovna will someday want to give her husband's virility further encouragement.

Or, conversely, Osip was actually Pyotr Petrovitch's son by a serf on his father's estate. He was very young at the time, a student perhaps, and didn't even know the girl had had a child, but it was known to a widow, also a very rich landowner, who wanted to marry Pyotr Petrovitch herself and who tried to prevent his marriage by telling Marfa Petrovna about the child. Marfa Petrovna wept—but not in front of the widow—and married Pyotr Petrovitch with undiminished love, and, out of respect for her dear husband, secretly freed his secret son, by this time a well-grown young man, and thus incurred an implacable debt of gratitude.

That's better. My god, that hair shirt was hairy. This is much quieter. Something might be made of it—in a minor key, of course. It's pure invention and doesn't solve any of the problems of the source, doesn't even satisfy my curiosity. But it does have the advantage of adding some sex to the story, which otherwise involves only a lady of a certain age, a gentleman even older, and a young man whose approach to marriage seems to be purely materialistic. A dim prospect unless you happen to share Lawrence's view that even buying a package of matches from a woman is a sexual encounter—and there is a good deal to be said for seeing things that way.

It might be just the thing to help me think up some explanation of Marfa Petrovna's action and settle down to that with no one the wiser. Perhaps one of these days I'll just give it a try with Osip as Pyotr Petrovitch's son or with the hair shirt even. Just writing it all down will give it substance, and that will be that. There stands the story of the peasant Osip. It might even be a good story. Why not? Who will ever sense the doubts and the difficulties, the hidden tributes to my skill?

Perhaps in time I will come to believe that I have hit on the right solution, hair shirt or what have you, that I have really explained why Marfa Petrovna freed Osip, but it will surely be a very long time before I can stop remembering that I was Marfa Petrovna and that I was Osip, that I was Pyotr Petrovitch and the stubborn young man and even the absent Ivanna Petrovna. I expect it will be a long time before I don't remember, as I consult my dreams on half waking, that while all of us were shouting It shall be so, part of me went off and quietly hanged itself. I wonder which part it was. I wonder if I shall miss it.

Look Homeward, Tourist

THE PRESIDENT said stay home, and Foster stayed home. So much for tourism. Secretly he was relieved. He had been losing sleep over the responsibilities he had been about to assume as a tourist, representative of his country. He knew he was unworthy, but he wanted to be loved.

Of course, his wife loved him, and his little girls loved him, but what he really wanted was to change history by smiling at a Russian on the Champs Élysées. Surely the Russian would know what he was like. Still, he was full of misgivings, and he stayed at home. Not, of course, in his own house. That wasn't the point at all. The point was to travel within the country and keep his money within the economy. Foster didn't in the least understand what that meant, but having helped elect the President, he felt a strong obligation to help support him whenever possible. He toured to Maine.

A friend of a friend knew of a little old lady who had a house on some property on a fine lake. The lake was fine and the property was on it, but the house wasn't. Between the house and the lake was a broad belt of impassible thicket, and even if you did hack your way through to the lake, you came out on bluffs that dropped sheer into the water. The only way to swim at all was to drive five miles in and out of ravines around the foot of the lake to a public beach.

The house itself hadn't been lived in for a long time and was certainly not a home any more—scarcely even a house. The chimney dripped honey into the living room. There were bats in the bedrooms and a snake in the attic. There had clearly been porcupines in the kitchen, and nothing at all could be done about the wasps that tunneled in the outhouse seat. The rent was very cheap, however, and it helped the little old lady. Foster hoped the economy would accept anguish in place of dollars, because there was plenty of anguish in making the house fit to live in—but that's another story.

Even when the house was settled into a routine, Foster found himself exhausted simply from living all day with his wife and children, and he fell into the habit of napping after lunch when the children napped. He was torn between different plans of how to spend the quiet time, but that was how he spent it. He napped or he dozed and he savored the quiet.

He was dozing one afternoon, vaguely aware that the children were waking up, that the sun was shining for a change, and that very soon he would have to cope. Each girl sang to herself when she woke up. The older two sang nursery rhymes and kindergarten songs. Cathy sang her own song. Foster usually made a point of listening to her, because sometimes he picked up clues about what was going to happen after nap; and, having a clue, he could get himself set.

"Cathy is awake," she sang. "The sun is shining. The sky is blue. There is a glass of milk and a molasses cookie and a tiny little bull. There is a red bathing suit and a red pail and a shovel and a sand castle and the giant says, Ho, ho, Cathy is a good girl."

Foster was glad he had thought about the sunshine, which automatically meant swimming, because he was even set for the song. The children fell silent and he drifted into sleep again. The next thing he heard was his wife saying, "Oh, no," and he pretended he hadn't heard that either. Almost at the same time he was aware that someone was standing beside his bed, and a piece of paper was being placed on his chest. He opened his eyes and saw that it was Barbara beside him. Barbara was the middle girl. Following an old custom in his wife's family, the girls were named alphabetically. First there was Alice and then Barbara and then Cathy.

"What is this?" he said, although he could see very well that it was a handsome Santa Claus with a very large Ho-Ho in a balloon just at his shoulder. "Is this his pack?"

"No, silly," Barbara said. "That says ho-ho."

"So it does," he said.

"It's an invitation," she said.

"An invitation? How lovely."

"It's to tea right now in our room."

"What a fine idea." He examined the invitation further and discovered that it was done on the back of one of the letters he had spent the morning typing—a pack of lies to save his face and his President's. "Where did you get this?" he said. "How many did you take?" He was surprised to discover that he didn't much care.

"We only took a few."

"Where are they?"

"Mummy got one."

She took him by the hand and he scrambled from the bed. When he turned toward the door, he saw his wife standing there. She was holding an invitation with both hands. "I see you got one, too," he said. He could feel his voice still muffled by sleep. His wife nodded and kept on nodding. "What's the matter with you, Gail?" he said. She looked like an actress portraying absolute terror, and he began to be alarmed, although there was nothing obviously wrong. "Has something happened?"

"No," she said, "no, of course not. Come on, Barbara. Let your father wake up."

"He's awake," Barbara said.

"He'll be along in a minute," Gail said. "Come on and get ready."

"I'm awake," he said, "but what's the matter with you?"

"Nothing," she said. "Really nothing." She turned on a smile. Barbara led them both into the children's room. The work table was laid with paper placemats decorated in crayon. The mats were clearly more of the letters. "You can have them back if you need them," Barbara said.

"Let's have tea first," Foster said. "They're too lovely to waste. I'll borrow them tonight and copy off what's on the back."

"You get to keep yours," Barbara said. "The invitation, too."

"I'll just run and bring up the pitcher of milk," Gail said. Foster wondered if one of them had gone crazy.

Foster helped build sand castles. He swung the children in great arcs in the water. He lay in the shallow water with a child on his back and scuttled on his hands like a crab—only he thought of himself as a dolphin. He kicked and splashed and played tag. And he sat on the wet sand and he rested.

The children built a wall around him, a sort of outwork of their castle. "Now the giant is shut up in the castle," they said.

"Please let me out," he said for the sake of the game.

"The walls are magic," they said, "and not even you can break them or step over them." Exhausted as he was, he was willing to believe in the magic of the walls and was a model prisoner.

Gail came and sat outside his prison. "Grapes or an orange?" she said.

"No feeding the prisoner," the children said sternly.

"You have to feed the prisoners," she said. "It says so in the Geneva Convention."

"But you can't get anything through the wall," they said.

"Grapes, if I'm allowed," Foster said.

"Magic grapes can," Gail said.

"Don't feed him too much," they said. "We want him to be a little weak." Foster wondered how much more they had understood of the farmer's explanation of why he kept a runt bull.

Three young men who had been displaying their muscles on the beach all afternoon came running and wrestling near the castle. Foster sprang up and bestrode the castle and fended them off, although they bumped him solidly. "Watch the kids' castle," he said. "Watch the kids."

"No English," one of the three said, and they passed turbulently down the beach.

"They're Canadians," Gail said. "I heard them talking French."

"Talk about American tourists," Foster said. He sat down again. The giant business was forgotten, and the children busied themselves in carrying out minor repairs in the approaches to the castle.

"What sort of man do you think I am anyway?" Foster said.

"What do you mean?" his wife said.

"I mean, what did you think I was going to do when I found out about my letters?"

"I don't know what you're talking about," she said. She was having trouble getting grapes out of a paper bag. The bag rattled loudly and nearly drowned her words. "I didn't think anything."

"My god," he said, "are all the women in your family crazy? On our wedding day—our wedding day, mind you—I heard your father saying to your mother, 'Grace, it's going to be all right. He's only going to marry her.' "

The bag sounded like a forest fire, but still he made out "—men are so violent. Have some grapes."

"Have I ever—" he said. "Did your father ever—"

"All right, children," she said, still without pausing or changing inflection. "Time to go home now. Wash yourselves off."

The children pretended not to hear. Their concentration on their play was intense. Their entire bodies were alert, heads bent, arms reaching, backs set. "First one for the speed-boat ride," Foster said. He grabbed Alice by the arms and ran with her out into the water. He held her by the wrists and swung her around in a circle until he got dizzy and fell down. They both came up sputtering and laughing, and he carried her out of the water and across the loose sand to a bathhouse where Gail stood in the open door ready to receive her.

The bathhouses were old wooden compartments, a row of

them set at the edge of the beach like a row of telephone booths. Foster set Alice down on the bench, and Gail gave her a towel. "Dry yourself and get dressed," Gail said, "while we get the little ones." They closed her in and left her.

When they came back again, each carrying a dripping, laughing child, Alice had not made the least progress in getting dressed. "What's the matter, big girl?" Foster said.

Alice looked stubborn, and Gail said, "What is it?" As Gail bent to put Cathy on the bench, Alice whispered in her ear. "Where?" Gail said. She glared at the walls and out the open door. Foster flinched. Alice placed her hand flat on the wall beside a wide crack in the old boards.

Gail banged on the wall with the side of her fist and shouted, "Hey, you in there, cut it out or I'll call a cop."

"For god's sake, what is it?" Foster said.

"There's some dirty old man in there peeking at my baby," Gail said.

"She's only a baby," Foster said. "Let's not make it into anything."

"It's disgraceful," Gail said.

"So it is," Foster said, "but you know you take her suit off on the beach to clean out the sand."

"That's different," Gail said. "This is dirty. Hey, you in there, do you hear me?"

There was a silence. Then a man said, "No English."

"Dirty Canadian," Gail said.

Foster stuck his head in the door and could see a bit of eye at the crack. It was amazingly alive and shining. "I'll look for another cabin," he said. But all the other cabins were in use.

Gail pounded on the wall. "Hurry up and get out of there," she said.

"Mother," Barbara said, "we can go home in our bathing suits."

"*Vous êtes malade*," Gail said. Foster and the children looked at her in amazement.

"*Ai, ma tête,*" the man cried. "*Ai, mon estomac.*"

"*Vous êtes un homme,*" Gail said with great difficulty and passion. "*Pour les hommes, les femmes, non les enfants. Malade, malade, malade.*"

There was a moment's silence. Then, "*No espagnol,*" the man said. There were shrieks of laughter.

"*No allemand,*" someone else said.

"*No russe,*" still another said.

"They're all in there," Gail said.

"I didn't know you were such a linguist," Foster said.

"They don't understand me," Gail said. She banged on the wall again.

"They understand all right," Foster said. "They're just a bunch of jokers."

Gail popped out of the cabin and seized the handle of the door of the cabin where the men were still laughing without control. "*Ouvrez la porte,*" she shouted.

"*No japonais,*" someone shouted.

In a fury she turned on Foster. "Are you just going to stand there?" she said. "Are you just going to stand there and stand for that?"

"But what can I do?" Foster said.

"You can break the door down."

"There are three of them after all," he said.

"All three of them together aren't half of a man that is a man," she said.

"Remember the children, Gail."

"You remember them for a change and be a man for once."

"A man—" Foster said. Now he was angry. He completely forgot the three men in the cabin.

She started to say something but stopped dead and turned to the door and shook it again. "*Mon homme,*" she shouted, "*vous frappez votre nez, votre dents, votre bras, votre jambes, votre tête—*"

A drawn-out howl was the first answer: "*A—lou-ette.*" Then

there was a chorus, half strangled with laughter. *"Alouette, gentille Alouette, Alouette, je te plumerai. Je te plumerai le ventre—"*

"Et votre ventre," Gail shouted, dancing with rage.

"Et la poitrine," they sang.

"Et votre poitrine," she shouted.

"Et le cul," they sang.

"Et votre cou, frapper, casser, tuer à deux pieces."

"No esquimau."

Gail began to cry with rage. "Come on," Foster said, "we'll take the children home in their suits."

"All right," she said, "all right. If that's all you're good for, carry the children to the car while I pick up here."

Foster got the children into the car and came back for blankets and towels and toys and bags of gear. "Now, I'm going to change," Gail said. Foster was going to protest, but she stared him down. She stepped into the cabin and closed the door.

When he was coming back for his last armload, there was a sudden flurry of shouts and cries of pain from the next cabin. The door burst open and all three men staggered out onto the beach. They clutched each other and headed for the water, running and falling in a parody of their former wrestling. They bumped into people and tripped over picnic baskets. The whole beach was in an uproar.

"Et votre yeux," Gail shouted after them.

"Here now, what's going on here?" An ancient constable had at last appeared.

"They were peeking at my wife while she was changing," Foster said.

"I threw sand at the cracks," Gail said complacently.

"Serves them right," the constable said. "They just will not learn our ways. I'll give them a good talking to now."

"You better speak French," Foster said.

"On parle français," the constable said. He went off down the beach toward where the three men were kneeling in the shallow

water, bathing their faces, the center of an angry ring of swimmers and picnickers.

"Ready?" Gail said.

"I'm ready," Foster said. He was very tired. Perhaps the President was asking too much.

A Day in Hamburg

You go burrowing through a mass of stuff, and everything is clear enough—unfortunately—and then you come upon this one thing. It's part of all the rest, but somehow it's different. It's bone of all the other bone and flesh of all the other flesh, and it should by all rights be just as much stuff and just as—well—clear as everything else.

Take, for instance, a cathedral. I don't mean to say a cathedral is stuff or clear, but it is a great place for burrowing. You go into the tall, light nave, all stained glass and glory, and you say to yourself, This is beauty. Then maybe you stretch out in a pew with your extra-strong bird glasses and spend the day studying detail work up in the roof where no one was ever expected to be able to see it. Or maybe you get down on your hands and knees and go crawling through the choir stalls with a flashlight to look at the carvings. And you say, Beauty and fun—or something like that. Then you go looking for the man with the key to the crypt: *Several especially fine Saxon capitals of doubtful origin, perhaps salvaged from the fire of 1135. So down you go—with your flashlight, of course, because without it you'd never see the capitals—and you pass in a daze from pillar to pillar, and you say, Wonder. Then at last over in a corner you come upon the wooden trapdoor. You lift it cautiously and flash your light into the pit. About six feet down you see a section of a stone disk set on a stone square, the base of a column of a Roman temple. And you are silent. You feel your hair move on your head and your flesh shake on your bones as if you were a horse.

Or take a Roman amphitheater you have walked all day to see, and there it is quiet and empty under the cold rain. You know all about it: smooth arcs of seats, sockets for vanished pillars, gaping graves of later date. You step into the mouth of a cave out of the rain to survey the site and to check off the proper emotions one by one. Before you leave, however, you throw your flashlight around the place. You see the smoke hole in the roof and the mangers carved into the rock of the walls. And your knees will scarcely hold your weight.

Or take Henry Ashley. There was a burrower. It was Ashley, as a matter of fact, who told me about the amphitheater and the cave. He is someone I met on a student ship westbound at the end of summer. It was a very old, very slow ship, but after all it was cheap. It was transportation, as we used to say about our worn-out cars. It was also transition, for the crossing took twelve days, if you can believe it. In that time I got to know Ashley very well indeed. Neither of us were students, and he had an ulcer; so he couldn't drink all that good cheap Dutch beer. So really there was nothing to do but talk.

We had a sheltered corner of the main deck where we stood and talked for three days until we found a couple of chairs there one morning, doubtless moved down by students late at night. Then we sat and talked for three days until one morning the chairs were gone again—perhaps moved back to the sun deck, perhaps thrown over the side in some frenzy of protest. According to the ship's newspaper, there was so much wreckage in our wake that other ships were always sending messages to find out if we were still afloat. Tables, chairs, a ping-pong table —everything went, and more and more every night as the whole dark pressure of our own continent began to make itself felt even at mid-Atlantic. After Henry and I lost our chairs, we stood and talked for the rest of the voyage. We were so much a fixture that the sailors joked about painting us along with the rest of the ship's gear.

We got through the easy preliminaries in the first few minutes of the first day. I had spent the summer in Oxford in a dingy room doing some work I could have done anywhere. Oh, I used the Bodleian, but any library in any East Podunk in the country would have served as well. So it might seem I could have stayed at home—nothing could be further from the truth.

As for Ashley, he had been wandering without plan all summer long. He refused on principle to make a plan in the face of his limitless hope for Europe. He had plans, he said, a whole box full of them at home. He made them during the years when he had no real hope of ever making the trip, when he had only maps and old Baedekers and tourist folders. He could take you anywhere you wanted on the London or Paris subways, but he never got to either city. "Why go to Paris," he said, "if you can't drink wine or eat a decent meal?" The ulcer, you know. And the one time he started for London he wound up in Amsterdam by mistake and did an improvisation on the Low Countries of which he knew relatively little.

He was a schoolteacher from a small town near Boston and had scrimped for twenty years on his lunch money and his tobacco money for this trip. His wife knew the subways as well as he did, and she knew the Louvre and the Prado better—at least as of their 1913 Baedekers. He was better than she on the Uffizi and the National Gallery. But there were still small children at home, and it was out of the question for them both to go. Another time, to be sure, but not now, not on this first wild exploration.

It should be some consolation to her that he speaks so well about his summer, for he does speak well, with almost always a curious objectivity as to his own motives and sensations. Look, for example, at how he described himself waking up that morning on the train to Hamburg.

He opened his eyes, he said, and looked at the ceiling. Although he was still keeping up the pretense that he had not slept all night, he wondered what had awakened him. The train was still rocking along gently. The compartment was still empty. There was no sound in the corridor. He remembered perfectly well the intrusions of the night—he had not been sleeping then either—when one figure after another touched his shoulder and said, "Passport," or "Customs," or "Money to change?" He scrupulously pointed out each time he told the story that the crowning irritation was—still was—that even asleep he should be spotted as American.

He studied his luggage in the rack overhead. No giveaway there, a cheap suitcase and a weathered rucksack, British Army surplus, bought long before at a rummage sale and carefully hoarded for this trip. Except on major moves like this one from Copenhagen to London he never carried both at the same time. He could appear as a traveler with a modest suitcase or a wanderer with a rucksack. It all depended on the friends he was visiting. Usually he said that only the luggage changed with his different roles, but sometimes he confessed to a secret preference for the rucksack man.

He glanced at the window above his head. A silver-gray light had replaced the dark, reflection-haunted night; so there would at last be something to see beside his own face brooding on him there in a second-class compartment hurtling through Germany where he had sworn he would never spend a dime or sleep a night. Why? Perhaps because he wasn't Jewish himself he felt he owed more respect to formality. He really didn't know. But since he was in Germany, for better or worse, he could at least sit up and see what was to be seen.

The white, wet fields were very still. The hedgerows and little woods were motionless. There seemed to be almost no light but he could see for a long way across fields—landscapes rather—accentuated by black-and-white cows. Wonderfully, all the fields were crossed by three long rolls of fog parallel to the track. At least he thought it was fog until he saw that the nearest roll was being laid down by the smokestack of the locomotive pulling his own train. The truth was no less wonderful, the silent mystery of the other trains leading him on to Hamburg. Who ever thinks of other trains except in terms of possible collisions? He must have been very tired, as if he had not slept, to ask himself such questions. His eyes burned and he was lightheaded. He took Danish bread and cheese from his rucksack and ate while he brooded on the world. At the far end of a long, narrow field, three red deer stood against a wood's edge, motionless, alert.

Then there was a highway beside the tracks. There were barns and houses. Thatched roofs still moved him, even more, perhaps, since he had taken his rucksack and wandered through the Danish countryside until he found a farmer who would let him sleep in the barn under the thatch after surrendering his lighter and cigarettes. He noted with professional eye that a thatcher had been at work in the neighborhood, for there were patches of bright thatch along the ridgepoles, and the trim boards at the gable ends were white and new.

Then more countryside. Some deer grazing beside the track wihout even deigning to look up. He rested his head on his hand. The train was standing in a large station.

He seized his luggage in a frenzy and ran staggering from the train. On the platform he stopped and looked around for a guard or conductor and was calmed by a large sign: HAMBURG. He had asked when he bought his ticket in Copenhagen and he had asked on the train if he could stop over in Hamburg, and he had been promised that he could. He was very well aware how he simplified his English when he asked the questions; so he had not missed the irony of the ticket agent's "Most assuredly, sir," and the conductor's "Quite right." There was no one in sight for him to ask now.

For a moment he was aware of his haste and panic and was ashamed of himself as he had been ashamed of the American girls who ran all night through the cars screaming, "Does this train really go to Hamburg?" and who had once, at some nameless station, actually abandoned the train and stood huddled and silent at last on the platform. He got up on his elbow then and peeked at them as the train slowly pulled away, but the train stopped and backed up, to add or drop cars, perhaps, and the girls scrambled on again. He lay down and stretched himself as on a tomb, feet crossed, while the girls began running and screaming once more. Awake, eyes open under his hat, he fought a rising terror, a senseless terror, for what did he care if the train went to Hamburg or not? He had no plans, no schedule. Although he did rather want to see the Kokoschka show at the museum at Hamburg, it didn't really matter if he wound up in Paris or Milan or London, not even if the only reason he had come this way was to stop for the day in Hamburg.

Calmer now, he walked into the station and then into the men's room. Cold water cleared his head and soothed his burning eyes and cut away the hoarded hallucinations of the night. He thought at last he could face himself, even if he looked as bad as he felt. He turned toward the mirror but he was not prepared for what he saw. Out of the mirror stared a face more familiar than his own face—for he had always believed that if he met his double on the street he would not recognize him. The face in the mirror was an unblinking nightmare face, a face as familiar to him as the palm of his hand, which he had pored over for hours on end as a boy, convinced there was destiny in the fact that the lines of his palm made h a, his initials. That was the right hand. The left hand said ah! or sometimes ah? He no longer thought it meant anything, but he had never forgotten the letters were there.

The dark hair was worn long. One lock fell over the forehead. Ashley instinctively tossed his head to put the lock in place. A small but very thick mustache. Mad and brooding eyes. "My god," Ashley said, "my god." He clutched at the washbowl and hung on. He became aware slowly that someone had been standing beside him, that someone had turned and walked away. He himself turned slowly and saw a man's back in the doorway and then gone. Again he turned to the mirror and this time saw nothing. "I'm getting out of here," he said. He seized his luggage and ran staggering back to the platform. The train had gone.

He forced himself to be quiet. He breathed deeply. "Angles of incidence and of reflection," he told himself. "If he was at one basin and I was at the other and the mirror was between us, I would see him and he would see me. A nasty shock for him as well." All this Ashley told himself and later told of himself, but neither then nor later did he believe a word of it. He was stuck, however, for the day in Hamburg, and felt that emergency situations deserved emergency rations; so he went into the second-class dining room and ordered an omelet, the one dish that seemed to be the same in all languages and never really poorly cooked. This one was excellent. He was a little reassured. His ulcer was also reassured.

He began to look about him then to see if many men were wearing the Hitler haircut and the Hitler mustache. That was just the kind of thing a traveler ought to bring back from abroad, the fresh, meaningful hint about how things really are. During the whole of his day in Hamburg, however, he didn't see another such mustache, nor did he gather very many facts although one very important fact did come home to him quite early in the day.

He stood in the fine cold rain before the station and studied a large glass-covered map of the city, trying to memorize the general layout, where the river was and where the park, his customary orientation points. From where he stood he could see the museum, but he still had two hours before it would open; so he began to walk, following in his mind's eye a cloverleaf pattern of four circles touching the station. He was surprised to see how many old buildings were still standing. He had so often heard aviators boast of what they had done to Hamburg that he was disappointed, but when he came to a ruined church he was still not pleased.

He was half an hour late for the opening of the museum, but that made little difference. In a new place he liked to make a short morning visit and then go on a long meditative walk through the city and then in the afternoon return for a more leisurely second look at things that had caught his eye. When he arrived at the museum, strengthened by his good breakfast, freshened by the cold rain, glowing with anticipation, he found the door locked and the building dark. He rattled the door savagely and stepped back. A policeman said, "I'm sorry, sir, I'm afraid the museum is closed on Monday." "Of course it is," Ashley said, rattling the door again. "But today is Monday," the policeman said. "*Donnerwetter*," Ashley said, glaring at the policeman, and he said no more because all the German he knew he had learned long ago from villainous Germans in boys' books.

And so the first fact that came home to him was that it was Monday. It was the first time he had known the day of the week since he left New York on Thursday, June 14. He stalked through the rain to the big map in front of the station to lay out bigger and bigger cloverleafs to take him through the day. "So be it," he said to himself, "so be it."

During the worst showers, he sheltered out of the rain in doorways and under arches. Once he sat on some stairs in an apartment house and ate his bread and cheese. Once he dived into a dank passageway to escape a deluge, and a woman dived in at his heels. She looked at him closely, with growing indecision. He wanted to shout *Donnerwetter* at her, but he had no idea what it meant, and he was close enough to tears without having his face slapped. She preferred the rain to him in any case.

Later he wandered through some new university buildings, very American in appearance. They were shoddy, as if corners had been cut and funds had proved inadequate both for finish and for maintenance. In one corridor student paintings were hung, mostly abstract except for the work of one girl who seemed to have a thing about small red deer alert against a wood's edge in some landscape of disaster.

Toward the end of the afternoon he strolled beside the river. He had no idea what river it was, but he still called it Charles as he had the first time he came upon it. The wide belt of grass and shrubs along the water and the good gravel path he called the Esplanade, perhaps because he had noticed on the big map near the station that somewhere in another part of the city there actually was a place called the Esplanade. In any case, during the day his wandering had several times brought him back to his Charles and his Esplanade, and more than once he had looked across the river for the M.I.T. buildings.

As he strolled, the rain was still falling lightly, but off in the west the sun was struggling against the clouds. The light was more than natural, as if in preparation for some incredible annunciation. The swans on the river were a white that would have been intolerable in full sunlight. Serenely, they hovered on the water, and Ashley more or less kept pace with them. He also more or less followed a woman being pulled along by a strong little dog.

There was a flurry in the water that at once subsided. The swans then settled down again to nonchalance. Again there was a flurry, and this time Ashley saw that one swan had overtaken another and seemed to attack it. The swan that was attacked vanished from sight entirely, and Ashley stopped in his tracks and stared. The attacking swan hovered as if equally amazed. Then fifty feet away, out toward midstream, a swan suddenly appeared on the surface of the water. The attacker beat his wings and paddled furiously to the attack. Now it was the turn of the other to hover until descended on furiously. Again the attacked swan sank and reappeared again unexpectedly. Pursuit, attack, six times repeated. Ashley was aware that on the gravel path very near him the woman with the dog was also watching.

Again the furious attack, but this time a white rush and a sudden blow, and the long defenseless neck is trapped by the fierce beak. There is no escape this time. The great wings beat. Both birds are nearly submerged, merged, and then they part. He preens himself upon the river, indifferent to all except that very feather he is straightening. She swims slowly to the bank and crawls up with some pain and rests.

The woman on the path turns to Ashley. Her mouth is open, her eyes are open, open all the way in, as he has never seen another woman's eyes. They stare for a moment at each other, and then she turns and runs down the slope toward the resting swan.

She runs as women do, knees close, arms up, elbows crooked like wings. Her little dog, left to himself, drags his leash along about some doggy business of his own.

Ashley, standing alone in the rain, hears himself say aloud, like a mad old man, "I am very happy."

Why? he would say each time he told the story. Why? He had gone burrowing through a wretched day in a city in which his very presence filled him with an agony of guilt only to hear from his own lips these incredible words. He had gone burrowing through his memory of the day time after time only to come back each time to the same irreducible facts: "I am very happy" and "Why?"

"Why?" he said once again, and we turned to watch a Navy patrol bomber swing wide of the ship and come bearing down on us, very low the way they always used to in the movies. We had been so long at sea that anything might have happened to the world. I was almost expecting machine-gun fire, but the nose lifted and the plane roared over the ship. As it passed, a barrage of beer bottles took off from the sun deck, and for a long time the air was full of seat cushions and towels and paperback books and a great savage howl.

The Moth, the Bear, and the Shivering Stars

A TELEGRAM. Who sends telegrams now? You still see an office in every city, and once in a while you see somebody standing on one foot at the counter or somebody else sitting at a small desk staring dimly over a pad of yellow forms. Usually, however, the office is empty except for the clerk. You wonder perhaps how the place manages to look so undeniably prosperous. You wonder what the clerk does with his time and what kind of person he is. You think of Saroyan or Henry Miller, depending on what kind of person you are at the moment, and you forget about it until you find the telegram in your mailbox one night after the bars have closed.

It's very peculiar, if nobody ever seems to send telegrams, that everybody knows what a telegram means—disaster. First and last the telegraph company must have spent millions of dollars to put across the idea of the birthday telegram and the flower telegram and the candy telegram and the money telegram and the singing telegram and the return-paid-telegram telegram. Very likely millions of people have received just such happy happy telegrams, but those same people will know at once what the poet means when he uses the image of a telegram slid under the door—disaster. Each generation gets its share of telegrams from the government apologizing for losing things they were supposed to take much better care of—that may be what keeps disaster fresh in the yellow envelopes. Who knows?

In our family, we know. I don't generalize, but for us a telegram can mean only one thing. No other news ever comes by
telegram, and news of a death never comes any other way. We
might need the speed of direct dialing or the fullness of a letter,
but we would send a telegram. If we met each other in the street,
we would not speak of it but would go and send a telegram,
craning on one foot before the dim yellow pad, filling in the
blanks according to our own ceremonial form.

So here I am late at night alone in the house with all the bars
closed and with a bunch of letters in my hand not quite hiding a
yellow corner. There's no good pretending I don't see it and
leaving the mail until morning—most mail will wait a day
without harm, that's one thing I've learned in seventy-five years
—but I don't open it either. I stand stock still, stone still, and
shudder as a stone would shudder.

It is almost certain that my Cousin Phillip has died. He had
a fall a month ago and smashed his hip, which is usually the end
for a man his age—a full ten years older than I. I've had a
month to steady myself, to think what I will say at his funeral
and again next summer when I, as next eldest, take his place as
family president at the big reunion back in Plymouth. Still, I
don't open the telegram. Visions of other telegrams come to me,
drowned men flashing before my living eyes. And one in particular, the first I ever opened.

I was living with Grandfather Warren at the time. Come to
think of it, he was then in exactly my present position. It was
his Uncle William who was head of the family then, a patriarch
of ninety-five who threatened to outlive the next two entire
generations and go on into the future mythic as Queen Victoria.
I know my grandfather was always grumbling about losing his
chance, and I very early got into my head an image of him as an
Aged Pretender broken by his mysterious wrongs.

As so often happens I never thought to check the image
against the reality I saw before me every day, the joyous old man
surrounded by his sons and daughters and their sons and daughters in turn. Even the way he played cards should have told me

better. I see him still fling down a trump or study the board, glitter within glitter of spectacles and eyes as he considers whether to take a card or stand pat. I should have known simply by the way he sat on a folding chair and administered a baseball game or a fishing party—it was after a fishing party, as a matter of fact, that the first telegram came.

Let me recapitulate. My Grandfather Warren and I were of the fishing party. His Uncle William, the patriarch of patriarchs, was off in Florida keeping warm over the summer. My Cousin Charles—ah, yes, he hasn't come in yet—my Cousin Charles was also of the party. Perhaps you will remember that I am all the while standing with letters in my hand—and a telegram which I expect to announce the death of my Cousin Phillip. Well, Charles and Phillip were brothers. Charles and I were of an age—we called ourselves twins—and Phillip, as I have said, was ten years older. He wasn't with us on the fishing trip, because he was already an important young man and was off somewhere about the world's foolishness. I don't any longer remember where he was or what he was doing, but he was very successful and rose from folly to folly to his heart's desire. But he wasn't around then and he doesn't come in at all—except for the telegram.

There were Charles and his father and Grandfather Warren and I and about six more men I don't really remember. I'm sure there was an uncle or two. Although it wasn't strictly a family affair, it would be hard to imagine such a group without uncles. The others usually seemed to be men they had been to school with or had been in the army with and didn't see as much as they should like. Still, each man wandered off by himself to fish as if they had all the time in the world and as if they had long ago said all that needed to be said.

My job, as always, was to serve as Grandfather's aide, not that I minded. There are many pleasures in fishing trips and I had found mine. I was always quite content to stay with Grandfather and not have any of the more adventurous fishing, although with Charles along I was doubly happy. People were always saying

Poor Thomas of me. I have even heard people who knew nothing of the matter at all refer to me as Poor Thomas, but I assure you they were quite wrong. Even when I went fishing by myself I acted much the same, often sitting for hours in a shady corner of the pond with an unbaited hook in the water.

When I was with Grandfather, however, my first job was to find a sunny spot for him. While he sat in the buggy and advised the men as to wind and weather and sent them off in all directions, I set up his folding stool on a good pad of grass and stabbed his glass holder into the ground on one side and his pipe holder on the other. I poured out a drink of whiskey to warm in the sun and had his lap robe ready to wrap around his legs. By then he had come slowly to the chair—I was most particularly not to help him, although it was a good idea if I quietly braced the light chair with my foot or knee while he eased into it.

Once I had him well wrapped up and had checked the actual convenience of glass and pipe and matches and tobacco, I took his hand line and baited it and strode down to the edge of the ripples and whirled the weighted end about my head and let it fly out into the mere (whatever that is). When the line had settled, I walked backwards to his chair, paying out more line as I went, and he was in action. My next job was to make sure the beer cooler was stocked and that whiskey and glasses and ice were laid out on the tailgate of the carry-all. There was no great hurry about this, because no one except Grandfather was allowed a drink until he had landed a legal fish. After the bar came a fire with water for coffee, frying pan, and so on. Of course all this was punctuated by having to check Grandfather's bait and throw out his line and take off his hook whatever he happened to catch. I remember eels in particular, which I always cooked for him and which he ate with great contentment.

With Charles to help, everything went much faster, and soon we were stripped to our bathing dress and lying on the grass near Grandfather's feet. I remember how glorious the sun was on my skin and how fond I was of Charles for choosing to stay with me rather than go off on his own. He needn't have. He had never had my opportunity to develop a philosophy of fishing, because he lived in the city and made only this one trip each summer. We talked quietly and Grandfather smoked, sipped, and moved his hand gently as if he were weighing the fishing line on his forefinger. Our only duties at the moment were to keep the fire going and to keep up the thin trickle of whiskey into Grandfather's glass.

"Does our talking like this bother you, Grandfather?" Charles said.

"Of course not," Grandfather said.

"Some people say that talking scares the fish away," Charles said.

"Superstition," Grandfather said as I had known he would. "Why, right this minute there's something mumbling around my bait, something very slow and thoughtful."

"An eel maybe," I said. Grandfather and I grinned at each other.

"I've never seen an eel," Charles said.

"Keep your eyes open," I said, "and trust Grandfather."

"He keeps bumping it and sniffing it," Grandfather said. "He even gums it a little now and then, but there's nothing for the hook to bite. Patience, Charles, and patience, Thomas—patience, patient Thomas—we must wait until he takes it in and tries to tip-toe away."

Charles laughed aloud at the notion of a fish tip-toeing and said softly, "Sorry."

"Superstition," Grandfather said. "However," he said, "my friend seems to have lost interest in the game. Thomas, if you please." He handed me the line and I pulled it in. The hook was bare. I held up the hook for him to see, and he acknowledged it with a little wave of his pipe as if to say, of course.

Once again I brandished the wet line about my head, a glitter of diamonds scattering in the sun, and threw the bait far out into the water. By the time I had paid out the line and put it in his hand, taut to the sinker, the myserious messages were coming through once more. "He wastes no time," Grandfather said. He gave a short quick pull. "No," he said, "patience."

"Father always tells me to be quiet," Charles said.

"For himself, not the fish," Grandfather said.

"That's interesting," Charles said in a curious way he had which suggested a piece of a puzzle being put in and locking with the oiled machinery of a bank vault.

"Try this," Grandfather said. "The two of you walk along the edge here until you come to a roach's nest. Wait a bit there. The roach will have seen you moving and will be out in deeper water, but if you wait it will come back very soon." I knew all this, of course, having caught my share of roaches in my time, but I couldn't see what he was getting at. "Then, standing very still, begin to talk."

"What will happen?" Charles said. I thanked him in my heart.

"I don't know," Grandfather said. "I'm just telling you how to find out. Then you can tell me whether it really is superstition. Your father likes to be quiet, so he says no."

"That's very interesting," Charles said.

"That's the scientific mind," Grandfather said. "I've always thought I had a scientific mind—scientific but lazy. And my scientific mind now tells me that, among all possible reasons I'm not getting any more signals from my mysterious friend, the most probable reason is that I have no more bait. Thomas, if you please."

He was right, of course. Once more I baited up. I spat on the bait for luck. I whirled the line about my head with my eyes closed (also so luck could direct my cast). I heard the whistling of the line through the air as it spun. I sensed the scattering of jewels in the air. I let the line go, and when I opened my eyes I saw the ripples where it had hit out at about the same place as before.

"Is he there?" I said as I handed Grandfather the line.

"Patience," Grandfather said.

"Is spitting on the hook—" Charles began.

"Superstition," Grandfather said. "Ah, he's back."

"Maybe he's too small to take the hook," I said.

"Maybe he's too wise," Grandfather said.

"Then let me ask you about this," Charles said. He had his billfold out and was rummaging among cards and clippings. "Here" he said, "listen to this. It's a long-range weather prediction."

"Foolishness," Grandfather said, "if not downright superstition."

" 'All signs indicate,' " Charles said, " 'that we are in for an unusually cold winter.' "

"Winters have been getting unusually colder every year," Grandfather said. "Don't mind me, Charles. Do go on."

" 'The pelts of fur-bearing animals are especially thick and warm this year. The walls of moth cocoons are especially thick. Moss blankets the north side of trees. Squirrels hoard unusual numbers of nuts. All known signs agree that this will be a terrible winter. A great hole in the Milky Way is letting in the cold of outer space.' "

"Eh?" Grandfather said, looking up sharply from the line, which he was delicately weighing. "Would you just read that last again, please?"

" 'A great hole in the Milky Way—' " Charles said.

"I thought I had been dozing," Grandfather said. "The ancients believed there were windows in the heavens. Rain came in when the windows were open."

"Is this foolishness or superstition?" Charles said.

"My scientific mind informs me," Grandfather said, "that the stars which seem to make up what seems to be the Milky Way are actually millions of miles from each other. I think it is probably safe to say that it might be a little draughty up there."

"Foolishness?" Charles said. I could hear the fine machinery start to move into place.

"Foolishness?" Grandfather said. "We must keep an open mind. It's right about the draught at least—but, wait, we've business closer at hand than all these stars." He moved his hand bruskly. "Caught," he said. He began to draw in the line. "Snagged," he said.

"Too bad," I said and reached for the line.

"Now, Thomas," he said without yielding the line, "what I want you to do is this. Walk as far as you can along the shore to the left, and when you have let out all the line, try gently to disengage the hook from the snag. You'll have a very different angle on it then and may be able to work it loose."

"Yes, sir," I said. Grandfather loved to explain that maneuver and must once have loved to carry it out as much as I did. When I came to the end of the line, I twitched it high and I twitched it low and I tried a slow steady tension, but nothing gave.

I saw Grandfather speak to Charles. "Come back," Charles called.

"Coming," I called. I went along winding up the line.

When I got back to Grandfather he said, "Go right." I went along unwinding the line. Again I twitched high and low and tried the strong and steady.

"Come back," Charles called.

"Let me feel it once more," Grandfather said when I had wound my way back to him. He took the line and twitched it as low as his knees and as high as his shoulders and gave the strong and steady with such concentration that I fancied the line would twang if I touched it.

"It's very heavy but it seems to move," he said. "Probably it's a water-logged branch. You might pull it out if you are very careful not to jerk suddenly." He passed the line back to me.

I went down to the edge of the water and even a step into the water and wound up all the slack. Then I leaned forward and grasped the line close to the water so as to lose as little as possible if it should break. I didn't have to turn around to sense Grandfather's approval. Then I put on the strong and steady and gradually built up tension until I knew the line must break soon. In my mind's eye I pictured a log half sunk in mud. I concentrated on the log to make it move. Sluggishly it did move. I gained line hand over hand. It was coming now, free of the bottom but still heavy. I expected to see a twig break the surface at any moment. Ripples from its hidden motion began to wash against my feet. Instinctively I stepped back out of the water.

Then I began to see the mass of it. My first thought was that it was an old wash boiler. I thought of a bolster from a bed. I thought of a great many things rather than think of the thing which many a night since then has swum evolving through my dreams, never surfacing but stinking even through the water and recognized, although decomposed beyond all recognition, even through the mists of dreams.

When it did at last break the surface I thought once more of a wash boiler. Then the head came up, too, beaked, snaky, primeval. I stopped gaining line and stared.

"Well, well," Grandfather said.

"A turtle," Charles said.

But what a turtle. It was easily the biggest I have ever seen outside of a zoo. We were all motionless, staring. The turtle included us all in a stare which chilled my blood, not because it was so personal, far from it, but because it was so very unblinking, so very much the same for all of us and for all possible objects as well. It had only the one look. The line was taut from its beak to my hand but no tremor came through of pain or fear or hate or anything else I knew.

"What are we going to do with it?" Charles said.

"Or what is it going to do with us?" Grandfather said.

"Can we make soup with it?" Charles said.

"First catch your turtle," Grandfather said.

I was already as close to that turtle as I cared to get. I had heard often enough of much smaller turtles snapping off a finger. I felt I was doing my share by just hanging on.

There's no telling how long Grandfather and Charles would have gone on making conversation while the turtle and I were Siamese-twinning it, but the turtle, apparently having had its fill of us, raised a claw to its beak and brushed away the hook and sank back into the water. It was gone before I realized that the line was dead in my hand. I drew in the few remaining feet and saw that the hook had been straightened completely and now looked like a tiny harpoon. I still have it in my desk.

"I thought animals weren't supposed to look you in the eye," Charles said. "It was looking right in my eye the whole time."

"So it seemed, no doubt," Grandfather said. "But it seemed the same to me, and I suspect that poor Thomas thought it was not only looking at his eye but at his fingers and toes as well."

"It would know any mouthful of me that I was crazy enough to put in the water," I said.

"A new hook, Thomas, fresh bait, and a try for better things," Grandfather said. "And I don't like to mention it, but in the heat of the moment my glass became empty. Charles, if you please. And then, if you please, my coat from the buggy. These late summer days are suddenly treacherous, you know."

That was the great event of the fishing trip itself. In the evening we rode back in the buggy. I could still smell the sun on our clothes and hair, and my right side, against Charles, seemed still to feel the sun's heat. We left Charles and his father at a small-town station to catch the late train for the city —they would be home and in bed long before Grandfather and I finished our ride, not that we minded. In fact we enjoyed a night ride. There was always a lot to talk about with Grandfather. Even our silences were companionable. Even when he dozed there was the steady movement of the buggy, the reassuring horse, the calm clear night, the splendid stars. Although the night had turned unusually cold, there were always enough robes in Grandfather's buggy to make the very cold a pleasure.

It was very late when we got home. In a kind of dream I put up the horse while Grandfather made his glacial way around from the barn. He wouldn't hear of my driving him to the door, so it happened that I was not far behind him in getting to the house. He was standing on the doorsill, looking at the telegram on the floor.

'Thomas," he said—I stooped and picked it up and handed it to him—"if you please." He didn't make any move to open it.

"Uncle William," he said. "I find, Thomas," he said and gave me the telegram.

I opened it and read it to him. I didn't realize at first that it wasn't about Uncle William at all but about Charles.

We learned later that as the train was coming into the station there was a very small accident. A car left the tracks and eased up onto the platform and touched him.

"Charles?" Grandfather said. He took the telegram, and the name got through to me when he said it. A flash of cold went all down my right side as if the blankets had come untucked on a winter's night. Indeed, the coat Grandfather had thrown over me as I lay on the hall floor did little to keep me warm.

And now once more I stand in a hall with a bunch of letters in my hand and the yellow corner of the telegram barely showing. I don't go so far as to put the wish on anyone in particular, but I do find myself praying fervently that it is not Cousin Phillip. Not Cousin Phillip at least. Not the last of all of them. The telegram when I touch it is like ice, like that thin sheet of ice we used to skim off puddles and pretend was window glass.

The Man Who Was Drafted

I

THE BUS DRIVER closed the door, and the man who had the papers, the man in the blue pin-stripe suit, began once again to check the roll. "Adams," he said. "Here." He answered himself and made a mark on the paper. No one laughed this time although they had all shouted with loud laughter when he did it up in the Draft Board office the first time they were all together and face to face. But they didn't laugh now that they were submerged in the bus seats and looking out the windows where they could see only whoever was there for a man to see when he was going off alone like this.

Robert Andrews saw Don and Betty Marshall. There was no one else within a thousand miles who could have stood outside that bus that day for him to see as he went off alone. He had asked them not to come but they had come anyway, still high from the party the night before and getting higher all the time by nipping at 7-Up bottles filled with martinis. Everyone else was quietly and decently waiting for the bus to leave, but Don and Betty, drinking martinis through straws, laughed and giggled and peeked at him between their fingers as if between bars. In reply he could only attempt to smile.

While the man in the pin-stripe suit, Adams, finished calling the roll, Don ran up to the bus and drew with his fingers— standing wildly on the guard rail he could reach well enough— in the light film of dust on the window, a ragged series of bars.

As soon as the driver released the brakes and the bus began to roll ever so slightly, all the people, except Don and Betty, turned their backs and began to file into the waiting room, but Don and Betty ran after the bus out of the station and into the street, laughing, waving their bottles and peeking between their fingers. Robert Andrews pressed his face to the pane and kept them in view until the bus turned the corner and hit the highway. Then he sank back into the seat and tipped his hat over his face and sat rigidly still, as he had wanted to do from the very beginning.

He wasn't able to stay long under his hat though. He could feel the bus dropping down hills and swinging around curves, and he could see in his mind's eye the woods and fields rushing past, and he wanted to see them really as he had seen them so many times along this road. He came out from under his hat along that stretch of road where you first smell the paper mill when you are coming into town, and he knew that he should any minute now be no longer smelling the mill, if indeed you can ever be said to stop smelling something you have been smelling for so long that you don't any longer know it stinks.

With one hand deep in the pocket of his old reversible coat gripping the fifth of special Scotch that Don and Betty had given him just before he got on the bus, he came out from under his hat and saw the brown land and the black trees rushing past the window—the land and the trees rising suddenly into hills against the sun. That was exactly right, at least for the time of year, and reassured he rolled his head back on the back of the seat and looked into the bus, still with his hand on the bottle. There was nothing to see. The seat across the aisle was empty. But he could hear laughter and talk everywhere. Slowly and carefully he slid his head up the back of the seat like a periscope. He saw a man in shirt sleeves, hat on the back of his head, vest unbuttoned, blow on his fist and take a quick step and throw like a bowler. "Eighter from Decatur," the man said. "What's on that other one?" he said. "One," someone said. The man grunted and reached for the dice. In the first seat Adams in the pin-stripe suit was reading through his papers. He underscored phrases with a silver pencil and constantly pushed back his coat and shirt cuff to uncover his watch although he never looked up from the papers. Robert Andrews swiveled his head around, again like a periscope, saw the group in the back seat passing a bottle from hand to hand, and slid back down into the seat with the whole picture to think about. In addition he knew that somewhere, slumped down and hidden by the tall seats, were the two men who had to be carried into the bus. He thought, not for the first time, that he had made a mistake in not going home to register for the draft and in allowing himself to be taken here among strangers a long way off. A man said, "Six. God damn it, six, where are you?" And in the back of the bus there was loud laughter.

The land was still brown and the trees black, but now there were houses and filling stations and off in the distance the black smoke of the mills at the edge of the first of the two big cities they would have to pass through. Robert Andrews rested his secret bottle on his thigh and took from another pocket of his coat a *Time* that Don and Betty had made him take in the bus station when they discovered that he had brought nothing to read. He had intended to bring nothing. They couldn't understand that. He had intended to go into this new life as nearly naked as the law allowed. Under his old coat, which should have been long ago discarded, he wore only an old sweat shirt and old pants frayed at the cuffs and thin in the seat. On his feet he wore torn tennis shoes. When he got his new clothes he could step out of the old and leave them where they fell.

He automatically noted the date on the cover of the magazine and as automatically thought, Already? but of course it was because there was no doubt in his mind what the date was on his induction notice. He riffled quickly through the pages and saw briefly the vanishing faces of famous men and maps of famous places, gains and losses, charts and graphs. He began reading at the back and read forward through books, art, movies, education, religion. He read always more and more slowly as they rode into the city, watching, always longer and longer, store windows, people walking, and the smooth silk knees of women driving beside the tall bus.

And then he turned from the window. Someone in the back of the bus was calling "Sergeant, sergeant, bring the soldier medicine quick. I got a bad attack." There was a loud laugh at this, and the whole group in the back of the bus began to shout, Sergeant, sergeant.

"OK," a man called from the front, "I'm coming." He staggered down the aisle waving a unmarked bottle of almost colorless stuff that could only be corn whiskey. He stopped at Robert Andrews' seat. "Was it you who was sick?" he said.

"I'm all right," Robert Andrews said, one hand on his private bottle.

Hardly had the man stepped away when someone said clearly, "Captain, you sure saved my life." And someone else began to sing, For he's a jolly good captain.

"Have a drink of mine, captain," someone said.

"Don't mind if I do," the man said. "I didn't get much of my own." There was a loud laugh from the group. "Stand back," the man said, "and give me room to lift this bottle." He staggered back up the aisle as far as Robert Andrews' seat. He lifted a half-pint bottle in salute and then drank steadily until it was empty.

"Hey, my whiskey," someone said. The rest laughed.

"That's no captain," someone said. "He drinks like a colonel."

"Colonel, hell, a general."

"Come on, general, give the man back his bottle." They all laughed.

"That's the last whiskey on the bus." They all groaned.

"Come on, general, let us smell your breath anyway." But the general was collapsing onto the floor like a rope that is slowly and gently lowered to the ground.

Robert Andrews frankly half stood up and watched them carry

the general to the back seat and lay him out. He was still there
when the bus stopped in the terminal, and they left him to sleep
while they all went directly from the bus into the restaurant
under the close scrutiny of the military police.

Once inside the restaurant, Robert Andrews found himself
seated in a booth with three of the men from the back of the
bus. All three wore zippered jackets, one with an athletic letter I.

"You played football in high school?" Robert Andrews said,
seizing on the most obvious conversational gambit because in
this compacted booth in this well-lighted restaurant he felt host
to these three others and obligated. Acually, he knew, his clothes
were like theirs but even shabbier, and he had no obvious right,
but he wasn't his clothes, and although he had dressed inten-
tionally he felt he must demonstrate to them that he wasn't
at all what he appeared.

"Me?" the man with the athletic letter said.

"Yes," Robert Andrews said, "the letter on your jacket."

"Oh, it's the general's jacket," the man said. "I never went to
high school."

"I remember him well," another man said. "He was years
ahead of me in Indianhead, but I saw him play often."

"I saw him play up here—" The third man looked around
quickly and was silent, for here was now hundreds of miles away.

"He would have shown them a thing or two if he went to the
university," the other said.

"I didn't ever hear of him," the man wearing the jacket said.
"I'm going next table with some friends of mine." He went to
the next booth and Adams came back in exchange.

"Welcome to our home, Adams," Robert Andrews said,
waving him to the one unoccupied space in the booth. Adams
slid in easily. He was perhaps the only one who had availed himself of the restroom to wash and comb his hair, and although it
was impossible he even looked freshly shaved. "I was about to ask
our friends if they would care for a small Scotch before dinner."

"Excellent, excellent," Adams said. "A small one." From the

motion of his shoulders Robert Andrews judged he was rubbing his hands under the table. "Excellent," he said again.

"I really need it," one of the men said.

"Me too," the other said.

Robert Andrews reached for the bottle in the inside pocket of his reversible coat, the inside pocket being always in the tweed side, not the waterproof side. When he first went away to school he had insisted on a reversible coat—to say nothing of saddle shoes—and had bought with his mother's help the coat with the beautiful piece of Harris tweed which, after the first time he turned it out to please his mother when he went off on the train, never again saw the light of day; and even then it looked like rain before he got to New York and standing in the car in the dark approaches to Grand Central he turned his coat—for the last time that coat.

"I always enjoy a quiet drink before dinner," Robert Andrews said, "and perhaps on this occasion not too small a drink either." As he worked on the bottle he smiled at Adams. Adams' shoulders continued to twitch with the unseen motion of his hands. "And now," he poured Scotch, a good double shot of his good going-away Scotch, into each of the empty glasses that had been ready on the table when they came in, "your very good health, gentlemen." He raised his glass. They clutched their glasses tensely, except Adams, who would, of course, have been to many a lodge banquet. "And success in your—shall I say our?—new career." He sipped slowly. Adams sipped slowly. The other two gulped without stopping.

"Oh, god," one said.

"Amen," the other said.

The waitress was setting the plates on the table. "Perhaps another drop?" Robert Andrews said. They both nodded. He gave them a scant shot more.

"Liquor, by god," someone said. "A whole god-damn bottle of liquor." The man wearing the general's jacket was looking over the back of his booth at Robert Andrews and his bottle.

Robert Andrews looked back at him. "Well, pass the bottle to me and my friends," the man said. "We're near dead for a drink." Robert Andrews was speechless and motionless.

"Give me the damn bottle," the man said. He stretched for it but couldn't reach it.

"I'm having a quiet drink with my friends," Robert Andrews said at last. "Please leave us alone."

"I'll take it then." He lunged across the back of the booth, but his friends grabbed him and kept him from diving headlong into the middle of the table. All four of them started to come out of the booth. Robert Andrews clutched his bottle.

"Break it up," the military police said, the biggest men Robert Andrews had ever seen.

The other two men ate their supper quickly and went out to the bus. Adams, who lingered behind, said, "You did right. You did absolutely right. They were drunk." But Robert Andrews ducked into the washroom and bought, as he knew he could, a bottle of corn from the attendant.

The interior of the bus was dark and the streets deserted as they drove out of the heart of the city. Robert Andrews slumped in his seat, his hands stuffed into his coat pockets, one hand clutching through the cloth the Scotch deep in the inside pocket, the other hand feeling cold and direct the corn, which he hadn't yet found any chance to give to the men in the back of the bus, and all the while the time when he could do it was growing shorter and shorter, ticking away like the street lights that flicked all alike but each different past the window. And then Adams came through the bus making another check. "Take it to them, Adams. You don't have to say it's from me."

"You shouldn't worry," Adams said. "You'll never see them after tomorrow."

"Someone else," Robert Andrews said. "Some other them."

Adams took the bottle and went on to the back of the bus.

"He can't buy us." And Robert Andrews slumped even further in his seat and pushed his hat over his eyes.

"To hell with him." It was completely dark inside the hat

except when a brief glow from a street light seeped around the edges. Robert Andrews felt and heard Adams go back up the aisle, but he didn't stop and he didn't bring back the bottle.

Robert Andrews felt and heard the empty bottle strike the arm of his seat and break on the floor. He smelled the whiskey too but he didn't move. He closed his eyes under his hat.

When the bus stopped, he opened his eyes and peeked out from under the brim of his hat, but he could see nothing. There was no light in the bus or outside. He withdrew again under his hat with his eyes open and watchful. He heard the bus door open and someone said, "Military Police." Then very loud, "All right. Anyone want to spend his first night in the army in the guardhouse?"

"Don't volunteer for nothing," someone in the dark bus said. There were two or three isolated laughs that were quickly stifled.

Glass crunched suddenly under heavy shoes, and a light came on so strong that Robert Andrews could see all the inside of his hat. "What about him? Is he for it?" This was said right over him. No one said anything and Robert Andrews couldn't somehow move his hands to take off his hat. Someone touched the hat and it rolled down his stomach and over his legs to the floor. The flashlight was full in his face. He tried not to blink. "Well?" He didn't say anything. "Stand up." He got up and stood in the aisle. "Name?"

"Robert Andrews."

"Sit down."

They went on down the bus. Robert Andrews sat bolt upright. His hat was gone now for good. In the back of the bus the same voice said in the same intonation, "What about him?"

"He's sick, sir," someone said. "The bus ride made him sick."

"Sure it's not whiskey?"

"No, sir, he's really sick, but he'll be all right when we get there."

"All right. Leave him."

They flashed their lights in Robert Andrews' face as they passed, but they didn't stop.

In the barracks a soldier told them they had twenty minutes to make their beds and get ready for the night. At the end of that time Robert Andrews, who had brought nothing with him, sat on the edge of his bed. The lights went out. Men shouted and cursed in the dark. Robert Andrews dropped off all his clothes and slid naked into the cold bed. In the dark he fumbled his bottle out of his coat and took a long drink.

The man next to him—he had carefully taken an end bed— was cursing and thrashing around in the dark getting undressed and throwing his sheets and blankets over the bed. Robert Andrews took another drink. The man next to him was in bed now, still cursing and groaning a little now and then. "What's the matter?" Robert Andrews said. He regretted at once having volunteered the question.

But the man only said, "Sick."

"Too bad," Robert Andrews said.

"I need a drink so I can sleep," the man said. "A good long drink."

Robert Andrews recognized the voice of the man called the general. He leaned over to the general's bed and felt for his hand. The general shied. "Put out your hand and don't say anything," Robert Andrews said. He touched the general's chest with the bottle. The general grabbed it and drank quickly. "Put it on the floor between us," Robert Andrews said, "and help yourself."

"You're my friend," the general said. "You think I'm drunk but I know your voice. You're my friend and I'll remember."

Robert Andrews took another drink, and when a little later he reached for the bottle again, it was empty. He folded his hands on his chest and went to sleep.

II

On the morning of the third day it was at last certain: the army was rejecting him. By noon he had been cleared absolutely from the reception center, and he caught a bus into town without waiting for the army to provide transportation back to the city where he was drafted. Strangely, though, he was in no hurry to get back to the place where his trunk was still sitting in the middle of his room, where his rent had two weeks to run, where his job was not yet filled, and where his friends went about doing the things they had all always done. He wasn't sure he wanted to go back, and if he didn't want to, he didn't have to. He had had his parties. He had said his goodbys. He had made his provisions.

When he got off the bus in town, he started to go into a hotel bar. It was a hotel of a chain he always patronized when he traveled, and he naturally started to go into this one. But he stopped at the doorway when he saw himself reflected in the plate-glass door, his reflection swimming strangely through the dim lobby. He turned away from the hotel because although he was Robert Andrews beyond a shadow of a doubt, even to himself he didn't look like Robert Andrews. Clearly and objectively now that the glamour of going into the army was off him he looked like a bum.

He went on down the street to a little place that was dim with the faint light of neon tubes around the mirror behind the bar and the dull glow of chromium strips hidden in the dusk. There he drank the lunch special twenty-five-cent highball right through the afterwork rush and into the slack when everyone had gone home to supper. All afternoon while he and the bartender were alone he drank steadily, with the bartender even throwing in one now and then on the house. And then when it was quiet again and they were almost alone in the bar, the bartender said, "Why don't you take a walk?"

"Oh, no," Robert Andrews said, "I'm not drunk."

"I know you're not drunk," the bartender said, "but you've drunk a lot of whiskey. Try a little walk."

"I really don't want to," Robert Andrews said.

"It would be good for you," the bartender said.

"If it will make you happy," Robert Andrews said.

"It won't make me happy," the bartender said, "but I think it's a good idea."

"OK, I'll take a walk around the block."

"And listen," the bartender said, "if you feel like drinking any more, come back here. Don't go anywhere else. They wouldn't know you from Adam, but come back here and let me take care of you."

"OK."

"You got that. Come back here, OK?"

"OK."

"Come back here," the bartender said. "I know what you're talking about. Lots wouldn't know but I know."

"OK," Robert Andrews said. And he walked out. He didn't know what it was that the bartender knew, but he knew about the bartender's boy dead already in the war, and he knew the bartender knew something even if it wasn't exactly what he himself knew if he could only remember it.

Out in the street he marveled at the amount of whiskey he had drunk and how clear his head was. He began to walk slowly around the block, holding the buildings at arm's length with the tips of the fingers of his right hand.

Once started, he just kept going around the block, and after a while he said suddenly, "This is enough." He was standing in front of an optician's shop. The bronzed, fit, handsome dummy head in the window smiled at him. Robert Andrews had scowled at the dummy and shaken his fist and said, You lousy bastard. And then he said, This is enough, because he saw as he said it an infinitely receding series of pictures of himself standing before the window, scowling, shaking his fist, and saying, You lousy bastard. He wondered how many times he had walked around the block and stopped in front of the window, but he didn't wonder for long. He only said, This is enough, and he knew that he had just to walk along the buildings until he came to the bar because he was sure, whatever else, that he hadn't crossed a street.

He was going along the back of the block, a dark street with warehouses and pawn shops, not paying much attention to where he was, when someone said, "How about a drink?"

Robert Andrews wasn't surprised to hear the voice suddenly out of the dark. His fingertips had told him already that they weren't touching brick, steel, wood, or glass. He hadn't got around to thinking about the fact, but he knew there was something there. When he turned his head he saw that his hand was resting lightly on the shoulder of a man's jacket. "What we need is another drink," the man said.

"I'm on my way to get one now," Robert Andrews said. "Come go with me."

"Got one right here," the man said, reaching for his hip pocket and staggering half across the sidewalk. "Alley up here where we can have a good quiet drink." He staggered off down the sidewalk, and Robert Andrews, trailing his fingers over the brick wall, followed along with him.

The man turned half around as he walked and staggered a few steps backward. "Come on," he said. "Just a little further."

Robert Andrews, straining his eyes to focus them farther ahead than they had been focused all day, saw the red arc of a cigarette thrown into the street apparently from the solid brick wall. Wondering he watched and saw a uniformed policeman step out of the wall and walk toward them.

The other man, still staggering and turning as he walked, suddenly saw the policeman not ten feet from him. He checked himself and walked briskly past the policeman and disappeared into the wall.

"Good evening, officer," Robert Andrews said, stopping but still holding the building at arm's length.

"Evening," the policeman said.

"A fine evening," Robert Andrews said, demonstrating flawless enunciation. "A little brisk but quite suitable to this time of year."

"I suppose," the policeman said.

"If you are cold," Robert Andrews said, "my friend and I were just about to step into this alley for a drink. Perhaps you would care to join us?"

"No," the policeman said. He moved on.

Robert Andrews found himself about to go past the alley without stopping. He automatically kept his right hand on one building and with his left hand reached across to the other. Spread-eagled like that he was obliged to look into the alley, so he remembered that this was where he was supposed to be. Forcing the buildings apart with his hands, he went on down the alley and out the other end without finding anyone. He was distinctly displeased but when he got through the block, there he was back at his old bar.

God knows how long he had been walking round the block without seeing it, but he wasn't at all surprised to find the bar as soon as he became aware that he wanted a drink. He eased into his old place at the bar.

"Ah, there you are," the bartender said. He set up a drink. "How do you feel?"

"Beginning to go to pieces around the edges," Robert Andrews said.

"Take a couple of drinks and go to bed."

"I'm just having a quiet drink," Robert Andrews said. "I'm not making any trouble, am I?"

"None at all," the bartender said, "but you need sleep." Robert Andrews nodded and set down his glass. "Did you have a hat?" the bartender said.

Robert Andrews felt his head. "No," he said, "no hat at all." He turned and drifted out of the bar with his head pulled down into his turned-up collar. He had no idea where he was, but he knew it didn't matter where he was. There was no place where he had to be. All places were alike. Even the place where his trunk stood in the middle of his still unrented room and his bare desk in the still unfilled office—even that place was like any other. It had no claim on him. He had broken all connection with the past, and now he was set down in a strange town where he could stay or move on as he pleased. There was no limit to where he could go. Miami, New Orleans, Chicago, Detroit, LA, Frisco, the banana republics—anywhere where no one knew him and where he could be someone else, someone reborn, washed in the blood of the tiger.

But he woke up on a bus with a ticket in his hand. The bus was dark and everyone else was asleep. He wanted to shout to the driver to find out where he was going, but he waited and when they came to a town and the driver put on the lights, then he could see that the ticket entitled him to a ride back to his room and his trunk and his desk and everything else—whatever it was—that had been everything until he got his draft notice and was forced to give it all up.

At the one transfer point, the only big city he had to get through on the way, he sat in the station while his bus was called and while it left and another was called and left. He was practically out just sitting there, but he didn't go to sleep, and when a policeman came through checking on bums sleeping in the bus station, he got up and walked out onto the street because not even his ticket could begin to explain why he was still sitting there.

The night, which had begun by being fine and cool, was now bitter cold and windy. He shivered inside his old reversible coat. He thought he could feel a cold spot on his body to correspond to each of the moth holes in the beautiful piece of Harris tweed.

He lingered as long as he dared over coffee and a barbeque sandwich and another cup of coffee. And a cigarette. And a—a —a phone call to a store across the street where there was no light. And another cigarette. And another try on the phone.

The night was colder than ever and the wind blew hard. As soon as he came to the first corner he changed direction to get the wind behind him. Even then he trembled violently with the cold and with fatigue. He had to get warm and he had to rest and he had to stay away from the bus station where the warm busses with the soft seats kept pulling out all the time all night long.

With the wind out of his face, he was able to lift his head a little from his collar and look off down the street, so he saw at

least half a dozen neon signs indicating small hotels, each up a
dingy flight of stairs. Without thinking about it, he climbed up
to the Hotel Bazaar.

There was no one sitting in the two straight chairs in the
lobby and no one behind the desk. There was no one loitering
beside the scrubby potted palm. He rang a bell a sign said to
ring, but no one came. He sat down in one of the chairs and
got up. He walked around the palm. The leaves were dusty and
there were cigar butts in the pot. He started off down a long
corridor that, other than the stairs, was the only way out of the
lobby. Under a dim light toward the end of the corridor he
could see the signs: Men—Women. He could smell faintly a
sweet medicinal smell.

A door far down the corridor opened suddenly and a woman
walked out and toward him. She wore a long robe that hobbled
her, and as she got closer he could see that it was a rich blue
silk, flowing, yet clinging as she moved, flattering too to her
yellow hair. When she was very close he stopped, but she passed,
brushing against his coat, without looking at him. He turned to
look after her. There was a long golden dragon coiling up the
back of her robe, its head resting on her shoulder. Trailing behind her was a blast of almost overwhelming perfume with a
strong undertone of the sweet medicinal smell he had noticed
before. He took a step after her, but she turned abruptly into a
room. One instant she was there, and then there was a swirling
robe settling about one bare heel raised for an instant out of a
high-heeled backless slipper, and then the door closed and there
was nothing.

He followed down the corridor but he wasn't sure which door
she went in, and he went on down the stairs into the cold street,
to the flashing neon signs, to the grit-ridden, paper-laden wind
at the corner.

Sitting stupidly in the bus he hadn't intended to take or at
least not yet, he watched the night weaken and a pillar of rosy
light erect itself over the spot where the sun lay beneath the
hills. He fingered the punched ticket entitling him to a ride to

the place he hadn't intended to go, not yet, the place where his room was, his trunk, his job, his friends, and everything he had ever wanted or a man could ever want.

Then when the flat red sun itself came up in a valley and slid for a while behind a hill and came up again in another valley, this time for the day, he knew he was getting close.

"Jesus," said a man behind him, "what's that stink?"

"Oh, that's the paper mill," another man said.

"How do you stand it around here?"

"Oh, you get used to it."

"How do you stand it until you get used to it?"

"You know you'll get used to it."

"Jesus," the first man said, "not me."

"Everybody gets used to it. You don't notice it after a while."

"Jesus."

It was full light in the town but early as he walked from the bus station to his room. There was little chance of meeting anyone he knew at that hour, but once he thought he saw a car he knew—Don Marshall's car—and he turned abruptly down a side street until it had passed. He would be able to get to his room and stay there for two or three days just lying on his bed and sleeping and thinking whatever he had to think about, a new man in an old town. With this in mind he bought bread and cheese and peanut butter and milk and a carton of cigarettes. And at another place he knew of he bought a dripping sack of beer cans pulled up by a secret rope from a forgotten well in a ruined cellar.

Then last of all he went down the steep driveway beside his house to the private door of his basement apartment that looked out directly into a savage ravine partially obscured by a heavy cedar thicket. He opened the door and went in. The room was still dark but he could make out his trunk in the middle of the floor. He could smell Betty Marshall's perfume still clinging to the room after the big farewell party the Marshalls had given him here and at their place and several other places along the way. He turned on the light.

Betty Marshall was sitting on the bed. "Hello," she said.

"Hello," he said.

"You're really back then. Don thought he saw you and called me from the plant to come over and see you."

The beer sack was dripping all over the floor. "I have to take care of this," he said.

She talked to him through the bathroom door. "I brought some whiskey," she said. "It's only the bootlegger special, not as good as the stuff we gave you to go away on, but tonight we'll really have a party."

"That's fine," he said, coming out of the bathroom with two wet glasses and taking the bottle that she had already opened for him.

The Gingerbread Man

Mason THOUGHT he had never seen anything like it before, and day after day he sat on his terrace wrapped in the sun and watched the men at work on the new building. At first he wrote long letters home about how different it all was. He knew a bit about construction back in the States, and he had friends who would appreciate the details he could supply. Other friends had to be content with the novelties of Moorish and feudal relics—castles and cathedrals and tiny streets—affairs which somehow seemed to hold his attention less than he had expected and which did nothing like so much as the new building to keep his mind off the fact that he had come to Mallorca to take a bit longer about dying.

It was the merest chance that he lived where he could see the work going on. He had been shown only the one house, a villa with a spacious view of the harbor, and he had taken it at once, fully furnished. For the first time in his life he was living like a rich man—buying the view he wanted, recklessly, price no object—and he liked it fully as much as he had feared during all those years when he used to tell himself that his private income wasn't really enough to live on, that, besides, he had to work to keep his self-respect. In a way he rather regretted not having realized long ago that he wasn't going to live forever.

He had brought almost nothing with him, so he was settled as soon as he had hired the first maid the rental agency sent

around, and he entered at once into the unrestricted enjoyment
of his view.

Patches of light on the sea, green and blue of water. Flashes
of light in the distance where the afternoon sun caught something in the hills beyond the bay. Gleams of white in the hills
off to the north. Not snow, surely. Perhaps marl. Who knows?
Rich clouds of a massiveness he wasn't used to. Yachts, fishing
boats in the harbor, and the entire waterfront dominated by the
only magnificently situated cathedral he had ever seen. The
castle behind him, he had noticed, was also well placed. Both
dated from the thirteenth century. This was the view he was
paying for and it was worth every peseta.

He turned his attention after a while to the view he wasn't
paying for, the kind of view he could have had even from the
cheapest apartment in town: roofs, chimney pots, walled gardens, orange and lemon trees, potted geraniums of giant size,
clichés of bougainvillaea tumbling over walls. He could also look
across his own garden into the next street down the hill. It was a
street with a fine passage of taxis, carriages, motor scooters,
children, horse carts, and donkey carts, and a quite tolerable
medley of street cries of which he could decode only the *Para
hoy* of the blind lottery sellers. *Para hoy*, seize the day. He could
see a good stretch of the street because there was a vacant lot
backing up to his garden wall.

The lot was rubble-filled, and he had at first the impression of
devastation but whether by bombs or time he couldn't say.
Around the lot there was a thin wall of flagstones stood on edge
and cemented and reinforced at intervals by square stone posts.
In places the wall had tumbled down. In other places it was
breached as if a small car had been driven through. He had seen
many such lots as he drove through the town, but he had been
assured that there was no bomb damage here and that nothing
in this section was at all old.

The lot, like his own garden, was much lower than the street
so that he had a plunging view into it from his terrace. It was
rather like an amphitheater, and it had a play of its own. He

first became aware of the play when two black goats ran down from the street. Shortly an old man appeared and sat on a fallen section of the wall and smoked a cigarette and looked all around but especially up at the terrace. He seemed to be used to finding there something worth watching. But the goats grazed only a few minutes before they scrambled up out of the lot and trotted down the street, snatching at bushes as they went or standing on their hind legs against a wall to reach a vine. The old man followed at a little distance as if they weren't really together.

Almost at once a dozen sheep tumbled into the lot. They were very much with a bearded man and a dog. The circling, barking dog was a very satisfactory sheep dog, and the man, carrying a small crook and cradling a tiny lamb in his arms, was a very satisfactory shepherd. They stayed no longer than the goats and were followed after a little interval by a boy with a flock of turkeys. Off and on, a man or a woman would creep along the face of a rubbish fill at one end of the deep lot. No matter how many times the rubbish was gone over, each new picker found something to put in his sack.

Late in the afternoon the stone of the cathedral brightened to its improbable limit and began to fade. Fishing boats moved out of the harbor. Their powerful motors throbbed across the still air. Somewhere a gun was fired several times as if in salute.

The cathedral faded and almost disappeared, and then sprang out of the gloom floodlighted. Well, it was made to be seen. Two old windmills, regular Don Quixote mills that he had seen from the ferry as his first landmarks, also reappeared—outlined in flashing neon. But even this was what he had come for, this continuity around him, and the whole idea of a pre-American age. He hoped he might find a bit of Roman marble—the smallest finger of a statue—or an amphora barnacle-encrusted from the sea, anything really that had been held in someone's hand a thousand, two thousand years ago, and that he could now hold in his own hand.

Out in the bay the brilliant lights of the fishing boats moved slowly across the dark. And that was the end of the first day.

For several days he took to the expected back alleys of the city, lay on the beach, went to the bullfights, which didn't, after all, make him sick, but on the other hand didn't much excite him except when he first stepped from his taxi and joined the crowd funneling toward the gate. Then, briefly, Hemingway and all that came flooding into his mind, and he stopped at a counter under the ramp for a Fundador, which he tried to drink with due ceremony. He went on up the ramp exulting into the sun to discover the ring.

Chocolate milk! That was the message on the gigantic bottle in the center of the ring. Chastened, he found a seat and sat down. The bottle stood there while the ring was sprinkled, and it seemed destined to stay throughout the fights, but just before the grand entry it put out legs and ran off accompanied by the most enthusiastic applause he was to hear all afternoon. Where the bottle had stood there was a round dry spot, and he seemed to see himself reading a story that ended—or began—Paco died where the chocolate-milk bottle had stood.

The fights were really rather dull although he didn't say that to anyone (nor write it in letters) and he shouted Olé when everyone else did. As a foreigner, however, he didn't venture to join in booing the bulls, which were entirely outclassed and died rather grubbily, trailing black *banderillas,* with nothing at all approaching a moment of truth. Perhaps another time, he thought, but he never went again.

He returned home late in the afternoon of a day when he was tired of walking and seeing and catechizing himself endlessly: Is it old? Is it good? Do I really like it? He settled himself on his terrace with a drink, which could no longer do him any harm. His view was admirably composed as always. The cathedral was just right from where he sat, and at that distance it didn't matter if the west facade was a nineteenth-century addition or which of the glass was really old if any. There was no need to question any part of what he saw although he did put it to himself that he might just as well, with all this spread out in front of him, have someone show him how to get started with paints. He had never before had time to paint although he had always wanted to be a painter. He thought he had the eye for it.

So engrossed was he in the great view that he did not at once observe that the theater in the sunken lot had added a new act. The two black goats were still grazing disdainfully along the foot of the rubbish fill, but at least half the lot was suddenly given over to a gang of men busily knocking together rough forms and pouring cement.

The area over which the men were working was uneven, but the level top of the low wall they were making was perhaps fifteen feet below the street. It was hard to tell really but he guessed about fifteen feet judging by the size of the men. The procedure struck him as strange, but never having built anything where the frost line was not a factor, he had to confess to himself that he just didn't know if they should have dug footings or not. He was, however, a trifle irritated to see no sign of lines and levels, no confabulations over spread-out blueprints.

Moreover, it surprised him at first that a house—if it was going to be a house—should be built so low, but he saw at a glance that other houses on the block were at least a full story below the street on the back and that the lower floor in each case gave directly onto a pleasant walled garden.

A carter backed his white horse and tiny cart off the street to the edge of the fill and dumped a fantastically small load of dirt into the lot. A few stones rolled to the feet of the goats, which seemed to make a point of not looking up. The cart, as Mason examined it, lurched forward and stopped. The carter swung the body back down against the shafts and locked it in place. A tipcart. Of course. It had to be. He hadn't seen one of those since he was a boy. He had thought there were no tipcarts any more. Regretfully he watched it drive away and then turned again to the workmen.

The rhythmic scrape scrape scrape of a shovel mixing cement focused his attention. That tableau was also familiar from his childhood: a man mixing, a man carrying pails of water, a man bringing cement, and another bringing sand. The man mixing was using the only shovel Mason was ever to see on the job, and he made his first acquaintance then with the flat baskets and the mattocks that Spanish workmen use as earth-moving equipment. He watched them brace the tilted baskets between their feet and use the mattocks to pull in the sand. When the cement was mixed, they carried it to the forms in black basins—perhaps rubber—exactly the same shape as the baskets, something like a dishpan. When the forms were filled, the men threw some large stones on top of the wet cement as if to hold it down. Then they went home.

The tipcart with the white horse had meanwhile come back twice in company with a cart with a brown horse. Mason visualized men digging somewhere and filling their baskets and tossing the dirt into the carts. He planned one day soon if this kept on to follow the carts to see where they came from and how long it took how many men to toss even that bit of dirt into a cart.

When they had all gone and the lot was deserted, he had a sudden image of a deep sand pit god knows how many miles and years away. There were some boys lying quietly in the sun on top of the pit just back from the edge. They were listening to two men at the bottom talking while they loaded a cart. Their shovels hissed rhythmically in the loose sand they had knocked down from the face of the pit. They were working steadily and laughing as if they didn't know that not a year went by without a man or a boy getting smothered in just such a pit. They surely didn't know that the boys had fled from the pit before they could be warned off and driven away. The boys might later roll stones down on them—small stones to tease them only—but it never worked out for the boys as it did for the Brave Little Tailor, who dropped stones on the sleeping giants and got them to fight each other. The men would yell and curse up at them, and once, when the stones were too big for a joke, they had silently climbed the sand cliff and caught the boys, but then they could think of nothing to do with them except threaten to tell their parents.

But in the image Mason had of the boys, they were not rolling stones but were lying still, their faces to the hot sun, listening to the voice of the world coming up out of the pit. The voice spoke of drink and women, common enough words, but somehow veiled now and promising something the boys couldn't even begin to imagine. They listened with their mouths open until the cart drove away and the pit was deserted. Then they started a small avalanche of sand that thudded hard against the bottom of the pit, and they ran and slid and jumped the last bit of the way down into the pile of loose sand they had created. "Hey, Joe," one of the boys said, "back that gol-darn cart in here right and give me a drink out of that gol-darn bottle, and I'll tell you what I heard about George Mason and the doctor's wife." He ended on a shriek, already rolling on the sand in an agony of self-approval.

Days passed. The low cement wall turned a corner and another corner and another corner and at last closed on itself as a rectangle. Apparently it was to be a house. It even began to add some inside partitions. But what baffled Mason completely was that there were no signs of door or window openings. The two carts, the one with the brown horse and the one with the white horse, came and went all day long. They were joined at times by a Chevrolet truck dating from the mid-thirties, not by any means the oldest truck on the island where Model A's were common and where two veterans of the Paris taxis' dash to the Marne still did an honorable business.

At first he resented the intrusion of the truck. Its monstrous loads of loose black dirt nearly overwhelmed the hard red clods brought by the carts, and the face of the fill was advancing alarmingly toward the growing cement wall. The clods were already rolling against it and settling in a red drift. Clearly there would be no sunken garden on that side at least.

But as he grew to know the sound of the truck's motor and the squeak of its hoist, he became reconciled to its presence and even liked it a little. He could lie in bed in the morning and pick out its voice from all the traffic of the street, and he would know that the work had been proceeding even while he slept. The first thing he did each morning was to check the progress of the work. Weather was no longer of prime importance as it affected the light in his view but as it allowed or did not allow the work to go on. Only after checking the work would he look at the sun on the sea and the shadow on the cathedral, the sharpness of the distant hills. Often the first thing he saw in the morning was a workman, his pants down, squatting against the new wall.

One morning he was awakened by the sound of the truck's motor laboring and the sharp cries of men. He didn't need to get out of bed to know what had happened because he had seen it happen before. The truck had undoubtedly backed too close to the edge of the fill and had sunk a wheel in a soft spot. They might be able to rock it out after a while, or they might call in a passing truck from the street, or they might hitch the horses to the truck if they came along first. It seemed no less a pleasant change for the workmen than it did for Mason.

He knew all that well enough and might in a moment get up to enjoy it, but he tried first to see it clearly in his mind's eye; and he did see—very clearly—a mired Chevrolet truck of the period of the mid-thirties and a group of shouting men around it. But to his surprise the truck was new, and the men, all of whom carried shovels, were shouting in English. The scene was vivid and familiar although he couldn't at first place it. Then suddenly he said aloud, "Medford." His next thought was of all the years since he had so much as remembered his first job and his first living away from home.

He had been hired in the cold winter of that cold year to work in a restaurant that was just being built. It was one of a chain of roadside restaurants and would be ready for the summer trade. However, he was to go to work at once in the company's training store in his home town. He would get no money while training and would have to furnish his own white shirts, but he would get three meals a day, a bunk in the bunk room if he wanted it, and a clean white uniform every day. He never told anyone that he wasn't being paid all those months, but he worked steadily and slept at home and was conspicuously missing from the neighborhood most of the time. His main object was to stay out of the way and let his father save a little money to send him away to school in the fall.

The waitresses—but he never liked to think about that afterward. He had gone straight to work from a high school where Post Office was considered a daring game, and he wasn't ready for the new games the waitresses wanted to play. At the same time he was fascinated by all the free and easy talk, and quickly advanced to petty grapplings in the stock room. Each night he walked a different waitress home, and he kissed them all good night. He thought himself a very devil at the time. It wasn't until years later that he realized they must have thought him a fool.

When summer began, the new store still wasn't ready, but the owner came around to meet his crew and offered them a chance to earn some money as laborers on the job to help speed things along. Their regular pay could start at once. Mason and the others were only too glad to grab a chance to earn some money. Mason himself had become desperate at the shifts he had been put to to get his shirts washed and ironed and keep up at home the illusion that he was being paid. By this time, however, he had developed such a preference for working in the kitchen where he could wear his uniform without a shirt that he was never to become really good at meeting the public.

The new work was hard. The restaurant was being built on the Medford marshes, and the yard still needed a lot of fill. All day the trucks came and dumped dirt, which Mason helped to spread with a shovel. Blisters formed and broke and turned to callouses. Now he was really away from home, living in a boarding house with the others. He learned to drink a little beer as if he enjoyed it. There were no waitresses around. It was a very good life. About this phase he had no regrets at all.

When the store opened, things were much as they had been at the training store, only better, because they were all in their own store now and all making a little money. Eleven dollars a week went a long way in those days when you got your room and board thrown in. There were waitresses again and there was even one waitress. Mason thought he was in love. He might very well have been, but whatever it was, it lasted all summer.

They both went away to college in the fall. They both wrote at great length, and then her letters gradually stopped. He wrote again and again and finally got one last letter. He could see that envelope for the rest of his life any time he chose. It was a light gray-blue with a thin piping of faint yellow. He couldn't see the letter itself ever again, but whatever it said, it meant the end.

They both worked at the store the following summer, but she never even spoke to him. That was a very bad summer and working there was never much fun again although he kept coming back every year until he finished college. Years later in New York he saw his old boss working in someone else's restaurant. They agreed it had been a good time and that it was a pity the restaurant failed. Neither had kept track of anybody. They had nothing further to say to each other. The old man couldn't pick up the check, and Mason couldn't tip him.

The whole thing faded from his mind after that. From time to time he thought in passing of the girl: someone would look like her—a toss of the hair, a gesture, a smile—or would have the same name, perhaps, a common enough one. He thought even less of all the girls he should have tried to make love to those summers at the store. And as the trucks of the period disappeared, he forgot especially that he had ever in his life worked with his hands and had been a young man among young men, drinking beer, singing in taverns, wandering the night streets of the town happily looking for something he didn't even know he wasn't finding.

The foot of the fill advanced to the foot of the wall and then began to climb. That explained, then, why there were no windows in the wall—at least if they were planning to fill on all four sides. The wall was now fully fifteen feet high on the side toward him but seemed less in other places. Well, that was certainly one way of getting a cellar without having to dig it. (He was pleased with this observation and repeated it in several letters to people who didn't know each other.) Yes, the fill was beginning to pass the corners of the wall and pile up along both sides.

The work on the walls, which never rose more than a few feet at a time, seemed to have been suspended with some of the interior partitions far short of the outside walls; and the center of activity shifted to the brook, which was so close under his garden wall that he couldn't see it as part of his view and had only discovered it when he walked out to inspect the work at night after the men had gone. Ah, that would be fine indeed, the brook all along that side at the bottom of a sunken garden.

The brook issued from a kind of cave under a wall on one side of the lot and disappeared into another cave under the street. It really wasn't much of a brook. Its bed was barely wet and he guessed that it was mostly used to carry off rainwater from the streets. Sometimes at night, however, he could hear it flowing briskly when there was no rain. He thought of rain falling hard on the distant hills and he was soothed. A busybody told him that hotels drained their swimming pools into it at night, but he found it easy to forget that.

He guessed from the way the men were carrying lumber up to his garden wall that they were making a cement channel to stop the brook's nightly erosions. He confirmed this after the men had gone, but all day long he watched the fragments of their actions and tried to complete the pattern in his mind without knowing really what was going on.

During the day, however, two new entertainments began in the lot. The horses came and went as before. The Chevrolet truck brought a load from time to time. The goats grabbed at the grass that was still beyond the reach of the fill. The sheep and their shepherds looked into the lot but passed it by. The turkeys came in their appointed hour and seemed to find something, as did the dump pickers, who kept to their schedules.

First, the Chevrolet truck came once with a load of dressed

stone rather than dirt. The men rolled the stones off one by one onto the top of the fill. The stones thudded heavily into the dirt. Mason could hear them even where he was. The stones were much bigger than a cement block, perhaps a foot by two feet by half a foot thick.

Two of the men who had been working near the brook appeared with hatchets in their hands and began hacking at the stones, which seemed actually to be very soft. (He felt them one night and found that they were gritty as if the surface were constantly turning to sand.) The men hacked all day and made shallow channels all around the narrow side of the blocks. Mason's first thought was that this was to keep a rope from slipping, but later he saw the men handle the stones without tackle of any kind, and he had to guess again. He could guess at nothing, however, and it was this groove as much as anything that made him send for someone to give him lessons in Spanish so that he could talk to the workmen.

In his Spanish lessons he learned to say, "Where is the American Express Company?" "I have lost my overcoat." "How much is it?" "When can I have it?" "I will be back tomorrow." At night, however, with his dictionary and grammar and phrasebook he worked out "I watch you from up there." "The work is very interesting." "The work is not like this in the United States." "What is this for?" He knew the foreman said, "I know it," but it hadn't occurred to him that it was one thing to sweat out a question but quite another thing to understand the answer. He began to look forward to talking with the foreman each day, but he never understood very much.

Another thing that happened on the same day the truck delivered the first load of stone was that the fill along one side came level with the top of the wall, and Mason was astonished to see them begin dumping dirt inside the foundation. Then he remembered that the ground was uneven, and he deduced that they were merely leveling up so they could pour a basement floor.

In the afternoon, other men left the brook and began laying

a course of the grooved stones on top of those sections of the inside partition that had been left much lower than the rest. Here they were clearly allowing space for doors. By the end of the day the stones were four courses high, nearly as high as a man's head, and the door openings could soon be closed at the top. They were clearly too wide to be bridged by any of the stones that had yet been delivered. Mason hoped the men would build arches for him although he had seen no arches on any new construction in town. He was almost too excited to sleep that night, but nothing further was done the next day on that section. In fact it stood that way for days on end, and Mason's Spanish wasn't up to asking why.

But the main event of that eventful day was the first appearance of an old army 10 x 10. Mason could scarcely believe his eyes as it backed over the sidewalk and dumped a colossal load of tan sand at the other end of the lot as if disdaining to share the petty work of horses and small trucks. Mason trembled at the thought of men with baskets and mattocks trying to load such a truck. Surely there must be a big shovel at work somewhere on the island. He could easily follow the truck in a taxi just to make sure.

The days passed without seeming to pass. The big truck came and went to some secret rhythm of its own. The brook ran in a cement trough all across the lot. The interior stone wall added two courses and stopped with the top stones reaching toward each other across the door openings. Mason thought that the projecting ends of the stones were beveled, and he guessed that a keystone might be used. It wasn't an arch by any means, but a keystone by itself was almost as exciting.

A low flat wagon delivered a load of something that looked like steel beams, and Mason felt somehow cheated. His imagination was deeply committed to the idea of a building made entirely without wood and entirely without steel. However, as he studied the beams through the glasses he had pretended to be buying for birdwatching (perhaps the clerk really believed he hadn't noticed that there were almost no birds) he saw that they were not red-leaded steel at all as he had thought but red honey-comb tiles a foot or so long cemented end to end to make up something that really did look, even when he knew better, rather like an I-beam. They must be going to use those for floor joists. There was nothing else in sight. Absolutely incredible.

The foreman on the job thought it was incredible, when Mason put the question to him, that anything else could possibly be used for floor joists. Mason had been too excited to work up the question properly and in despair fell back on "These? There?" pointing to the beams and gesturing across from one wall to another. "Of course," the foreman said. "Strong?" "Very strong." "Very interesting," Mason said. "In the United States, wood," he said. "Wood?" The foreman tapped a plank that had been used for the forms. "This?" "Yes, wood." Mason turned the plank up on edge. "Wood, so." "Is it cheap?" "Very cheap," Mason said.

He saw, while he was talking with the foreman, that new forms were being built on top of the cement trough of the brook, arched forms supported from within by piled stones. Cement was already plastered over part, and it could only mean that they were planning to bury the brook completely. That night he listened sadly to its small torrent. In his head the thing that would some day turn him off like a light slept. He slept.

Except for his tours of the new building he rarely went out any more. He visited no one and no one visited him. The few people he had met in his pension when he first came to town had all long since finished their vacations, and he was left, as he had been warned by a traveled friend, with a choice between his own company and the company of "the kind of people you would go miles out of your way to avoid at home." He tried it both ways and in the end decided he was much less gregarious than he had ever believed. There were his letters and his building.

His maid—she was a shred of a woman old enough so that he didn't feel obliged to think about her—cleaned the house while he sat on the terrace, and while he ate his lunch she swept the terrace and emptied his ashtrays and mislaid his binoculars. After his nap she straightened the bed and disappeared, leaving something cold for his supper and a constant supply of the red wine he was delighted to find himself enjoying with all his meals. For all this he paid her much too much—exactly what she asked for when she first came to him. She also cheated him in small ways. He learned to check the market prices in the morning paper he couldn't otherwise read much of so that when they faced each other across the kitchen table with the groceries spread out between them he would know when and how much she was cheating him. He never said anything to her about it. He was satisfied with her cooking and was secretly ashamed of how little he paid her—about $14 a month as a matter of fact although he never mentioned the price to anyone for fear of being branded "one of those Americans who are overpaying for everything and ruining the place for the rest of us." He probably took as much pleasure in her minute peculations as she did. He wished he could watch her on the morning she let herself in and found he wouldn't need his binoculars or camera or cash-on-hand any more.

When he first learned that he was as good as dead, he had been afraid to close his eyes at night and had resented having to open them in the morning to face, across another day, another night of falling asleep. That was long past now as was the period when he said, half in drunken jest, each night the child's "Now I lay me down to sleep," and awoke each morning with an almost heartbreaking sense of the beauty of the world. After all, that sort of thing can't go on forever although he did know of a man who, under a year's sentence of death, left behind in his room three hundred and sixty-five empty whiskey bottles. But now with his letters and his building, Mason's days passed without seeming to pass and always with a sense of fullness. He was never bored.

He thought once of the time when the building would be finished, and he sent for a man to show him how to paint with oils. They sat side by side a few days and painted the harbor, the light, the light, the endless light, and then Mason dismissed him and began painting the colors of the fill, red and black and tan, the geometry of the disappearing wall and the blocked pattern of the interior partitions. Although it wasn't art, he would always know what it meant, and once he had begun to paint he forgot that he was painting for any particular reason.

He also thought that if the building went more than two stories high, he would have no view. At the moment, however, he was not concerned about that.

One Sunday, having exhausted his enthusiasm for the grand view and having sent out into the world more letters than he ever got back, having checked with a steel tape the accuracy of his bird-glass approximations of the building materials—he had in fact been far off on the dressed stone, which turned out to be 15 x 30 x 10, and quite close on his guess at the tiles which made up the joists, eleven inches where he had guessed a foot—having done all this and arrived only at lunch time (red wine, cheese, and a can of sardines), he bethought himself again of the world.

He remembered then that he had heard there were trotting races every Sunday after lunch "if one cares for that sort of thing." He wasn't sure actually that he did care for that sort of thing, but he knew he didn't care for *futbol* or *jai alai* or the last bullfight of the season. He knew he didn't care to go down to the Plaza Gomila—or anywhere else—to drink with Americans. He hadn't been to trotting races since he was a boy, and he hadn't liked them then, but they used to be part of the autumn fairs that fell about his birthday, just past without observation, and they seemed to be more what he wanted than anything else.

He allowed himself to be deflected slightly from his purpose because he had been experiencing pangs of guilt at having become one of those Americans who make no real effort to learn the language. He had developed, it is true, a fairly workable construction vocabulary—the foreman enjoyed teaching him the names of things—and an adequate household vocabulary, which he and the maid used less and less as they knew each other better. So in order to force himself into a position where he would have to speak Spanish he decided on the austerity of a bus rather than the usual taxi. In a way it was a relief for once not to have to re-mind himself piously how cheap taxis really were.

Getting downtown on the bus was relatively easy. He was crowded into the back near the door. The ticket seller stood up and looked pointedly around. Mason had a small bill ready in his hand—he didn't know how much the fare was—and stretched toward the ticket seller. The man took his money and looked at him. Mason held up one finger. His ticket and his change came back to him through several hands. And that took him down to the Glorieta where he would have to do something about getting another bus.

Fortunately, "Where is the autobus for the hippodrome?" was exactly the kind of thing his Berlitz phrasebook was up to. Before he approached the bus starter, he practiced it twice to himself, following with care the easy guide to pronunciation. "Straight ahead along the Borne, sir, then to the right," the starter said in careful English as if he had practiced at least a dozen times. "Avenida Mola?" Mason said. "Yes," the starter said, "just at the corner of the Borne and Mola Avenue." "Gracias," Mason said doggedly. "You're quite welcome," the starter said. "Just follow the crowds."

Mason was somewhat taken aback to discover that there would be crowds. He had got the impression that racing here was a kind of hole-in-the-wall affair. Still he joined the crowd strolling along the broad, shaded Borne. Everyone was well dressed, and many carried flowers.

Three crowded buses passed before he could get on one. He had a long ride to the end of the city, but he could see very little from where he stood. He thought he really ought to rent a car some day and drive out to see the island.

He got off with the crowds and automatically followed along as they funneled toward an ornate marble entrance up ahead. This was exciting. Better than the bullfights because he knew what was ahead and wasn't nervous about how he would react. It was like going to a football game. He wished he had brought a flask and his bird glasses. It was like going to a fair.

He shuffled through the gate with the crowd, but he saw no sign of a place to buy a ticket. It must be up ahead somewhere because the crowd moved more and more slowly. He tried to peer over heads but he could see little. Off to the left there were the roofs of a series of small but very elaborate buildings. Some were like mosques and some were like banks. There were bits of stained glass in some. He caught flashes of color through the crowd, massed flowers everywhere. "What a horse race," he said aloud to himself.

To his right there was a high wall—fifteen feet perhaps— stretching away for a hundred yards or more. The wall was marked off in squares about three feet to a side. Each square was decorated with flowers so that for a moment he thought an art show was being held in conjunction with the races, a high, mad, jumbled wall of floral paintings. But of course there was always a flower show at the fairs and he was always taken into the flower tent or building, as the case might be, to shake hands with the ancient man he was named after, a noted flower fancier, whom he never saw under any other circumstances. And then he realized that he was in a cemetery.

Because of the crowd there was no hope of turning back, and he moved slowly ahead with a part of the crowd that was splitting off to walk along the wall. Lamps hung from the wall in places, flaring pale in the breeze and smoking black. Candles flickered on brackets. The crowd flowed slowly, held up from time to time as someone stopped to admire a particularly tasteful exhibit. It eddied around a family group sitting on folding chairs and eating a picnic lunch and visiting gaily with neighbors. One woman sat crying beside a new grave. A group of ragged gypsies stood together barefoot before a dozen huge candles stuck into the mud. Except for that, it was like walking around to see the fraternity decorations at Homecoming.

The crowd split again at the head of some stone stairs. Mason was carried down into a kind of vaulted cave that divided continually until he was able to move independently at last. Here the same high walls of flowers were on both sides of him. They were dotted with candles, brighter now in the gloom. Strolling, Mason tried to make out the inscriptions but found his Spanish inadequate. He persisted, however, and at last successfully puzzled out an inscription that stated in plain English that a couple from Columbus, Ohio, were buried there. There was no decoration on that stone.

At the end of the alley he found a stone elaborately decorated with ancient and dusty flowers. The ribbons were in tatters and the wreaths trailed long cobwebs. Preferring not to philosophize on that, he turned back, reading inscriptions as he went, and found himself face to face with a gaping hole.

After his first startle he was aware that, although it was indeed an empty grave, it was being used as a dump. It was full of broken glass, tin cans, and withered flowers. Near the front edge there was an inexplicable yellow chrysanthemum, very fresh. Hardening himself against the thought of the dispossessed tenant of the grave, he took the flower and wandered with it until he found again the couple from Ohio. There he left it.

Above ground he was carried along past gaping crypts down the steep stairs of which he could see candles, flowers, and gleaming altar cloths. Past graves covered with flower-petal mosaics. Past the tombs of rich families which put their trust in marble rather than in flowers. And at last he found himself gently rejected by way of a side gate.

He stepped into a taxi and asked in English to be taken to the race track. "Are you kidding, Mac?" the driver said. "It's just across the street." Mason apologized and went at last to the races. He was much too early, having forgotten that after lunch for him and after lunch for the Spanish were very different things. However, the bar at the track was open and he improved his Spanish.

The work on the building went on steadily. It had reached one of those stages where nothing seems to be happening. The walls didn't seem to get any higher. The fill didn't seem to advance in the least. There was as much activity as ever, and Mason enjoyed it as much as ever, like the familiar business of a favorite play— in fact he wouldn't have had it otherwise, but even so he was aware that his mind wandered. He thought often of his resolve to get out to see the island, and on the following Sunday he did rent a car and drive out to the far end of the island to see a Roman theater he had read about.

He left the car on the highway and walked up a narrow road following signs for the Teatro Romano. He passed some men working on a new house, but the house was in advanced stages, closed in and secret. He passed a well. It was one of the classic Moorish wells, a long horizontal sweep to which a horse could be harnessed, an endless chain of clay pots passing over a big wooden wheel. He wished it had been in operation. He stepped into the field and leaned against the sweep. It moved easily. He took a step with it. The whole mechanism creaked and rattled, and the pots began to go over the wheel. Water splashed in the well. With each step the load became heavier, the sound of water louder. At last a streaming pot appeared and then another. A pot passed over the wheel and spilled its water into a trough. He stopped. He felt like a horse. He felt like a slave. He felt historical. He felt good. He released the sweep, and the pots sank slowly back into the well.

The theater, after the well, was somehow an anticlimax. It was exactly what he expected: stone benches cut into the hillside facing a good-sized acting area with the side of someone's barn as a backdrop. Dotting the flat ground and even cut into the benches themselves were rectangular pits. He studied his Spanish guidebook and then his dictionary and found the pits to be (probably) graves of a somewhat later period. He sat on one of the benches. The air was mild. The view around the barn was gentle, but he couldn't feel like a Roman at the theater. Idly he probed the cracks in the seat with his pocketknife. He found no coins or earrings lost at performances long ago.

There was a cave, the guidebook told him. He opened to the map and turned the book slowly and heavily, feeling himself swinging slowly into orientation like a sluggish needle. Now, with the stage in front of him, the cave must be behind him. Yes, there it was back at the top of the hill. He had come in just beside it but hadn't noticed it at all. It was supposed to be even older than the theater—probably.

He climbed up to inspect the cave. There was a circular chamber with a sort of alcove at the back, a hole in the middle of the roof, and all around the walls a trough cut into the rock, certainly a manger. This he would like to paint. He stood at the mouth of the cave looking in. Out of the smoke-blackened rock and the word *manger* he could make something that not all the Nativities of the Flemish, German, Italian, French, Catalan—

Voices woke him, American voices, a man and children, just behind the hill on the path leading to the theater. "How much farther?" a child said.

"Not far."

"Can we work the well again on the way back?"

"Of course you can. And try to remember how it works because it's just exactly the kind of thing the Moors used hundreds of years ago when they were here, and before that it must have been used for thousands of years all over the East. Why, it must be exactly what Samson was chained to after Dalila betrayed him." The man cleared his throat and Mason could imagine him taking a stance to declaim.

> Why was my breeding ordered and prescribed
> As of a person separate to God,
> Designed for great exploits; if I must die
> Betrayed, Captived, and both my Eyes put out,
> Made of my Enemies the scorn and gaze;
> To grind in Brazen Fetters under task
> With this Heaven-gifted strength? O glorious strength
> Put to the labor of a Beast, debased
> Lower than bondslave! Promise was that I
> Should Israel from Philistian yoke deliver;
> Ask for this great Deliverer now, and find him
> Eyeless in Gaza at the Mill with slaves,
> Himself in bonds under Philistian yoke;
> Yet stay, let me not rashly call in doubt
> Divine Prediction; what if all foretold

Had been fulfilled but through mine own default,
Whom have I to complain of but myself?

"I love to hear you recite poetry, Daddy," a child said.

"Yes, Daddy," another child said. "What poem was it?"

The voices were coming nearer now, and Mason sank back into the cave. This was a new kind of American all right but certainly no improvement.

"A poem about Samson by John Milton, an English poet. He was blind himself and—"

"A stage!" a child screamed, a full-bodied dramatic scream. There was the sound of running feet. "Take a seat, Daddy. We're going to put on a play." Two little girls in dungarees and scarves leaped over the seats like goats and ran once around the stage and stopped stage center.

After a brief conference, the older took a step forward and spoke to a large audience. Her father was seated off to one side near the entrance, but she spoke left and right and up to the cave where Mason hid. "Ladies and gentlemen, today we are going to bring you our own version of *The Gingerbread Man*, written, directed, and starred in by Jean Hawkins—ahem, that's me."

The other little girl stepped in front of her sister. "And co-written, co-directed, and co-starred in by Debbie Hawkins—that's me, heh, heh."

If he hadn't been trapped in the cave, Mason would have sneaked away at that point, but in the end he was glad he had stayed. The girls turned out to be real actors, even to their failure of taste when they weren't under the discipline of a part.

The play progressed, with the smaller girl playing the gingerbread man throughout and the larger girl playing in succession the little old woman, the little old man, the boy, the girl, the field full of mowers, the barn full of threshers, the bear, the wolf, and the fox. In each episode there was a lot of stylized running with big, slow, moon-running steps. In each episode the two came together to sing a chorus of "I ran away from the little old woman, I ran away from the little old man, I ran away from etc.

etc. and I can run away from you, I can." And in each episode there was so much excitement and so much high good humor that Mason found himself caught up and tempted again and again to shout *Ave* or something.

At the end of the play, the father went backstage to congratulate the players. Mason hastily scribbled a note on the back of an envelope—after tearing off his name and address—"This is for my ticket to *The Gingerbread Man*. Sorry I didn't have time to get one beforehand. Thanks for a memorable performance." He left the note with two five-peseta bills in the middle of the floor of the cave and made his escape. The children were shrieking and laughing and lying down in old graves.

On his way back to the highway, he saw that the well was in operation. He stopped, hypnotized, as a blindfolded horse tramped around and around and around and around and around and around and

The sound of the children coming down the path sent him hurrying to his car.

He awoke one morning to the sound of the Chevrolet and the 10 x 10 snarling at each other from opposite ends of the lot. He threw on his robe and walked out onto the terrace. The Chevrolet was actually backing over the top of the wall and extending the face of the fill as if there had never been a wall there at all. The 10 x 10, even with its infrequent loads, had brought its share of the fill up to that end of the foundation and was working around on the side toward Mason. His own garden wall cut off his view in that direction, so he couldn't see exactly how far the work had gone, but he guessed that the foot of the fill must be nearly up to the arched tunnel that hid the brook completely now from side to side of the lot. He didn't know what he felt as he saw—or seemed to see—all the work going under. He was certainly sad. He was certainly a little terrified. He turned his attention to the interior section with its unfinished doorways. Surely that part was not going to be buried. He was also more than a little impatient.

Off to one side, two men were using a two-man saw to cut one of the dressed stones. The cut wasn't quite deep enough yet for

him to be sure, but it looked very much as if the cut wasn't verti-
cal, as if they were tapering a keystone.

The racing of the motor of the 10 x 10 to hurry up the hoist
caught his attention. He knew the sound of that motor well, not,
of course, in the same way he knew the sound of the motor of
that particular Chevrolet, but generically because the 10 x 10 was
to him the symbol of his time in the army.

He went into the army directly from college. He neither asked
for nor was offered a commission. He knew well enough that the
end of college was the end of a world for him, mater, alma mater,
and all that, but still he wasn't anxious to meet the new world
more than halfway. However, the new world for its part advanced
to meet him in the form of a 10 x 10 truck that bundled him together with a mob of others off to basic training.

After basic training he had his only intimate contact with the
big trucks when he was in a searchlight battery on an island in
Long Island Sound. That battery had had only seacoast lights in
fixed positions, and they were suddenly given four antiaircraft
lights and nothing more. They were expected to invent their own
ways of moving them around.

Mason was one of the men assigned to the new lights, but he
invented nothing. He went along with a work party to the scrap
heap and helped carry two channel irons to the blacksmith shop
to be cut to length and bent on the ends to make a ramp for
loading the lights onto a regular 10 x 10 from the motor pool. He
mashed a finger badly on that job, and later, when the ramps
were ready to be used, he quite literally ruptured himself the first
time they tried to horse a light into a truck. The army fixed his
rupture for him, but he would have been entitled to a small dis-
ability if he could have brought himself to claim it. There wasn't
much he remembered of that post except beginning with the
lights and then the night the lieutenant committed suicide.

He had been right there himself but only learned about it
later. He was on the control station, turning a little crank to
match the pointers that moved as the sound horns traveled.

When the pointers were matched, the light was supposed to be automatically pointing at whatever the horns were listening to.

That night the target plane had been delayed as usual—often it never came at all. The men on the horns were passing the time by listening to trains over on the mainland, going vicariously to New York or Boston with the trains. Mason was keeping the pointers matched so the whole thing wouldn't go out of orientation. The light, of course, was following along, and when the command In action was suddenly given, the light flamed through the main street of a town like the light of judgment. They got the beam out of there at once, but the lieutenant caught it from the captain as usual. Mason could still see him standing at the field telephone saying, Yes, sir, and No, sir, and the sweat streaming down his face. Later that night they found his clothes in a pile on the beach.

Later, a very long way from Long Island Sound, standing to night after night with a light set up back in a field, Mason would listen to the pulse of convoys throbbing on the highway. The sound of the trucks would sometimes remind him of his first post, and that would sometimes remind him of the lieutenant. Then he would tell himself that he had only been keeping his pointers matched. It was true, and he believed it every time. He also believed that he had somehow muddled through the army where the other—so many others—had failed.

The sawyers stayed with their stone through the morning. It was quite clearly going to be a keystone, and he found himself impatient for the act of magic that would hold it in its place against all reason. The Chevrolet came and went. A boat whistle blasted in the harbor but he couldn't spare a glance. The 10 x 10 appeared once more. The horses came steadily and were joined by a gray. They were carrying rubble now. Mason could see shattered plaster and even broken ornamental tile. The foundation was on the point of disappearing.

The workmen began to lay out long iron rods along the top of the foundation. Four of these rods were being shaped by the use of wire into a long skeletal box perhaps eight inches square in cross section. Mason was aware that he didn't now feel cheated of his all-stone building. He was even excited as the box grew along the exposed top of the wall. Something new and unexpected was surely about to happen.

He leaned eagerly out over the amphitheater, his hands and chest pressed hard against the rail. The snarling of the two trucks was fading. The lights were fading. The carters shouted at their horses as if from a great distance. Clearly something was about to happen. Something very important. Perhaps the whole point. The two little girls were hurrying to stage center. Ah, they knew their business, those two. Sound and light had almost vanished as they opened their mouths. Gripping the sweep, he soared out and out and out and out with the searchlight flaming always in his eyes.

In the Hands of Our Enemies

So far Mason's map-reading had been flawless. He had come over Hampstead Heath, past Boadicea's tomb (legendary), past Jack Straw's Castle (reputed), past The Spaniards (notable for associations with Dick Turpin, if you like highwaymen, and with Mrs. Bardell, if you like Dickens—he himself liked both), through the grounds of Kenwood, stately home-become-museum, and now he sat on a bench in the yard of The Flask, finishing a pint and poised for his final descent to the cemetery and the grave of Karl Marx.

Why Karl Marx? Mason himself didn't know. In fact he had been surprised, when a friend mentioned the grave, to hear himself say, "I must see it." But he had known then and he still knew that he would have to present himself before that massive bust and retreat step by step (for perspective) until he stood against the Thomas family tomb (his information was meticulous) kept polished by the backs of the faithful. He wondered if he had ever, perhaps in the enthusiasm of the undergraduate moment when he first read *Das Kapital*, bound himself to this pilgrimage. He toyed with the last of his pint, putting off from moment to moment the enjoyment of the final taste, the decisive setting down of the mug.

There would be a park on his left hand going down the hill, flowers and close-cropped, well-rolled grass. A play might be seen there on a lucky summer evening. On the right would be the wall of a part of the cemetery but not the part he was interested in. That was farther along on the left, just after the park.

High brick walls on both sides of the lane closed him in, and he was so busy peering ahead for his first glimpse into the park that he almost missed something just beside him. In his mind's eye he was already confirming with great pleasure the shortness of the grass and the smoothness of the turf, the freshness of the flowers and the impeccable order of the flower beds. He was noting the baby carriages and the old men nodding on the benches, which might some day bear their names In Loving Memory. He caught out of the corner of his eye, when he was almost past, an opening in the wall across the way, a gate which was neither on his map nor in his briefing. He slowly crossed to face it.

It was a large iron gate, somewhat rusty, and gave the impression of not having been opened for a long time. He had seen such gates at Saratoga, still guarding the privacy of long-dead millionaires, but it was another image that forced itself on him: the camera passes through the locked gate and follows up the ruined drive. The moon is behind a cloud, and the great house stands in all its ancient splendor. He hears himself say, " 'Last night I dreamed I went to Manderley again,' " and the moon comes out and shines through the shell of the burned-out house.

The drive behind the gate was so broken and neglected that it showed only in patches the remains of a macadam surface. Trees and bushes crowded in from both sides and left only a glimpse along the gently curving avenue of tombs. Tall grass overwhelmed the smaller stones, and the whole place was so utterly ruinous that he felt an urge to visit it, to savor its melancholy and, perhaps, who knows, find the images of the tombs translating themselves into words and beginning the dance that would sooner or later crystallize into a poem. In the long run, he had more faith in broken macadam than in Karl Marx. But he continued down the hill and turned in at the gate on the left, noticing as he did so, however, an open gate on the right that would let him find his way back into his view from the upper gate.

Now that Marx was no longer his goal, he went on impatiently and with little desire to look about him. He stepped aside for a large party of pilgrims returning from the shrine, hung about with cameras, light meters, containers of film, returning now, all vows fulfilled but with stern joy or none at all. He thought at first they were Americans—what Americans?—but they weren't right, just not right, too stocky perhaps even for some leftish union. And their language was nothing he recognized at all. Usually he guessed an orangutan in such cases, but a woman trailing along behind them was explaining to a couple who looked actually like part of the group that it was "the Russian delegation." That pleased Mason more than the actual grave, although he rubbed against the Thomas tomb and felt with his fingers behind his back the letters of the name even as he confronted the massive head. He thought again of the Russians going sternly home, their cameras loaded with spoils, thinking each in his heart, Why must our holy shrines be forever in the hands of our enemies? He had seen the same expression on crusaders' marble faces in country churches all over England.

Across the lane, the gate was grudgingly ajar. Signs forbade him to bring in either a camera or a dog. All to the good, one place at least he needn't walk as if he were afraid he would rupture himself, skidding over the film of dog shit that covered all of London in wet weather. Still, he was tense as he stepped through the gate to begin his search for whatever it was that must not be snapped up into a camera and carried off in triumph.

He saw at once which way he must go. To his right a drive led uphill and seemed to parallel the wall he had followed down on the other side. But he stood a moment to make sure the secret wasn't hidden just there in the most obvious place of all. To his left was a sort of courtyard, again of broken macadam, bounded on the street side by a shabby chapel, Victorian, he guessed, and facing the chapel an arcade of dingy brick, brick that had not mellowed with time but looked exposed to view unexpectedly, like a bombed celler, and merely dispirited. The inner wall was leprous where memorial plaques were missing.

As he turned his attention back the way he would go, he saw, even before he took a step, that the broken macadam gave way to grass just a few yards up the hill, and as he committed himself to the drive, walls sprang up on either side. There was no gradual introduction. All at once the rows of monuments began, marble foundering in grass and trees, no space left that was not marble foiled in greenery foiled in darkness. At first paths led off into the vacant jungle but even these soon disappeared, and there was no exit anywhere except here and there the hint of trodden grass scrambling between two stones and disappearing with a twist behind one of them. It was all darkness but he could only try. Cautiously he left the drive and climbed the bank and passed behind the stone. Darkness and jungle. Gradually he made out shapes of marble beneath the grass, within the bush, behind the vine. Gradually the marble city took shape in his mind, a Chichén Itzá, an Angkor Vat of the imagination, although the one date which stood clear before him was barely fifty years old. Less than his own age. The dead branch he was staring at turned into an iron rose. He tried to clear the grass away with his hands and pricked his thumb on a real brier. Overcome by sadness and the sudden urgency of his beer, he respectfully pissed against a tree. "A second-hand libation," he said, "but sincere."

There were no real paths—a bit of scuffed moss on a slab, branches broken back at the corner of a tomb, these were the hints he was following as he scrambled over the stones, fleeing like Eliza over the ice—or pursuing perhaps—each new darkness promising to open into hope or despair. At the very least he expected to discover a body, victim of some horrid crime. For some reason he saw the murder taking place during a blackout, but it was not a skeleton he expected to find. He also thought it not unlikely that he would discover the Three Witches (the ghosts of Christmas Past, Present, and To Come) summoning up over all his protests the most discreditable passages of his life. It was with a delicious fear that he turned each terrible corner and entered every shadow.

He was so thoroughly expecting some awful sight that he was

unprepared for the howl. He was not even terrified. It was very unlikely, after all, that any animal had escaped from the zoo and found its way across London back to its native jungle. Probably some dog had slipped in unobserved and hurt itself in this remote place. There must be someone to whom it should be reported. He pressed forward with great stealth. Even a hurt dog can turn nasty. Tracking the sound, he passed from stone to bush, and parting still another screen of leaves found himself about to step on the long-expected body.

There were no signs of wounds about her, although her hair and clothes were in great disorder. Of course, corpses didn't make sounds like that, but the flattened grass all around her suggested terrific struggles and very likely death throes. Then he saw the marker she clutched with both hands. It was a freshly varnished wooden shield nailed to a stake in the ground. He withdrew more cautiously than he had approached. Finding a fresh grave in this wilderness was more disturbing than anything he had imagined. On the way back to the drive, he turned his ankle and wrenched his back, skidding on a slab of marble made slippery where his piss had run down the tree.

The hurt was not serious, however, and the absolute desolation of the scene restored his good humor. He came upon a sunken avenue of splendid tombs, the doors awry, paint flaking, iron flaking, inverted torches almost burned away by the slow fire of rust. He could make out on some doors the late addresses of the families and knew them now as rooming houses or blocks of new flats. The avenue branched left and right, a circle with an island in the middle. He followed around to the right, peering in at the coffins and at the ranked nests of the columbarium. On one door he saw a modern plaque and was pleased to find that he had made a pilgrimage to the tomb of Radclyffe Hall, who in the face of all this was memorialized with "I shall but love thee better after death." Poe? It had a Poe-ish ring about it. "Ligea," perhaps? "The Assignation"? Then he remembered all those southern girls doing their recitations and all chosing "Hayow do ah luv theee? He had thought he would never forget Mrs. Browning.

Before he had quite completed the circle, he climbed up out of the trough by a flight of broad shallow steps to investigate a great mausoleum he saw towering above the sunken tombs. Through the broken glass he could see, even from a distance, the glint of gold and patterns of inlaid marble high on the wall. The effect was splendid. Cautiously he put his face to the gleaming edge of the glass and started back from the stench. But when he investigated his snapshot memory of the interior, he discovered that the stench was only pigeon shit with very likely a dead pigeon or two thrown in, another sort of columbarium. Cautiously he put his nose to the smell and looked again. Towering to the ceiling on each side were broad shallow compartments intended for coffins, but there were only two coffins and one urn in all the place. Round them and about the lone and level pigeon shit stretched from wall to wall. "Vanity," he said, "vanity." He saw himself lying there through the slow years, listening to the mutter of the doves and tasting the strong thick stupefying stench of the rising tide of pigeon shit. "I'm trying too hard," he said. "Mustn't force it."

A fine mist of rain quickly worked itself up to a sharp shower and made him think of shelter. Some of the tombs below had rather deep doorways, and surely somewhere around the circle he should find a sheltered spot. He started hastily down the steps and slipped, wrenching his ankle painfully. He thought that this time he might even have succeeded in breaking it. The sudden waves of pain sickened him. He felt the rain hiss on his flaming face. He slipped down and lay along a step almost asleep.

Voices woke him. He would do well to verify them in case he really needed help. It might be days before anyone came this way again. With skill and cunning and great care, he slid down the steps and worked his way to his feet. His ankle wouldn't bear his weight, but he was able to hop on one foot along the wall until he could see what was going on. A young man and woman were making love standing up in a sheltered doorway. It seemed to him about where he had seen the plaque commemorating Radclyffe Hall. Yes, he saw a corner of the plaque over the young man's shoulder. Stealthily retreating, he imagined her in marble on her tomb with all her armor on her, feet crossed and resting on a little dog, and that expression on her face. He sank down in a doorway and waited.

The rain cut down suddenly to a fine mist and imperceptibly stopped. He listened to their commentary on the progress of the rain and checked it critically against his own observations like a suspicious Cardinal fan sitting in Busch Stadium, watching the game and listening to his transistor to check Harry Carey's "great plays" and "close decisions." The big pine tree—it wasn't a pine—above him glittered in the sunlight. He too thought there might be a rainbow and would also have climbed up to look if he had been able. They were coming toward him, hunting for the stairs.

"Hello," he said while they were still out of sight. "Hello, can you help me? I've had a fall." He listened to the dripping of water onto water, onto stone, onto sodden earth. Remarkable what a little anxiety could do for the senses. He listened again. They must have stolen off—or vanished. "Hello?"

"Where are you?" the young man said.

"Keep on around the circle," Mason said, and almost at once they stepped into sight, the young man in front, leading the girl and holding in the other hand a particularly jagged bit of concrete. "Ah, yes," Mason said, "it would look that way, wouldn't it? Not much use, though, if I were a ghost."

"Are you alone?" the young man said.

"Alone and hurt," Mason said. "I think I've broken my ankle. I'm at your mercy."

"I hope so," the young man said. He hefted the concrete in his hand. Mason hadn't thought of that. They had sounded very decent and looked all right, although he still responded much better to short skirts on girls than to long hair on men, but having just made love should gentle them in any case.

"I mean," the young man said, "in a place like this I'd rather have you at my mercy than be at yours."

"Yes," Mason said, "I was just thinking that."

"You don't seem too badly hurt," the girl said.

"That's so," the young man said. The jagged concrete showed fresh signs of life.

"I'll tell you what," Mason said. "You go down to the gate and tell them I'm up here with a broken ankle."

"I shouldn't like to leave you all alone," the girl said. "I'll stay with you. You go down, Sam."

"No, I'll stay," Sam said. "You go down—no—"

"I don't need a hostage," Mason said.

"Let's take a look at that ankle," Sam said. He tossed aside his piece of concrete and knelt and gently lifted the injured foot. He cradled the heel in the palm of his hand. "It's what the trainer used to do," he said. He rotated Mason's foot, and Mason passed out.

When he came to, there was a raincoat under him and a raincoat over him. Sam was squatting beside him. Mason looked around for the girl. "Sally went for help," Sam said. "Take it easy, man. You feel OK? Want a cigarette?" Mason nodded yes and no. This was one of the times he regretted giving up cigarettes. The decision not to smoke had revealed that he was no longer confident he would live forever, and he badly needed reassurance now. Sam was already smoking, and the drifting smoke was delicious to Mason. In fact, he was rather drifting himself, inert but curiously happy. Sam was large and close and real but he himself felt small and very far away.

"Sure you're OK?" Sam said. Mason nodded. "Can you talk?"

Mason made an effort. "I can," he said, "but I don't want to." He easily sank again to a great distance.

"Shall I talk to you?" Sam said. Mason shrugged his eyes—or imagined he did. "My name is Sam Hall." Mason gave a great jump wholly contained within his skin and, because Sam didn't add "god damn your eyes," relapsed. "My girl friend is Sally Brooks. She's an American but she's doing her thing at the L. S. E." Mason was already so light, so small, so far away that even the London School of Economics lost its usual power to diminish him. "That's why we're out here today looking for the grave of Karl Marx." Sam looked at his cigarette and took a drag, looked at it again and shifted his grip. "It's been uphill work, man, swimming up this current of vegetation all the way and then finding this backwater and a tomb with the name Hall on it—did you notice that one? Perhaps some ancestor of mine." Mason was glad he had chosen silence. He would never have been able to select a remark. "We'd been looking for Marx, you see, but found something better, amost by instinct, you dig?" But Sam didn't seem particularly interested in whether or not Mason understood. He too was going away. Mason was afraid, in fact, if much more of him went he would become transparent.

"It's funny," Sam said, "all of us being Americans." It depressed Mason unreasonably that lying unconscious he should be recognized as an American. He was usually able to pass for Canadian or Australian or even Irish in England, and on the Continent he passed for English. "When we thought you were dying we went through your pockets—good thing you didn't wake up then or you would have been sure we were out to rob you at least." That was a relief and there was really nothing else they could have found in his pockets. He didn't carry anything to identify himself as an academic. If anything, he was more anxious to pass for a writer than for an Englishman. And the package of safes he carried on general principles was quite fresh—he had only recently replaced the scruffy mass of dingy cardboard and perished rubber. He was as satisfied as he thought of his pockets now as his mother used to be as she thought of the elegance of her underwear: one should always be fit to be found dead in the street. There was his age, of course, on all his documents, but that would certainly be as incredible to anyone else as to him. And there was nothing more for anyone to steal.

"You may wonder," Sam said, "how come a young guy like me is free to travel at this time of year. How come I'm not teaching or in the army." Mason didn't mind wondering that now it had been offered. "I mean, I'm too young to be having a sabbatical, and besides my hair's too long for me to stay anywhere long enough to work up sabbatical time, the bastards. As a matter of fact I do have six years in—at four different schools —I'm older than I look—but the place I teach now is on the quarter system and this is my quarter off. Low man on the totem pole teaches summers—god, those midwestern summers —and takes the fall off, the one season that might reconcile you to the Midwest. So here I am. I met Sally coming over on the boat. We both came on the *France* for the food." He brooded a moment. "It wasn't that good," he said. "The service was lousy."

Ah, well, Mason said to himself, that's just the way it is. The things you look forward to disappoint you as often as not, and then something totally unexpected more than makes up for it. He could see himself so clearly in Sam that he was quite disarmed. God, how it all came back. The outrage, the relentless outrage, the generous outrage he had known then. "But you found the tomb of your ancestors," he thought. Or it seemed to him he thought it.

But Sam said, "Of course, it isn't all economics. Oh, you're talking."

And having begun to talk, Mason said, "So it seems."

"How's the ankle?"

"I feel like the man who died of a toothache in his heel. Tell me some more to take my mind off my troubles." Sam didn't seem to hear him. "What do you teach for instance?"

"Math," Sam said. "I'm a topologist and I get to teach Introduction to Algebra in teachers' colleges if I'm lucky."

"You have a Ph.D.?" Sam nodded. "I'm not going to ask you to explain topology if you don't mind," Mason said.

"You're a gent," Sam said.

"I've had it explained dozens of times," Mason said, "and it has never helped a bit to be told that topology is the science of making a hole in an inner tube and then pulling the entire tube through the hole or constructing a bottle that has neither inside nor outside or taking your vest off without removing your coat.

In fact, don't offer to explain Introduction to Algebra. That would be just as bad."

"At least you've heard of topology," Sam said.

"Cheer up," Mason said. "If you have a degree and have been teaching six years, you must be pushing thirty, and soon all those people you can't trust now will suddenly trust you and you'll wind up in an endowed chair."

"I won't be thirty till I think I am," Sam said.

"Splendid," Mason said. "I won't either."

"It's no joke," Sam said angrily. Then he laughed and said, "But cool it, man, cool it."

"Gladly," Mason said, although it irritated him that Sam was clearly willing to cool it only because he was convinced communication was impossible with such a fossil. Damn it, he knew as much about youth as anyone, and he longed for a dream gesture or floating word to prove it. "I thought mathematicians could pretty well write their own ticket," he said rather more cruelly than he intended.

"My problem," Sam said, apparently anxious to be conciliatory, "is that I was too deeply committed to the student power movement to make a very distinguished academic record. I think of myself as brilliant but erratic, although that's probably not what's on my record."

No students had been threatening anything Mason was interested in, so he was disposed to be benevolent. "It's no use counseling moderation?" he said.

"I'm afraid not," Sam said.

"And it's much too late anyway, I suppose?"

"Much too late."

"And you're over here now to stir up revolt in English universities?"

"No, man, no. I'm over here to write a couple of papers and consolidate my academic base."

"Very sound," Mason said, suppressing a smile.

"It really bugs me to have to take the time, but there's a

superstition among mathematicians that if you don't make it by thirty you don't make it at all—I'm twenty-nine. No one will take me seriously if I don't get something out at once."

"And you're over here to avoid distraction?"

"This is a distraction but I mustn't be distracted from it," Sam said. Both the tone of his speech and the tone of his silence convinced Mason that he wouldn't be.

"Absolutely," Mason said. "The more impressive your academic credentials, the more effective you'll be as a student leader."

"It won't sound like sour grapes, anyway," Sam said. "Christ, what idiots. Maybe something does happen to the brain at thirty after all." He shut up his face as if he were going out of business for good, but he opened long enough to say, "Present company excepted, of course."

"Of course," Mason said. He was only too glad to settle for common politeness. But he *did* understand. He could prove it by—he could—he really could. Look, he said to himself, look— "Look," he said to Sam, "since you except present company, I hope you won't mind if I ask why you're so sure that no one over thirty can understand what's bugging you." Mason winced. It was a matter of principle with him to stick to his own vocabulary. Sam, however, left it all up to him. "You must know that there are a lot of us who agree with you entirely on matters of personal freedom and curriculum reform and representation on university committees." Again he looked to Sam for encouragement but got none. He had quite sincerely forgotten that the last time he got a job offer from another university there wasn't much left for his own university's counter offer. They had run out of rank to tempt him with: Mason was already a research professor with no contact with students whatever. Money had long since been irrelevant. The only move left had been to relieve him of all committee assignments. Now, from his remote position, the desire of students to get involved with committees seemed silly, although he still sympathized with their desire for a better education, a curriculum that fell somehow between the irrelevance of the traditional education of the gentleman of leisure and the deadly relevance of the traditional tooling-up of the man of labor.

"You want the university turned back to you," Mason said, "and quite rightly, for your education, not continued as a stamping mill for social units labeled Artificially Aged—Guaranteed Safe—Can Be Used At Once—Need Not Be Stored Until Thirty."

"Then why don't you do something?" Sam said.

"Do?" Mason said.

"Do," Sam said. "What did you do when you were a student? Run for student senate or write furious editorials for the student paper about lack of school spirit or debate passionately in the student union something like Resolved: we should clear out of the UN—"

"League of Nations," Mason said. "You all think the world began with you."

"Which was it?" Sam said.

"As a matter of fact, we drank," Mason said. He was not encouraged by seeing Sam suppress a smile.

"Tell me, man," Sam said, "were they as tough on whiskey in those days as they are now on pot?"

"You could get kicked out of school all right," Mason said, "but after Prohibition it was hard even for them to be too hypocritical."

As Mason spoke, he again felt the beginning of rapport, but Sam said at once, "And what did you do in addition to drinking?"

"We grumbled. We hid ourselves in the library and read things we wanted to read. We believed, perhaps, in some professor and followed his lectures. We told ourselves we could get an education in spite of them. What I mean to say is that although we were as full of savage indignation as the next man it was somehow impossible for us to think the thought you all find so obvious—simply that the system can be reformed if it doesn't work as it should."

"Not exactly perceptive, you must agree," Sam said.

"No," Mason said. "No, I don't agree at all. Look at Columbus and the egg."

"Come again?"

"It's an old story," Mason said, making an automatic and highly professional attempt to keep the condescension out of his voice. "Briefly—"

"Of course I know about Columbus and the egg," Sam said. "What do you think I am, some kind of idiot?"

"I have no way of knowing, have I?" Mason said.

"That sounds like student debating—you sure you didn't?"

"Let's stop with insults even."

"Nothing, neither way," Sam said, finessing a last point, which Mason was willing to let him have. "What I meant was," Sam said, "what about Columbus and the egg?"

"Yes," Mason said. "Columbus and the egg, yes."

"Yes," Sam said. "What about Columbus and the egg?"

"Yes," Mason said. "I seem to have lost the drift, I'm afraid."

"It doesn't matter," Sam said.

Stung by Sam's compassion, Mason plunged into his class-room manner. "The story of the egg teaches us," he said, "that the flights of the most extraordinary minds become at once laboratory demonstrations even for the dunces of the class. Ah," he said, "I have it. You don't suppose their Catholic Majesties were dunces, do you?"

"I have no way of knowing, have I?"

"You must have learned your debating from a woman," Mason said with great pleasure, but he hurried on to avoid interruption. "Of course they weren't dunces. You know it and I know it, but—" At this point he became aware that Sam was also talking, and since he was losing the drift again, he thought he might as well listen.

"I only mean," Sam said, "that it seems to me that the egg was standing there in front of you all the time."

"Of course it was," Mason said. "I can see—now—that the egg was standing there, that the Emperor was naked, but there was something else that I could see even then. I'll tell you about it. It's probably a parable or something."

"I'm really very fond of parables," Sam said.

"One day in the fall," Mason said. He felt that perhaps he had lost the drift again, but the parable—or whatever it was—was insistent and he really didn't much care. "This was a southern university by the way, and please don't say it figures—"

"You mustn't think I'm a complete pig," Sam said.

"Sorry," Mason said. "I wouldn't have mentioned it except to explain the weather. And it does figure really and I don't like it. But the weather was fine. Falls were glorious there—and long. Anyway, one day some of us—there must have been eight, let's say—rented a couple of boats and took a picnic up the river. We used to go on the river a lot, a slow muddy southern river with muddy banks and with trees and undergrowth white with mud to very surprising heights above the ground. There was really no place to land but there used to be barges loaded with beautiful white sand anchored in a reach well up into the woods away from town. We used to go there and sunbathe and pretend we were down on the Cape—some of us. Some pretended Coney Island. It was quite idyllic.

"Well, on this particular day we took a couple of six-packs of cokes and a couple of lemons and a big earthenware pitcher we had picked up once on a walk in the country when we discovered a potter at work. We stopped at the bootlegger's for a couple of pints of rum. This was our picnic, you see."

"And that pushes you farther back than you have admitted," Sam said. "Perhaps into the twenties. Anyway, before 1933."

"I see," Mason said, "that you do know some ancient history, but you've overlooked sociology, the phenomenon of local option. The churches and the bootleggers conspired—as they often do—to keep the university county dry."

"Surely even you must have seen that injustice," Sam said.

"We felt it keenly," Mason said, "believe me, but I'm afraid we loved even more to go to the bootlegger's." Sam's eyes flashed but he kept quiet. "Thank you," Mason said. "So we got into our boats and rowed up to the barges. It was lovely there. Hot and still. We took off all our clothes and lay in the sun and drank in turn from the pitcher, passing it from hand to hand. I don't know that we said anything very important. We wished we had brought more rum, and we wished we had brought something to eat, and we wished we had brought some girls. Not that we knew any girls. We might as well have been monks. It wouldn't have cost us anything to take the vows. We lay in the sun and sweat and dozed and drank. Sometimes I think that if I had to take a pen and mark an *x* on the time I was happy, I'd mark that day. I don't know why. I just remember it that way. Sun and sand and water and the others just there. I can see it and hear it and smell it. I haven't drunk a Cuba Libre for thirty years— can't stand them—but I can still taste that pitcher, and it's just as marvelous as all the rest.

"Of course someone remembered we had to get back for supper, so we got dressed and started back, drugged by the sun, relaxed. Sooner or later, however, somebody in the other boat naturally got splashed a little by one of our oars and splashed back harder. You can imagine the rest. It wound up with all of us in the water and the boats swamped—I saved the pitcher when we went over and still have it. I pass it off as an example of native American craft.

"We were able to swim the boats to the bank without much trouble and even got them bailed out in the shallow water, but the mud was over our knees and we were a real mess. Finally we found a place where a fallen tree gave us a bridge over the mud, so we washed the boats and ourselves and went up and built a fire on higher ground to dry our clothes. We stole some potatoes from a field and feasted and lay half the night around the fire without saying much. Then we all pissed on the fire to put it out and rowed quietly home."

"I dig that scene," Sam said.

"It was happiness," Mason said. "Funny."

"I dig."

Again Mason felt a flash of perfect sympathy. "But it was crazy," he said.

"Crazy, man."

Mason was brought up sharp. "No," he said. "I mean *my* crazy, not yours. I mean insane, illegal, immoral, and stupid."

"What *do* you mean?" Sam said. He, too, seemed to have run into an unexpected wall.

"I'll tell you what I mean. Just think of the danger. An accidental bump on the head as the boats were going over and somebody gets drowned. How did we know we all could swim?"

"Oh, for god's sake," Sam said.

"Or we might all have gone over the dam while we were struggling with the boats."

"You didn't mention the dam," Sam said.

"It was there just the same, at the locks."

"How far?"

"Perhaps a mile from where we were."

"Jesus, man, you're worse off every time you get into a car—or go prowling around cemeteries by yourself. You're a real Clever Elsie."

"I'm sure that's not a compliment."

"You mean you don't know about the Clever Elsie? I thought everybody over thirty loved fairy tales."

Mason wanted to meow like a cat but humbled himself. "Could I have a cigarette?" he said, and when Sam had given him a cigarette and lighted it for him, he said, "Tell me about the Clever Elsie."

"Once upon a time," Sam said, "there was a girl called the Clever Elsie. One day when her boyfriend, Hans, came to call, her father sent her down into the cellar to draw a pitcher of beer—a German folk pitcher, by the way—and she happened to notice a hammer lying on a beam over the barrel, so she sat down and cried her heart out. When her father and Hans came to find her—they had grown very thirsty—she explained that when she saw the hammer, which, I forgot to tell you, had been left there by the carpenters when they built the house six generations before—she explained that she had suddenly realized that if she and Hans got married they might have a son and they might send him to the cellar to draw a pitcher of beer and the hammer might fall and it might kill him. 'Oh, what a Clever Elsie,' the admiring menfolk said."

"I don't think the cases are at all similar," Mason said. He had been lying very quiet and barely listening in order to concentrate on the point.

"If you stay in bed all the time, you can avoid a lot of trouble," Sam said, "but if you really want to be safe, why don't you just let me pry open one of these doors and slide you in? My god, man, you didn't even get a cold, did you? You've just told me the day was happiness."

"But leaving aside silly risks"—Sam snorted—"we might have lost the man's boats, we were trespassing on the sand barges, we stole the potatoes, we wasted a meal we had already paid for—"

"You can be sure some Black children remembered you in their prayers that night," Sam said.

"That is something, isn't it?" Mason said. "But the whole thing is so messy."

"That's what we call life."

"It's what I call a mess."

"You just called it happiness."

"That only makes it messier," Mason said. "For all I know the whole thing may have been reeking with latent homosexuality."

"Very likely," Sam said.

"My god, doesn't anything revolt you?" Mason made a violent and impatient movement and did not stay for an answer but passed out again.

"We've decided to adopt you," Sam said as he and Sally tucked Mason into his bed. "They didn't want to keep you at the hospital and were willing to toss you out, cast and all, so we thought we'd better look after you. Finders keepers, you know."

"For better or worse," Sally said. She arranged the covers over him, and the sheets and blankets fell away in great marble rhythms to the floor when she was done. She placed a hot water bottle at his feet, and his soles reached toward it and were warmed. Drowsy, he drifted, smelled the good smell of good strong soup, heard the muttering scales of the piano student upstairs. He was nearly happy but thoroughly perplexed.

A Note on the Author

For this collection of sixteen short stories, Curley won an award in the National Council on the Arts Selection Program. A member of the English department of the University of Illinois for fifteen years, he was a Fellow at the Center for Advanced Study at the University from 1968 to 1969. From 1955 to 1960 he was one of the editors of *Accent*, a literary magazine published at the University. He taught at the Bread Loaf Writers' Conference in 1958, and won a Guggenheim Fellowship for the academic year 1958–59, which he spent in Palma de Mallorca and Oxford. Since 1947 he has published two novels, *How Many Angels?* and *A Stone Man, Yes*; a collection of short stories, *That Marriage Bed of Procrustes*; criticism, poetry, and several plays.

UNIVERSITY OF ILLINOIS PRESS